## 'What are you ...g

As he removed his shirt, Raoul studied her with obvious amusement, liking the fire he saw in her grey eyes. Hortense hissed in exasperation and bit back an oath.

'I can see you're not going to give me the pleasure of watching you get out of the water,' he chuckled. 'I suppose I'd better turn my back before you turn completely blue. Here!' He tossed his shirt on to the bank near her. 'You can use this to dry yourself. I don't want you catching pneumonia.'

His blue eyes studied her appreciatively as he walked towards her across the grass. Stopping in front of her, he reached out to smooth her cheek. 'There's no way you could pass as a boy. I've known you were a female from the very beginning. Don't you think it's time you told me who you really are?

Truda Taylor grew up in Okehampton, Devon and now lives in Desborough, Northamptonshire, with her husband John, and children George and Amy, and a selection of cats and hamsters. She teaches seven-year-olds and enjoys encouraging them to use their imaginations and write.

Five years ago, she made her first visit to the Vendée, and it was her fascination with the history of that area that eventually led to her writing historical fiction.

Previous Title

HAZARDOUS MARRIAGE

This one is for Dad

# HEARTS OF THE VENDÉE

## Truda Taylor

First published in Great Britain 1991
by Mills & Boon Limited

© Truda Taylor 1991

Australian copyright 1991
Philippine copyright 1991
This edition 1991

ISBN 0 263 77495 3

Masquerade is a trademark published by
Mills & Boon Limited, Eton House,
18–24 Paradise Road, Richmond, Surrey, TW9 1SR.

Set in 10 on 11 pt Linotron Plantin
04-9112-79631
Typeset in Great Britain by Centracet, Cambridge
Made and printed in Great Britain

# PROLOGUE
## Paris, August, 1793

THE walls of the prison cell were running with conden-
sation and the air stank of unwashed bodies. The young
man sitting quietly on the floor in the corner brushed the
beginnings of mould from his blue uniform jacket and
smiled wryly. A year ago, like most of France's pro-
fessional soldiers, he had worn white, and on that the
mould would not have shown at all. He had only been in
that accursed place a week and already the stench of it
seemed to have seeped into his every pore.

He stretched his cramped limbs and, for the first time
in days, suffered no pain. He had been a fool to resist
arrest, and the beating the soldiers had given him had
been excessive. It was not often that they had an officer
at their mercy, especially one who commanded in a
regular regiment and had therefore not been elected.

A child aged about two or three toddled across the dirt
floor and sprawled on its face near the soldier. With
surprisingly gentle hands the young man set it on its
feet. A pretty young woman smiled her thanks and,
taking the toddler's hand, led him away to join her
friends at the far end of the cell. Raoul Duchambray
could understand why other prisoners were wary of him,
for in that autumn of 1793 the new uniform of the
republic was feared by the aristos.

Duchambray watched the young woman as she
attempted to amuse her two fretful children and, in spite
of his contempt for the aristocracy as a whole, felt
nothing but compassion. Ruthlessly he tried to suppress
the emotion, for it was compassion that had brought him

5

to this God-forsaken place and now he was likely to die with those he despised. And yet that young woman didn't look nearly as cold and implacable as the uncle and cousin he had loathed. Neither had Thierry, he reflected. Their friendship had survived both timing and their differing political views, and when Thierry had asked his help to get his wife and children out of Paris, Raoul had hesitantly agreed.

Poor Thierry had gone to the guillotine a few days ago, but at least he'd had the consolation of knowing that his family had been smuggled to safety. In spite of being caught, Raoul did not regret the act. He staunchly supported the Revolution and even understood the need for a certain amount of bloodshed, but he had ever been one to let his heart rule his head.

His musings were cut short when the cell door opened and everyone fell silent.

'You've a visitor, Duchambray,' the guard jeered. 'It seems you're to be allowed to speak to him in private. You must have some important friends.'

Duchambray climbed stiffly to his feet and followed the man down the long cobbled corridor. The fellow gestured to a door at the end and, not knowing what to expect, Raoul entered. When the door closed behind him he found himself confronting his natural father, a man he hadn't even known the identity of until his eighteenth year.

Thomas Beaulieu studied his son, noting his dirty uniform and dark, dishevelled hair. With such colouring one would have expected eyes of a dramatic brown but instead they were a startling cerulean blue that could sparkle with laughter or chill a man to his bones. They were the only physical legacy the boy had acquired from his beautiful, wayward mother and one of the reasons Beaulieu found it so hard to accept him. It was unsettling to see Felice's eyes staring back at him from a replica of his own face.

In fact, he didn't think he would ever completely get over the bitterness he had felt when she'd refused to marry him. Oh, she had loved him in her way, he supposed, but not enough to defy convention and her family. . .and yet she had done just that for her baby son. She had insisted on keeping him and persuaded her mother to recognise him, but then that had not necessitated her leaving Ramboulard and her pampered lifestyle.

The familiar blue eyes challenged Beaulieu and his mouth twisted in a wry smile. In spite of his predicament, the boy held himself proudly. Whatever his parentage and looks, he was every inch a Duchambray; so much so that Beaulieu resented the responsibility he felt towards him.

'You've been very foolish, Raoul,' the older man finally said, 'throwing away all you have achieved for the sake of two aristo brats and their degenerate mother. I cannot understand such sentimentality, unless, of course the woman was one of your lovers.'

The young man shrugged and moved over to look out of the office window, drinking in the feel of the sunlight on his face. 'She was the wife of a friend. Not all the aristos are the monsters you Jacobins make them out to be.'

'If you are renouncing our Revolution,' Beaulieu replied harshly, 'then there is nothing I can do for you.'

'I don't expect you to do anything,' Raoul replied. 'I'm quite prepared to face the consequences of my actions. . .but, for the record, I am still a committed Republican. True, the execution of the King left a nasty taste in my mouth, but I can accept the necessity for it. Jeanne Raveneau, however, and her two children, represented no danger to our illustrious Revolution.'

The sarcasm in the son's voice annoyed Beaulieu. 'You betrayed the trust placed in you when you used your uniform and authority to get your friend's family out of Paris. You can imagine how the Committee for Revolutionary Surveillance will view that!'

Again the young man displayed an irritating indifference. 'You don't need to warn me. I know what to expect. I'm only sorry that it's the civil authorities who are holding me. I'd sooner face a firing squad than Madame Guillotine.'

'If you can convince Commissioner Carrier that you are indeed a true Republican then you might not have to face either. The fact that you are a Vendean could be very useful.'

'So things are still going badly in the west.' Raoul turned and permitted himself a smile. Republican though he was, he still felt a wry amusement at the way the people from his home area had unexpectedly opposed the call for liberty.

'You'd better wipe that smile off your face,' Beaulieu snapped angrily. He took a seat at the scarred wooden table and gestured to the chair across from him. 'Come and sit down.'

When Raoul obeyed he continued. 'I don't suppose it will grieve you to learn that your uncle and cousin are both dead or that your grandmother is grievously ill.'

A momentary shadow crossed the young man's face. He didn't care about his uncle and cousin but he was fond of his grandmother in spite of her arrogant ways.

'It is a good time for you to return to Ramboulard,' his father told him. 'You are needed there and would be welcomed with open arms. It would be only natural for you to join the Vendeans. Your political activities have always been low key, so there is no reason for anyone to suspect your Republican sympathies. You would be in a unique position to help us.'

'Are you asking me to spy?' Raoul asked.

Beaulieu smiled coldly. 'It's that or the guillotine. . . Come, my boy, it's not as if we're asking you to act against your beliefs. It will be dangerous, I know, but you've never shied away from that. Your commanding officer speaks most highly of your courage.'

Still Raoul hesitated. He had inherited his mother's pride but not her pragmatism and, although he had his father's intellect, it was without that coldness of heart. When he finally agreed it was because he could see no valid reason to refuse, not when he considered the alternative; and yet he did not feel at ease with the idea. Intrigue and subterfuge were not his style.

# CHAPTER ONE

As HER horse cantered across the bridge Hortense Claviere glanced down at the swirling waters of the Loire. The tide was in and the great river rubbed high against the stone arches, its colour reflecting the rapidly darkening sky. For two days she had been following it, using it to guide her west, but at Saumur had decided to cross it and strike out towards Cholet.

It was getting late and once more she had to decide whether to camp out or look for a suitable inn. There was an autumn chill in the air and she longed for a wash and a warm bed, but she placed little confidence in her boy's disguise. Obviously she couldn't share a room, and when that had been the only option at an inn in Vendôme her hurried departure had drawn unwanted attention. She had experienced worse in Tour, where she had been propositioned by a gentleman with a partiality for beardless boys, and her emphatic and horrified denial had greatly amused the inn's unsavoury patrons.

Not for the first time she wondered if it would have been safer to travel as a girl, but respectable young ladies just did not ride across country on their own and she could not afford to draw attention to herself. What she needed was speed and, above all, anonymity, so that no one would suspect the fortune in jewels hidden in her saddle-bag.

Continuing on through the small town, she decided to opt for a night in the woods and resigned herself to sleeping only lightly with a loaded pistol close at hand. She was regretfully riding through the outskirts of the town when she noticed an inn on her right, its courtyard swarming with the hated blue coats of Republican soldiers. For a moment she was almost swamped with fear and had to remind herself that they could not know of her flight from Paris or her intention to join the Vendean rebels.

When she rounded the next bend there were more of them milling around at the roadside. She should have been expecting them, she supposed, because she was approaching the limits of the Vendean insurgence, but their presence still upset her. The soldiers who had dragged her father from his house had been wearing that same uniform.

Once again her heart boiled with hatred for the perpetrators of the Revolution and all who supported it. To begin with her quiet, rather scholarly father had been quite willing to coexist with the Republicans and had even had some Girondin friends. Not that it had done him any good in the end; he had gone to the guillotine less than a week ago and his so-called friends had done nothing. Obviously the fortune he had acquired through judicious investment in the capital's expanding construction trade had earned him more enemies than he had realised.

At least now Hortense knew why they had lingered so long in the capital. Appalled by the carnage there, Emile Claviere had finally decided that he could no longer sit back and let events take their course and had quietly and systematically been changing what assets he could into jewels and gold. Not, she had discovered on reading his last letter to her, to provide for himself in exile, but to take home to the Vendée to help buy arms and ammunition. Victory by the Royalist Vendean army was the only way he had seen of putting an end to the present reign of savagery and terror.

At any moment Hortense expected the soldiers to detain her, to at least stop her and question her loyalty, but they were too occupied with their own concerns. When the Republicans were a fair way behind her she began to relax and, slowing her horse, scanned the woods that bordered the road for a suitable camping place. Noticing what appeared to be some kind of barn showing through the trees, she turned off and headed towards it.

It was a dilapidated three-sided structure that had lost part of its roof, but at least one corner of it appeared dry. There was even a small pile of hay that would serve as a comfortable bed and, on seeing it, the girl's spirits rose. There had been times on her lonely journey when she had felt close to tears. Now, suddenly, she sensed that the worst was over. Just one more day, two at the most, and she would reach her destination.

Almost cheerfully she began making preparations for the night, unsaddling her horse and gathering some twigs and straw to make a fire. Finally, having spread out her blanket, she rummaged in her saddle-bag for what remained of her food—a piece of sausage and some stale bread. It wasn't much, but she consoled herself with thoughts of the culinary delights to come; at her cousin's château they always ate well.

She was just licking her fingers and trying to decide whether to throw away the crust of stale bread or force it down when she heard the sound of snapping twigs. Freezing, she listened intently, but the only sound was the rapid beating of her own heart. Then she heard the unmistakable whinny of a horse, closely followed by a man's soothing whisper.

Reaching for her pistol, she scurried into the shadows, well away from the fire. There she forced herself to remain still for what seemed like an eternity, until finally a shadow materialised from the shelter of the trees. She tensed and struggled to contain her fear as the man, still leading his horse, cautiously approached her. Resolutely she primed her pistol and, at the sound of it, he froze.

'Move forward into the firelight,' she commanded. Inside she was shaking like a jelly, but her voice remained gratifyingly steady and calm.

Dropping the reins of his horse, he lifted his hands to show that he was unarmed, and slowly complied. For a moment the girl was able to study him. He was quite tall and the dancing flames of the fire highlighted features that were both handsome and strong.

'Who are you and what is your business?' she demanded.

'I'm simply a traveller on my way home.' He smiled wryly and she caught a glimpse of even white teeth. 'As you are no doubt aware, all the inns in Saumur are full. I'd rather sleep here than in a field. . . I'm prepared to share my food with you in return for shelter.'

An uneasy silence stretched between them as Hortense frantically considered her options. She did not want to share her camp with him but was afraid of his reaction if she refused. In fact, the safest thing to do was to shoot him, but she doubted she could be as ruthless as that, and supposing she missed? What would he do to her then?

Glancing at the slight figure holding the pistol, Raoul Duchambray was very much afraid that he had miscalculated. He had decided to ask for shelter, not caring whether his companion was a Royalist or a Republican; he was in a unique position to ingratiate himself with either. What he hadn't expected was to be confronted by a nervous youth who, without any discussion, seemed set to blow him to kingdom come.

Coolly he considered his chances of disarming the boy. Obviously he was at a disadvantage standing in the light, but the barrel of the pistol seemed none too steady. He had more or less decided to take the chance when the cry of a screech owl momentarily distracted Hortense. As Raoul sprang forward the pistol exploded, and he felt something burn across his arm. Then he was upon the struggling figure and it was like trying to subdue a tiger cub. Hortense scratched and kicked and even turned her head to bite Duchambray's hand.

'For God's sake, be still,' he hissed, finally managing to trap his opponent's arms. 'I mean you no harm.'

They were both breathing heavily, their bodies pressed tightly against each other. Incredulously Raoul felt the stirrings of desire, an involuntary reaction to the softness he felt pressed against his chest. It was at that moment that he realised that he was dealing with a girl, and a deliciously curvaceous one at that.

Slightly dazed, he lifted his hand to caress the soft curls that framed her face. 'I'm not going to hurt you, brat. I only want to talk.'

Hortense glared at him as he moved to sit by the fire.

'Come on,' he encouraged. 'I won't punish you for shooting me.'

She could only stand and stare as he removed his cloak and then his dark jacket. Up until then she hadn't had the faintest idea that she'd hit him.

'Damn,' he grumbled, feeling in the pocket of his breeches with his good hand. 'I'm bleeding like a stuck pig. I don't suppose you have a handkerchief?'

When she shook her head he gave a grunt of exasperation and yanked off his cravat.

'Can I help?' Hortense asked hesitantly, kneeling beside him and wondering why she should feel so guilty. After all, it was his own fault he was hurt; he should never have rushed her.

Wordlessly he handed her the cravat and then extended his right arm. The pistol ball had cut a shallow furrow near his elbow. Although only a superficial wound, it was bleeding badly. With gentle fingers Hortense began to bind it with the cloth.

While she was concentrating on her task Raoul took

the opportunity to study her. She was a pretty girl, he thought, far too pretty to pass for a boy. She seemed to have cropped her hair as part of her disguise, but the cap of copper-tinted curls was surprisingly attractive. It would be glorious when it grew, he decided, something a man would ache to run his fingers through. Her features were delicate, her cheekbones high and her delightfully cleft chin definitely stubborn. She was also blessed with wide, intelligent eyes. Raoul Duchambray liked what he saw. He liked it very much.

Sensing that she would feel easier with him if he continued to treat her as a boy, he decided not to let her know he was aware of her disguise.

'Would you have shot me if I hadn't rushed you?' he asked curiously.

'I don't think so,' she replied, ripping the cravat and tying a knot.

'You don't think so,' he grumbled. 'In that case I'm glad I didn't wait to find out. You're a bloodthirsty little devil, aren't you?'

'Actually, I'm sorry now that I did so,' she admitted, finding his wry smile undeniably attractive. 'You don't seem at all threatening. I'd be glad to share the shelter with you.' She grinned. 'Particularly if you have some food.'

He studied her thoughtfully for a moment and then nodded as though coming to a decision. Getting slowly to his feet, he went to tether his horse and then returned, carrying a canvas sack. When he opened it the savoury aroma made the girl's mouth water. With a knowing smile he drew out a roasted fowl, some crisp fresh bread and a bottle of wine.

'It smells delicious,' Hortense groaned. 'Where on earth did you get it?'

'The inn I stopped at was full, but I was able to charm the landlady into letting me have some food.'

I just bet you were, Hortense thought, gratefully accepting the chicken leg he offered her. You could probably charm the birds out of the trees.

True to his word, he generously shared everything, watching with some amusement as she ate ravenously. Apparently she wasn't as adept at taking care of herself as she would like him to believe.

When they had eaten their fill he carefully wrapped what was left and then offered her the wine. 'Sorry, I haven't a glass.'

'Don't worry. I'm used to roughing it.' She shrugged and answered with what she hoped was boyish nonchalance, but the effect was rather spoilt when she choked on the rough red liquid.

Struggling to hide his amusement, Raoul patted her on the back enthusiastically.

'It's all right,' she snapped, feeling foolish. 'You don't need to pound me to a pulp. In fact, I'd just as soon you kept your hands to yourself.'

'Whatever you say, brat,' he answered coldly. 'I don't know about you, but I'm ready to turn in for the night.'

In strained silence they spread out their blankets as far apart as the sheltered corner would allow.

'We'd be a lot warmer if we shared,' he suggested reasonably.

Hortense stifled a gasp of horror and searched around frantically for a reason to decline. 'I don't think we'd better,' she finally managed to say. 'You wouldn't like it. I'm afraid I kick.'

He grunted something that she didn't quite hear, then, to her relief, settled down alone.

She thought he was asleep, and was dozing herself, when he muttered, 'My name is Raoul. . .what do they call you, boy?'

'Henri,' she replied, borrowing her cousin's name.

Then, after thinking rapidly, added, 'Clisson; Henri Clisson.'

The sound he made was suspiciously like a laugh. 'Goodnight Henri. . .Clisson.'

It was a moment before she realised she had made the mistake of naming herself after a town that was close by. She was cursing her foolishness, and wondering if he would have the nerve to question her further, when she fell asleep.

The barn was filling with watery sunlight when she finally awoke, feeling stiff and cold. For a moment she could not think where she was, then, remembering, sat up and looked around. There was no sign of her companion and she was conscious of a feeling of disappointment. He could at least have had the manners to say goodbye. Climbing to her feet, she looked outside and saw him coming towards her through the trees, carrying a musket.

'Where have you been?' she asked irritably.

'Testy in the mornings, aren't you?' He grinned, and for the first time she noticed that his eyes were incredibly blue.

In fact, he was even more good-looking when viewed in the daylight, and the dark stubble on his jaw did nothing to lessen his appeal.

'I was going to shoot us a rabbit,' he continued, 'but there's a lot of activity on the road and I thought it unwise to draw attention to ourselves.'

'Republiclans!' Raoul did not miss the contempt in her voice and it told him just what he wanted to know. She was a little rebel, and cultivating her friendship could prove useful.

'I've been thinking,' he said later as they were finishing off the remains of the chicken. 'If we're heading in the same direction then we might as well travel together.'

Hortense frowned and considered the matter. It would

be nice to have company, and as long as she kept her boy's identity there could be little harm in it. True, she had no idea of Raoul's political views, but then she had no intention of sharing her own secrets with him either. He seemed harmless enough, apart from the fact that he was so disconcertingly attractive.

'I'm heading towards les Herbiérs, to Château Claviere,' she finally admitted. 'My brother works for Henri Claviere.'

For some reason this seemed to surprise him. 'Then we are going in the same direction,' he confided. 'My family live near St Fulgent, at Rambouland.'

'The Duchambrays!' she exclaimed without thinking. 'They own Rambouland. You're a Duchambray!'

'That's right.' He answered coldly, only Hortense was too pleased by his disclosure to notice. If he was a Duchambray then his allegiance would be the same as her own.

She would have liked to question him further about his family but was aware that in her present disguise such curiosity would seem out of place. Instead she searched her memory, sure she must have met him before, but the Duchambrays, she remembered, were all fair. . . Then she placed him. He was Felice Duchambray's illegitimate son! The black sheep of the family in more ways than one.

The knowledge of his identity cheered her immensely and she felt almost light-hearted as they continued on their way. Raoul, on the other hand, seemed to be brooding, and she wondered if he regretted revealing so much about himself.

Eschewing the road, they cut across country, Raoul leading the way. It was a nice day and, as the strength of the sun increased, Hortense became rather warm. Raoul removed his jacket, then, flashing her an amused glance, suggested she did likewise. When she saw the way the thin material of his shirt outlined the breadth of his shoulders and the contours of his chest she knew she didn't dare, and instead declared that she did not feel at all uncomfortable.

Around noon they stopped to rest the horses and finish what was left of the wine, then, rejoining the road, carried on towards Cholet. This turned out to be a mistake, for they had not gone far when they spotted four blue-coated soldiers approaching along a track to the right.

'Leave this to me,' Raoul snapped, not seeming unduly perturbed. 'I can talk our way out of it if you'll just follow my lead.'

Hortense thought of the jewels in her saddle-bag and decided not to take the chance. Turning her horse, she kicked it hard and headed back the way they had come. For a moment Raoul hesitated, then realised he had little choice but to follow her. Reaching the woods, she turned to see the soldiers spurring after Raoul, swords in the air. Horrified, she watched as his horse seemed to stumble and he pitched headlong to the ground.

There was a loaded pistol in her saddle holster and, in spite of her reluctance to use it before, she knew she was a fine shot. When she saw Raoul drag the musket from his limping horse and use it to down one of the Republicans she clawed out the weapon and turned back. Thumbing back the cocking piece, she prayed that it would fire.

Raoul had no option but to wait for the other soldiers, holding his musket like a club. The odds were hopelessly against him and he thought himself as good as dead. The soldiers, however, made the mistake of being over-eager, one spurring well ahead of the others, and they were so intent on their quarry that they failed to notice Hortense.

She stopped her horse and, lifting the heavy pistol, fired. The leading soldier threw up his hands and tumbled to the ground. At the same time Raoul neatly side-stepped and, swinging his musket, brought another man crashing down.

'Catch his horse,' he shouted, and she hurried to obey.

The fourth soldier slowed uncertainly, then, pulling out his own pistol, discharged a poorly aimed shot at Raoul before deciding on discretion and turning away. Hortense leant over to retrieve the pistol from the saddle of the captured horse and calmly took aim at the man's back. She was both surprised and annoyed when, at the last minute, Raoul knocked her arm aside, causing the shot to go wide.

'Why did you do that?' she demanded. 'I could have brought him down. It would have been one Republican fanatic the less.'

'Republican fanatic be damned!' he snapped. 'He is probably some poor devil who was forced into the army so that his town could reach its quota of so-called volunteers.' He was blazingly angry, she realised. His face was pale and his blue eyes positively sparked. 'My God, woman! You nearly got us both killed!'

Turning away, he bent to examine the foreleg of his dejected-looking horse, and swore vehemently. 'I won't be able to ride him, but I'm damned if I'm leaving him here.'

Almost snatching the reins of the Republican's horse from Hortense, he swung into the saddle and, collecting his own beast, set off towards the trees, leaving her to follow. At his behaviour her own temper flared. Damn him! She'd just saved his life! She was just brooding on his ingratitude when she realised that he had referred to her as a woman, and she cursed him again for allowing her to continue with her charade. No wonder there were times when he had seemed so amused!

When they were once more in the shelter of the woods Raoul dismounted. Hortense watched in fulminating silence as he took the saddle off the horse he was riding and replaced it with his own. His movements were brisk and jerky, she noticed, revealing a barely suppressed rage. Tossing the spare tackle under a bush, he mounted again and, gathering up the reins of his own horse, set off without saying a word.

Hortense glowered at his broad, stiff back and tried to sustain her own anger. As usual the emotion had flared in her and then just as quickly died away, and she found the silence that stretched between them horribly constraining.

'Have you had your horse long?' she finally asked when she could stand it no longer.

'He went through the Austrian campaign with me.'

'You were a soldier?'

He glanced at her coldly. 'Yes; a few weeks ago I was wearing the blue uniform you so despise.'

'A Republican!'

Raoul saw the horror in her face and cursed himself for letting his true feelings show.

'No,' he snapped, 'merely a soldier for France. I was in the army before the Revolution, and until recently I had no reason to get out. No doubt you would have approved of me when I was all decked out in white!'

Ignoring his sneer, Hortense asked curiously, 'Is that why you wouldn't let me shoot that man?'

He shrugged. 'I just don't like killing for killing's sake.'

It was a strange attitude for a soldier, she thought, and for the first time realised that he was not so wholeheartedly Royalist as she. It was just as well she hadn't mentioned the fortune she was carrying. In spite of the fact that she felt drawn to him, she had the uncomfortable feeling that he was not all he seemed.

When they came out of the woods beside a wide river the sun was already low in the sky, and Raoul suggested that they make camp. Hortense was disappointed, hoping to push on and reach Cholet, but he refused to continue after dark. He had further to travel, he insisted, and he was stiff and sore from his fall.

Together they worked to make themselves as comfortable as possible. While Hortense collected wood for a fire Raoul lashed some larger branches together to make a rough shelter. Then, taking his musket, he went off into the woods to hunt for a rabbit.

With nothing else to do, Hortense wandered down to the river. Although the sun was beginning to set, it was still quite warm. She felt hot and dirty and the gold-tinted water looked particularly inviting. Glancing back at the campsite to make sure that Raoul was nowhere around, she quickly removed her clothes. She knew it would have been safer to find a more secluded spot, but she dared not wander too far from her saddle-bag.

The water was cold and she gasped as she edged in gradually, then, when it was just lapping her breasts, lowered herself to swim. She splashed about for a few minutes and ducked her head to rinse her hair. She was so engrossed in her pleasure, in the feel of the cold water like silk against her skin, that she failed to notice Duchambray strolling back along the riverbank.

Raoul was feeling happy and relaxed, enjoying the warmth of the sun on his face and the satisfaction of a successful hunt. Catching sight of the girl, he stopped dead in his tracks, momentarily mesmerised by the enchanting picture she presented. Her skin was as pale and smooth as alabaster, and the setting sun had turned her hair to molten gold. He knew he shouldn't stand and watch, but he just didn't seem able to draw his eyes from her lovely young body.

When she stood up and turned unwittingly towards him he felt a fierce throb of desire. Her eyes met his accusingly as she modestly lowered herself back into the water, but not before he had noticed the soft white fullness of her breasts. Feeling like a child who had been caught stealing sweets, he decided to brazen it out, and sauntered over to her as if it were the most natural thing in the world.

'What are you doing here?' she demanded, the colour rushing to her face. 'I thought you'd be ages yet.'

He grinned and held up his kill. 'The rabbit was most obliging.' Placing it on the bank, he began to unbutton his shirt.

Hortense could hardly believe what he was doing. 'Stop that! You can't possibly come in! If you were a gentleman you'd go away.'

As he removed his shirt he studied her with obvious amusement, liking the fire he saw in her grey eyes. Hortense hissed in exasperation and bit back an oath. By now the water was freezing. Her toes were numb and her calves were beginning to cramp from crouching low enough to keep the water level with her chin.

'I can see you're not going to give me the pleasure of watching you get out,' he chuckled. 'I suppose I'd better turn my back before you turn completely blue. Here!' He tossed his shirt on to the bank near her. 'You can use this to dry yourself. I don't want you catching pneumonia.'

Moving away to wait under a nearby tree, he assiduously kept his back turned, and a nice back it was too, Hortense thought; broad and smooth, with a beautifully marked indentation running down his spine.

Aware that she could not remain in the water forever, she struggled up on to the bank, praying that he would not turn around. As she wiped herself briskly on the shirt she noticed that it still held the heat of his body. It smelt slightly of sweat too, yet, rather than offending her, his scent was pleasing to her. As soon as she had buttoned her shirt and breeches she called out to him.

His blue eyes studied her appreciatively as he walked towards her across the grass. Stopping in front of her, he reached out to smooth her cheek. 'There's no way you could pass as a boy. I've known you were a female from the very beginning. Don't you think it's time you told me who you really are?'

'I'm Hortense Claviere,' she admitted. 'Henri's cousin. As I was travelling alone it seemed safer to dress as a boy.'

He nodded consideringly. 'Yes, I thought that was who you must be. Henri doesn't have many relatives, and you certainly don't speak like a peasant. Besides, we visited Château Claviere a couple of times when I was growing up, and I think I can recall you. You were a skinny little thing, all legs and hair.' He grinned. 'That's certainly changed.'

Hortense smiled, remembering that particular summer, one of many she had spent growing up on her uncle's estate. Henri had been like a brother to her, and her aunt, until her death, had tried to substitute for the mother who had died giving birth to her. Even when, at the age of fourteen, Hortense had gone to live with her father in Paris she had continued to think of the château as her home and to regard herself as Vendean. Henri owned the estate now, her uncle having died two years before, but she knew she would be made just as welcome. In his letters he had often urged her to return, and only the love she had felt for her father had kept her in the capital.

'I thought you insufferably arrogant,' she confided to Raoul. 'You refused to play with us younger children and spent all day fishing with one of the men.'

His smile was charming, not so much in itself but in

the warmth it brought to his eyes and the way it softened the lean lines of his face. 'So you remember me too.'

'Yes, you're the Duchambray. . .' She stopped, appalled by what she had been going to say.

'Yes,' he answered drily, the sparkle disappearing from his eyes, 'I'm the Duchambray bastard. I've been aware of the fact since I was five, and my cousin and uncle never let me forget it.'

'I'm sorry,' she admitted candidly. 'I think none the less of you because of it. I didn't mean to insult you. It's just what everyone called you.'

He shrugged and, pushing his hands into his pockets, walked back to the water. Picking up a pebble, he skimmed it expertly across the pool before sitting down on a wide moss-covered boulder. Much to his annoyance, the memories came flooding back. All too vividly he remembered his cousin's taunts and the resentment he had felt at being denied a father. That resentment had increased tenfold when he had finally discovered why his parents had never wed. He felt little for his father and had loved his mother, yet he could sympathise with Beaulieu, whom he saw as a victim of the pernicious class system that had been stifling the country. Yes, he reminded himself fiercely, the Revolution was the best thing that had ever happened to France.

As Hortense moved hesitatingly to sit beside him she resisted the urge to run her hand across his bowed head.

'I can remember your uncle and cousin too,' she confessed after a while, 'and I didn't much like them. Philippe used to try and lord it over Henri simply because Ramboulard was so much bigger than Château Claviere.'

'That would be just like him.' He shrugged. 'They are both dead now you know. Philippe was killed in the recent fighting, and my uncle died of a heart attack last year. That leaves only Paul and Grandmère.'

'I don't really remember Paul.'

'That's not surprising; he was scarcely out of leading strings when we used to visit Henri. He's more than a dozen years younger than I; only eighteen and not really up to running Ramboulard.'

'So you are going home to help him,' she added with sudden insight, 'in spite of the fact that you don't really want to.'

He sighed deeply before turning his head to look at her, disconcerted that she could read him so well. He was going to have to be extremely careful when he was in her company. In fascination he watched the sunlight play across her face, casting the curve of her jaw and her delicate nose into shadow. The fiery strands of her hair looked like silk, and he wondered if they would feel as soft. He was losing perspective, he realised with a feeling of panic; in fact, his sense of purpose had been threatened since the moment they had met.

'I've never felt so ambivalent about anything,' he surprised himself by admitting. 'I both love and hate the place.'

The sympathy and understanding he saw in her face made him feel extremely guilty. He knew he was attracted to her but he didn't want to like her. He couldn't afford to when their aims and ideologies were so far apart. He had a job to do and he refused to let her distract him, yet he couldn't remember when he had felt so drawn to a woman. He hardly knew her and yet he wanted to throw her down on the grass and take her there and then.

'I think I'd like a swim too,' he said rather abruptly, standing and moving away from her in an attempt to shatter the disconcerting effect she was having on him. 'Perhaps you'd better make yourself scarce.'

His sudden withdrawal puzzled Hortense. One moment he seemed prepared to open his heart to her, and the next he had pulled back behind an emotional wall. She had always liked to know exactly where she stood with people, and his capricious nature irritated her. Returning to the shelter, she busied herself making a fire and tried to ignore the splashing coming from behind her. All too quickly he joined her. With his hair still wet and without his shirt he presented a perfect picture of male vitality.

She had seldom seen a man wearing so little and could scarcely draw her eyes away as he knelt down beside her and began preparing their meal. She was fascinated by his strong masculine beauty, by the pleasing symmetry and hardness of his body. His chest was firmly padded with muscle, as were his shoulders and arms, and his flesh had a smoothly sculptured look. The dark hair on his chest was not thick but tapered invitingly down to his belt, and she wondered whether it would feel as soft as it appeared. In fact, he was altogether too attractive for her peace of mind.

With the meal finished and the shadow lengthening they began to think of settling down for the night. As they spread their blankets out inside the makeshift shelter she was all too well aware of his proximity, and when she accidentally brushed against his bare side the contact seemed to burn.

Sharing her discomfort, Raoul muttered something about a last walk and, collecting his still damp shirt, left her to get ready alone. Returning to the river, he stripped off his clothes and swam until he was ready to drop, knowing it was the only way he would be able to banish the image of her deliciously naked body from his mind.

They resumed their journey early the following morning and passed through Cholet before the town was really awake. They were too far west now to have anything to fear from the Republicans, but it was some miles before they saw any Vendean troops and then it was only at a distance.

It was another mild and sunny day. Hortense found the smell of the hedgerows and the sounds of the crickets marvellously familiar, and she wondered if Raoul, too, was experiencing the restorative sensation of coming home. Noon found them passing the three windmills that topped the hill just outside les Herbiérs. It was a superb vantage point and they were able to look out across the surrounding countryside for miles. Away to the north-west they could just make out part of an army bivouacked beside a wood.

'More Vendeans,' Raoul muttered unnecessarily, standing in his stirrups and squinting into the distance. When he turned to face Hortense his eyes were shadowed with concern. 'With the Republic bringing up reinforcements there's going to be some pretty heavy fighting and, from what I can see, this area is going to be right in the thick of it! You certainly picked a fine time to return home.'

Hortense was a little disconcerted by the bitterness and frustration she sensed in him. She knew it was partly due to his family situation, but there was more to it than that. He resented the fighting too fiercely. She would have put this down to cowardice, but, having seen him face mounted soldiers with nothing but an empty musket, she knew it couldn't possibly be that.

Heading down the hill, they entered the small town and stopped at an inn for something to eat. While the landlord was serving them they asked for news of the war. At first the man was a little reticent, but once Hortense had given her family name he visibly relaxed and chattered away quite freely.

Things had been going well throughout the summer, he informed them, but a couple of weeks ago the Royalists had suffered a severe defeat at Luçon. A man passing through yesterday had insisted that Republican troops were in Nantes and that Monsieur Charette was headed north to prevent their advance. Hopefully he would be able to teach those outsiders a thing or two.

'The Republican regiment you are talking about are the Mayençais,' Raoul commented dispassionately between mouthfuls of veal pie. 'They are well disciplined and ruthless. Charette won't find them easy to defeat.'

Hortense glared at him then sighed unhappily. Luçon, Nantes, Saumur—the Republicans were massing at the three points of a triangle with the wooded area of the Vendée at its centre. Things didn't look good, and she grudgingly admitted it.

'What did you expect?' Raoul asked, more harshly than he'd intended. 'The Republic can't afford to let the Vendée defy it. Now that things are easier on its frontiers it's going to attack with everything it's got. Kleber, Haxo, Marceau, Travot—some of its best generals have been sent here; generals of great experience who served before the Revolution.'

'But we have some excellent generals too,' the innkeeper protested. 'The Marquis de Bonchamps is a brilliant tactician in spite of the fact he gave up his military career. De Lescure too, is very able; and then there is le Chevalier de Royand. Having spent most of his life as a soldier, he is the most experienced of all. As for Charette, they say his men are more like brigands than soldiers, but he always fights well. . . And what of you, *messieurs*? Will you be joining our army? The Vendée needs all her sons now.'

'It's what I came home for,' Hortense answered, living up to her boy's disguise.

The innkeeper glanced questioningly at Raoul.

'Yes,' he replied, with a marked lack of enthusiasm, 'I shall be joining the army too.'

The innkeeper nodded. 'If I thought my wife could manage here I would join up myself.'

Raoul made no comment, and Hortense was still feeling oddly disappointed in him when they resumed their journey and headed out of town. Now the road was familiar and she was filled with a pleasurable anticipation, knowing she was only a mile or two from home. When they reached the fork in the road where their paths diverged she pulled up to take her leave of him, but instead of stopping he turned left towards Château Claviere.

'Having come this far,' he informed her, 'I intend to see you right to your door.'

The road narrowed until it was no more than a track, with the trees on either side of it meeting overhead to form a cool tunnel. The horses' hoofs were silent on the moss-covered ground, and the only sounds were those of birds in the hedgerow and small scuttling animals disturbed by the passage of humans. Of one accord, the travellers did not speak but let the peace and tranquillity of the place wrap around them like a rejuvenating blanket.

There was no evidence of the château until the ancient arched gateway opened up unexpectedly on their right. Only then was the house visible. Built of muted grey stone, it somehow looked as if it had grown there along with the bushes and trees. It was not a large place, for the Clavieres were only small landowners, but Raoul had always envied its rustic tranquillity. Laughter and love had been apparent there, and even now it seemed to ooze from every stone. But there were changes. The gardens, which he remembered as being so well cared for, now looked slightly overgrown. The main doors were in need of a coat of paint and a couple of tiles were missing from the single rounded tower.

For a moment Raoul studied the girl, enjoying the

delicate curve of her cheek and proud tilt of her chin. He was unexpectedly moved by her silent appreciation of the house, and felt unwilling to disturb her.

'Well, brat,' he muttered, half hoping that the teasing term would make her seem less of a woman, 'I suppose I'd better be on my way.'

She drew her eyes reluctantly away from the panorama in front of her and smiled at him. 'Surely you'll come in?'

'If I do I won't reach Ramboulard before dark. Remember me to Henri.'

She took a deep breath, unaccountably reluctant to let him depart. 'Will I see you again?'

He nodded. 'I'll ride over in a few days.'

When he turned his horse away she called after him. 'Raoul, will you really be joining the Vendeans?'

His smile was wry and a little sad. 'I expect so.'

She shook her head as she watched him ride away, not at all sure what to make of him. Somehow he reminded her of a flickering fire, always changing; being close to him could be warm and satisfying, or it could bring pain. He was lonely, she realised, and, in spite of the arrogance with which he carried himself, oddly vulnerable. He was obviously intelligent, possessing a political tolerance she did not share, but there was something else too—not exactly a lack of honesty but a determination not to reveal too much of himself. She wished fervently that he wasn't so damnably attractive; that she didn't feel so ridiculously protective towards him. Dear heaven, but they had only been together for a couple of days! If she felt like this now, how would she feel later?

# CHAPTER TWO

HORTENSE stood in the kitchen doorway, savouring with the delight of a returned wanderer the scene before her. The air was fragrant with the smell of baking bread, musky with the scent of spices, and for a moment she was transported back to her childhood. How many times had she stood in that same doorway hoping to scrounge a tasty titbit?

At the scrubbed table in the centre of the flagged floor the cook was preparing the midday meal, while Marie Claviere busied herself filling a pitcher with freshly squeezed lemonade. A fire glowed and flickered in the ancient hearth that had a blackened oven beside it, and skimmers, ladles, skillets and pans, many of them burnished copper, hung from racks around the walls. On the broad mantelpiece stood spice jars and a salt box, while flitches of ham and curing pheasants hung down from hooks in the rough plastered ceiling.

'Oh, Marie,' Hortense spoke her thoughts aloud, 'it's so good to be back here.'

Marie Claviere lifted her fair head and smiled. She was a charming woman, as gentle as she was beautiful. Henri had fallen in love with her when he was just nineteen and married her as soon as he was able. That had been more than six years ago, and since then his only regret had been her inability to bear him a child. Yesterday Marie had confided to Hortense that she thought she was pregnant. It was too soon to tell her husband in case she later had to disappoint him, but she desperately hoped it was so. From time to time she would get a faraway look in her soft brown eyes, and the other girl would know exactly what she was thinking.

Henri had been away from home when Hortense had first arrived at the château, but Marie had welcomed her warmly and, in the few days since she had been there, the two of them had become firm friends. With Henri's return the peace of the château had been shattered, for he had brought with him nearly a hundred men, untrained but willing to risk everything in the Vendean cause. It seemed to Hortense that they trained incessantly in the field beside the château and, watching them, she could not help comparing their enthusiasm to the apparent reluctance of Raoul Duchambray. In fact, it was a source of irritation to her that she should think of that man so often.

Placing the pitcher of lemonade and half a dozen glasses on a tray, she went out of the back door and walked sedately across the cobbled courtyard. Instead of continuing on to the small, formal garden she turned left towards the gateway that led into the neighbouring field. A young peasant, leaning negligently against the wall on the far side of the gate, moved swiftly to open it for her and, smiling her thanks, she headed across the grass, completely missing the look of appreciation that followed her. In her green riding skirt and neat white blouse, and with the sunlight burnishing her curls, she presented a charming picture. In fact they were the only clothes she had brought with her from Paris, and she had been forced to borrow from Marie while the village seamstress was making her some other garments.

Skirting the tents and a group of men being instructed in the use of the bayonet, she headed towards the corner of the field where she had last seen Henri. He was talking to two men who had their backs to her, and when he saw her he waved. Although he was not a tall man, Hortense thought he looked dashing in his green uniform coat with the sacred heart emblazoned on its pocket. It complemented his brown hair and eyes. He said something to his companions, and the taller of the two turned to look at her. Hortense felt her heart give a strange little flip-flop when she recognised Raoul Duchambray.

'You're looking well, Hortense. Being here must agree with you.' His smile was warm, but she thought he looked tired; much more tired than he had on their journey. 'Let me present my cousin Paul,' he continued.

The Marquis, a fair, fragile-looking youth, no taller than herself, bowed awkwardly over her hand. His blue eyes were the same colour as Raoul's, she noticed, yet somehow lacking that intrinsic fire. His smile was hesitant but rather sweet, making her realise that, Marquis though he was, the Duchambray arrogance had quite passed this young man by.

'Would you like some lemonade?' she asked. 'I went to fetch it for Henri but there's plenty for everyone.'

Taking the tray from her, her cousin gestured towards a grassy bank. Raoul removed his coat and spread it out for her to sit on. The gallant gesture surprised her, but the challenging look in his eyes dared her to make any comment.

'I haven't thanked you yet for seeing this hoyden home,' Henri told him as they all settled down on the grass.

Raoul smiled as he accepted a glass of lemonade and leaned back on one elbow. 'I'm sure she would have managed on her own.' He glanced at Paul. 'Did I tell you she actually shot me?'

Henri nearly choked on his own drink as Hortense answered, 'It was his own fault. Only a fool rushes someone with a gun.'

'I don't see it as foolish,' Raoul replied teasingly. 'You admitted you were in two minds of shooting me. I don't think I've ever met such a bloodthirsty woman.'

'That's hardly surprising,' Henri added, 'considering what she was carrying in her saddle-bags. My uncle had converted most of his fortune into gems. His last wish was for Hortense to bring them home to be used in the war effort. It was generous and characteristically idealistic of him, but they belong to Hortense and I refuse to accept more than a quarter of them.'

'I've told you, I don't want them!' Hortense snapped. 'If you won't take them then I'll give them to one of our generals.'

'You never said a word,' Raoul accused, realising, with a surprising lack of bitterness, that, in seeing her safely home, he had unwittingly aided the Vendean cause.

'I didn't know you well enough,' Hortense replied. She did not add that she still wasn't quite sure of him.

'Henri's right,' he told her. 'Don't risk it all on the war.'

'I would give everything I have to defeat the Republicans!' she snapped, her eyes flashing. 'Everything! They murdered my father. Not that I expect you to understand!'

An awkward silence followed her outburst, and then Raoul spoke quietly. 'I'm sorry, Hortense. I had no idea.'

His kindness made her feel like a spoiled child; even worse, she was experiencing a strong desire to cry. She hadn't really had time to grieve properly, and now she wanted to scream at the injustice of it all. Her gentle father had never harmed anyone.

Swallowing the burning lump in her throat, she struggled for control, determined not to disgrace herself. 'Papa wanted you to have the money, Henri. He wanted to feel that he had done something to help, to atone, because at first he supported the Revolution. It was his last wish and I want to see it fulfilled. Besides, if the worst happens I still have that property in Louisiana. Nobody was interested in buying that.'

'All right,' Henri replied, wrapping his arm around her and giving her a rough hug, 'I'll think about it some more.' Hoping to change the subject, he glanced at Paul and asked, 'How's your grandmother today?'

'She's dying,' the boy admitted. 'The doctor thinks it will only be a matter of days. Raoul sat with her through the night, but she seemed little better this morning.'

So that accounted for his haggard appearance, Hortense thought, both surprised and touched by the information. She hadn't expected him to be quite that caring.

'I was hoping you would see your way to joining us,' Henri said, turning to Raoul. 'My men and I are frighteningly inexperienced; but I can see that now is a bad time.'

'Things are difficult at the moment. It's not just Grandmère. There's a lot to be sorted out at Ramboulard.' Raoul tried to sound sorry but, in truth, he was glad of an excuse to postpone his involvement with the Vendeans. He didn't relish the part he had to play and would just as soon not take advantage of a man as decent as Henri Claviere. Yet some sort of commitment was obviously expected of him.

'If I get the time I'll ride over and help,' he finally promised, 'but as yet I cannot be tied.'

That seemed to satisfy Henri. 'I understand,' he replied, 'and I'll be grateful for anything you can do.' He nodded towards his men. 'What do you think of them?'

Raoul placed his glass on the tray and climbed slowly to his feet. 'Let me have a closer look and I'll tell you.'

Hortense watched as the two men walked across the field. Raoul was almost a head taller than Henri but they both moved with the same lithe grace. Every so often they stopped to converse with the men, and she couldn't help noticing how at ease he appeared. As he laughed and joked all his arrogance seemed to have deserted him, leaving only a man who appeared confident and concerned.

'It's done him good to get out,' commented Paul. 'Since he's been home, Grandmère's been rather clinging. She never used to be like that, but I suppose she's old and she's had more than her share of grief over the last year.'

'I'm sorry about your brother,' Hortense told him.

His blue eyes darkened and he surprised her by saying, 'I'm not. Philippe was a pig. He had a nasty sadistic streak and I think that even Grandmère was beginning to notice it. He mistreated the servants and used to ride his horses into the ground. I suppose I should be thankful that, on the whole, he ignored me. Raoul was the only one who stood up to him and he hadn't much success with my mother and father so firmly on my brother's side. I wasn't surprised when he left to join the army.'

He plucked viciously at a tuft of grass and mangled it between his fingers. 'Do you know, he was the only one who ever had any time for me? My mother and father didn't even like me. Grandmère was obsessed with Ramboulard, and Aunt Felice, Raoul's mother, died soon after I was born. I can't tell you how glad I am to have him here. I don't want him rushing off to join our army.'

It occurred to Hortense then that Paul was rather young for his age. Not only did he lack the Duchambray arrogance but also that core of steel. He never mentioned joining the army himself, and yet he was quite old enough, even if he did look too soft and fragile to fight. The Duchambrays had more to lose than most landlords, she thought bitterly, and yet they seemed all too willing to let the others do their fighting for them.

When Raoul and Henri returned the four of them went up to the house to see Marie. Raoul had never met her before and, like most men, soon fell under her spell. What did surprise Hortense was the irrational jealousy she felt. He smiled and said all that was appropriate, exhibiting a surprisingly polished charm, and she felt miserable. He was treating Marie as he would any beautiful woman, yet he still seemed to see her as a boy, alternately teasing her and ignoring her completely.

When it was time for the Duchambrays to take their leave he paused in the doorway. 'I'll ride over when I can, Henri. I'm not promising anything, but I'll try to make time.'

For a moment his eyes lingered on Hortense but his expression was quite unreadable. In fact, he was calling himself all kinds of a fool. He had spoken, hoping to gain her approval, yet knew it was a desire that could only lead to disillusionment and pain. She was his enemy, for God's sake, and if she knew of his duplicity would denounce him without a qualm!

Hortense felt oddly restless after he had gone and found it impossible to settle to anything. Somehow he kept intruding on her thoughts. She accepted that she was attracted to him, but it was more than that, and she was annoyed because she could not quite put her finger on what it was about him that so disturbed her. She only knew that she was looking forward to seeing him again and that, without him, the day seemed rather dull.

As things turned out she was denied his company for quite some time. The following morning a message arrived from Ramboulard informing the Clavieres that Lisette Duchambray had died in the night and that Raoul was tied up with administering her estate. The funeral was held at the end of the week, and Henri and Marie, together with Hortense, drove over to attend it. There was a massive turn-out of peasants as well as friends of the family, and afterwards the more élite went back to Ramboulard, where Raoul and young Paul acted as charming, if somewhat sombre hosts.

Hortense watched them both in concern. Paul looked as though he had been crying and, on more than one occasion, she saw his cousin give his shoulder a reassuring squeeze. Raoul did everying that was expected and necessary, but he looked desperately tired as though he had not slept well for days. She could not help wondering why he seemed so deeply affected when he had not been home for years. Unlike others, she could not condemn him, for she knew how difficult his life at Ramboulard had been. More than once his eyes stared out across the sun-washed garden, and she had the distinct impression that he was seeing more than the fading roses and hydrangeas.

There was a noticeable lack of young men at the gathering, most of them being absent with the Grand Army, and automatically the talk turned to the war. Henri, because he was currently serving under Bonchamps, was called upon to verify the news of a Vendean victory at Torfou.

'It's quite true,' he informed them all with a broad smile. 'I received word this morning. My general thinks that one final, concerted push will finish the Mayençais troops. In about four days I shall be marching to join him.'

'Henri!' Marie exclaimed, her lovely face paling at this unexpected revelation. 'Why didn't you say something before?'

He did at least have the grace to look suitably apologetic, but Hortense could see that he was eager to march. He was so excited by the prospect that he could not conceive that his wife might feel otherwise.

'I'm sorry, my dear,' he told her. 'I was going to tell

you when we got home. At least you'll have Hortense to
keep you company.'

'I didn't think your men were ready,' commented
Raoul quietly.

Henri shrugged. 'They will just have to make up in
enthusiasm what they lack in skill.'

'That's the spirit!' one of the older men exclaimed,
then turned pointedly towards Raoul. 'Although a
number of them followed Philippe, there are still plenty
of able-bodied men around here. All they need is someone to lead them. You took your time coming home,
boy. I hope you'll act honourably now.'

Raoul's jaw clenched as he bit back a cutting retort.
He thought Monsieur Rolland was a doddering old fool
and he ached to tell him so. The room was suddenly
uncomfortably quiet as his neighbours waited for his
reply and, for a moment, he was tempted to tell them all
to go to the devil. Even if he had wholeheartedly
supported the Vendeans, he would still have resented
Rolland's attitude, having seen too much of war to
approach it enthusiastically.

His glance swept the room before finally coming to
rest on Hortense. The look she sent him was half
sympathy, half challenge, and he knew that to prevari-
cate further would place his whole mission in danger.
For days he had been struggling to maintain his Republican convictions but, reason as he might, he could not
quite kill the reluctant sympathy he felt for his neighbours. They were not like the majority of landowners in
France, treating the peasants as if they were beyond
contempt; yet the fact remained: the attitude in the
Vendée was the exception rather than the rule. In the
rest of the country the people had suffered badly beneath
the aristocracy's yoke.

God, how he abhorred the old regime! Not only had it
denied him a father, but it stifled ability. He'd seen

enough of that in the army, where able officers had been passed over in favour of those with high titles and no aptitude or intelligence. Ultimately it was the men who suffered, who had to endure death and defeat because they were commanded by imbeciles.

Suddenly he was uncomfortably aware of the attention he was drawing and, for one heart-stopping moment, wondered if those around him had been able to read his mind.

'I'll see how many men I can recruit and join you the day after tomorrow,' he told Henri. 'We can ride north together.'

This statement was greeted with applause, and he smiled thinly in acceptance of it. He seemed to warm more to the idea when Henri went across to embrace him, but Hortense suspected that she was not the only one to notice his restraint.

This was confirmed when Monsieur Rolland leant close to her and whispered, 'Anyone would think he was afraid. Bad blood, you know.'

'No, I do not know!' she snapped, unconsciously echoing Raoul's thoughts of the old gentleman. 'I've had first-hand experience of his courage. Perhaps, as a soldier, he appreciates the danger more than most.'

Turning her back on the man, she stared out of the french windows, across the impressive grounds. A hedge divided a formal rose garden, in itself the size of Château Claviere, from a vast area of shady walks and fountains.

'Quite spectacular, isn't it?' Raoul muttered, coming to stand at her elbow. 'Were you wondering what the Duchambrays did to deserve it all?'

'I was more concerned with how you've managed to maintain it. Most of our servants have gone to war.'

His eyes narrowed at the hinted criticism, but instead of snapping back at her he sighed. 'That old fool Rolland is right; there are still many able-bodied men around here. Not surprisingly, few of them liked Philippe enough to follow him to war.'

'But they'll ride with you?'

He nodded seriously. 'Yes, as a matter of fact, they've already asked me to lead them. I only hope they know what they are getting into.' He glanced at the autumn sunshine. 'It's pleasant outside. Would you care for a short walk?'

Hortense considered the matter. She desperately wanted to get away from the oppressive gathering but wasn't sure she should go off with him on her own. In view of the time they had already spent together, bothering about propriety seemed a little ridiculous, but, for Marie's sake, she didn't want people to talk.

'Why the frown?' he asked, running a finger lightly across her brow.

'Won't your guests think it rude if you disappear?'

'That's the least of my troubles,' he admitted honestly. 'Most of them already consider me quite beyond the pale. But, for the sake of your reputation, we'll stay within sight of the house. Come on, at least I can talk to you.'

Opening the french windows, he guided her out on to the terrace, then, slipping her arm through his, led her down some steps into the rose garden. In spite of the lateness of the season, there were still plenty of blooms and the air was fragrant with them. Raoul absently reached out a tanned hand to touch one of the flowers and it crumbled beneath his fingers.

'Grandmère used to love this garden,' he confided. 'She supervised the planting of some of these bushes when she was just a girl.'

Glancing at his face, Hortense thought he looked as if he was carrying the cares of the world.

Unconsciously her fingers curled around his arm. 'You're looking tired; haven't you been sleeping well?'

He smiled, gratified by her concern. 'I've had things on my mind and Paul has needed a lot of support.'

He didn't add how worried he was about the boy. Paul had always been rather timid but not so unhealthily clinging and demanding. He still wasn't really reconciled to Raoul's joining the Vendeans and tonight would make no end of excuses and objections.

'If you're so worried about him who don't you tell everyone to go to the devil?' Hortense suggested. 'Someone else could lead your men.'

'Isn't that a change of heart?' he asked wryly.

'I suppose so,' she admitted, 'but I can see what he's like. I can understand why you feel so protective of him.'

'If he were stronger physically I would take him with me. It could even be the making of him. As it is, he wouldn't last five minutes. There have been other problems too.' He was silent for a moment as he glanced back at the impressive house. Hortense waited patiently for him to continue. She sensed his need to talk, and knew it would be best not to hurry him.

'I don't want this to go any further,' he continued, 'but Philippe left his finances in a terrible mess. He'd been gambling and he'd made some disastrous investments. Monsieur Saurin and I have been working night and day to set things right. Thankfully we seem to have sorted it out. It will mean selling some land, but if he's sensible Paul ought to be able to manage. I'm only grateful that Grandmère died without realising how bad things were.'

Hortense was swamped with sympathy and something more—a vast, overwhelming relief. Now she could see why he had been so reluctant to commit himself to the Vendean cause. How awful it must have been to have people pressing him when all his thoughts had been centred elsewhere.

Raoul saw the understanding in her eyes and felt a

complete fraud. What he had told her was perfectly true but it was his mission that had been the cause of his losing sleep.

They walked on, saying little, but Hortense was acutely conscious of his presence at her side. He was so tall, so devastatingly handsome, and yet it was the depth and kindness she sensed in him that drew her most of all. Raoul sighed and for the first time in days felt some of the tension drain away from him. There was peace in the garden, the homely peace of flowers and fountains and singing birds that was like a balm to his over-stretched nerves.

Hortense stepped away from him and bent to sniff at a flower. The sunlit sheen of her hair blended beautifully with the plant's bronze-tipped foliage, and he thought again how lovely she was, and how totally unaware of it. Reaching out, he snapped off a flawless pink bloom and placed it in her hand.

'Thank you.' She smiled shyly up at him and the movement of her neck and hair sent a warm wave surging through him. It was followed almost instantly by something like despair as he realised the impossibility of what he had begun to contemplate.

Hortense too was experiencing a kaleidoscope of emotions—pleasure, hope, embarrassment, fear—and she could come to terms with none of them. She only knew that here was a man who could come to mean so much to her, more even than a friend. She had seen the warmth in his eyes as he had given her the flower, yet now he was drawing away from her again, distancing himself in more than a physical sense.

'I think we'd better be getting back,' he told her in a voice devoid of all emotion.

As they turned towards the steps Paul came out on to the terrace, his expression one close to panic.

'I didn't know where to find you,' he complained to

Raoul. 'I've been looking for you everywhere. It's not proper for you to go off with Hortense like this.'

Raoul's eyes narrowed, revealing his irritation, but he answered pleasantly enough. 'We were always in sight, and what you want cannot be that important.'

'The cook wished to know if anyone will be dining with us tonight, and I didn't know how to answer her.'

'Then why not ask our guests and find out?' Raoul told him with strained patience. 'I suspect most people will want to return home before dark, but it is only polite to issue the invitation.'

"Oh!' The boy smiled uncertainly. 'I wasn't sure if that would be all right.'

'It's your house now, Paul,' his cousin explained. 'You don't need anyone's permission to invite guests.'

As expected, most of the mourners left soon after this, the Clavieres among them. Once they were settled in the coach Henri grinned across at his cousin and asked, 'Do I sense romance in the air?'

Hortense felt herself blushing and promptly told him that he was mistaken. She was fond of Henri but she knew how he could tease.

'Raoul is a charming man and extremely attractive,' Marie commented, 'but materially he has little to offer. I doubt that will weigh with you, Hortense, but you should bear it in mind.'

'It seems to me that it is more a question of whether he is the kind of man to settle down,' Henri continued thoughtfully. 'Don't misunderstand me, Horry; I like the fellow, I always have, but he's incredibly self-sufficient and has always kept his feelings to himself. It's a trait that appears even more pronounced in him now than it was when he was younger.'

'There is nothing between us,' Hortense protested. 'At least not in that way, but, for what it's worth, I think his self-sufficiency is stretched a little thin. He's lonely and I would like to be his friend.'

The only trouble is, she thought wryly, you shouldn't actually desire your friends, and that was certainly what she did when she was around him.

Later that evening, when Paul had retired to bed, Raoul once more went for a walk in the grounds. Although it was a dry night, the moon was playing hide and seek with the gathering cloud, and there were times when it was difficult for him to see his way. He walked purposefully, knowing his destination, and yet his thoughts were troubled. Conflict raged within him, and he hated what he was going to do.

When he came to the old summer-house beside the boundary wall he slowed his pace, his eyes searching the darkness.

A shadow appeared in the doorway of the building and a voice called out, 'Is that you, Duchambray?'

Raoul had not been quite sure whom he was going to meet. He had expected a stranger but had the distinct impression that he had seen the man before. There was something vaguely familiar about the narrow sloping shoulders and thin face with its long jaw.

'It's a dark night for a meeting,' he said, using the agreed introduction.

The man gave a grunt of satisfaction. 'You're late, brother,' he complained. 'I've been waiting in the cold for nearly an hour.'

'Then let's go inside and conclude our business,' Raoul snapped. He had recognised his companion as Michel Saurin, the lawyer's son, and he resented the familiar form of address. He was also suffering from a surprising amount of indignation; the Saurins had been employed, and most lucratively, by the Duchambrays for over thirty years. Raoul could remember Michel as a spotty youth accompanying his father to the château on business, and he decided he had never liked him.

'Have you got anything useful for me?' Saurin asked, stepping back into the darkness.

For a moment Raoul was tempted to tell him nothing. Adjusting his cloak, he stared out at the shadowed trees and wondered why he should feel so resentful and guilty. Hell and damnation, but he didn't want any part of this war!

'Henri Claviere marches to join Bonchamps in a few days and there will be others like him,' he admitted after a moment. 'General Bonchamps is collecting his forces for a last push against the Mayençais. As you are no doubt aware, they are considered some of our best troops, and if he finishes them it will be a severe blow to our morale, not to mention the strategic advantage he will have. You can tell our masters that an offensive in another part of the Vendée might just divert some of our opponents and give the Mayençais a breathing-space.'

'And that's it?' Saurin demanded impatiently.

'It's the best I can do at the moment,' Raoul answered curtly. 'When Claviere marches north I shall be joining him. I will be in a position to discover more then. Somehow I will find a way to pass on anything I find out, but Citizen Carrier will have to understand if my reports are somewhat sporadic.'

'I don't trust you, Duchambray,' the other man replied nastily. 'I'll make no bones about it. In my opinion, you should have been sent to the guillotine. Cross us and it will give me great pleasure to see you dead.'

The darkness concealed the loathing and anger that flashed in Raoul's eyes, but it was quite apparent in his voice.

'Don't threaten me,' he answered coldly, 'not if you value your life. I'd run you through as soon as look at you! As for your opinion, it matters nought! We may have to work together, but as much as possible you are to keep out of my way. I don't like you. I never have!'

Turning abruptly, he walked back into the night, not caring what Saurin might do. He couldn't more adequately have demonstrated his contempt for the man and yet it afforded him no satisfaction. The information he had passed on had been scanty, but he still felt a bitter self-disgust. Responsibility lay like a dark cloud over all his thoughts, and it was forunate that at this point he did not know what a severe blow he had dealt the Vendean cause.

# CHAPTER THREE

THE château grounds seethed with martial activity, the clash of steel on steel punctuated only by the occasional musket volley as the men drilled and trained for battle with the dedication of medieval knights. The time was short and Henri was determined to cram as much experience as possible into this last day.

Hortense watched Raoul as he instructed a group of men on the use of a bayonet. Although the day was cool, he had removed his coat, and his hair was appealingly dishevelled. He was a surprisngly good teacher, answering questions with a patience and humour that did not falter, even when a particularly burly peasant charged him with a force that sent him sprawling in the dirt. In fact he used the incident to demonstrate the superiority of skill over brute force as his own weapon hovered within inches of his assailant's belly.

For a moment anger and frustration clouded the big peasant's face, but Raoul dispelled it with a good-natured grin. 'You're too enthusiastic, Letouc. Use your brain as well as your muscle.'

Finally satisfied, he dismissed the men and sauntered over to where Hortense was standing. She smiled at him but received only a frown in return.

'What's that for?' he asked, gesturing towards her musket.

Her lips twitched in amusement as she registered his disapproval. 'Henri is setting up some targets. I thought I'd practise too. He won't mind, I assure you.'

'Most of the men are already pretty good shots,' he told her curtly, 'but we need to do some more work on the volley. A real battle is quite different from target practice.'

'Then I'll learn that too,' she informed him sharply, walking off to where Henri was setting out a row of up-ended logs.

Raoul swore to himself as his gaze followed her. She was wearing breeches again, and they highlighted the graceful swing of her hips; then he gave a wry smile and shook his head. She had spirit, sure enough, and an appealing lack of guile. It wasn't her fault that he found her so damnably attractive.

He watched her practise her shooting for nearly half an hour and saw the men fall, one by one, under her spell. It wasn't that she flirted with them, and neither did she remain aloof. Instead she treated them with the easy affection of a sister, making them feel that she liked and appreciated them all. She had treated him the same way, he realised, and irrationally wished that it had meant something more. Knowing it was pointless to stand and brood, he moved forward to take charge of the training session.

Hortense was enjoying herself, revelling in a freedom to mix that had been denied her in Paris, and when Raoul began to explain the advantages of the volley over independent fire she remained with the group. She watched in fascination as he ran through the routine of load, fire, clean, with a military precision. He had a gentleman's hands, she noticed, and yet they were tanned and capable-looking.

Loading their muskets with powder but no shot, they doggedly practised the routine until their volleys were no longer ragged and they had reduced their loading time to well under a minute. Finally, beaming with satisfaction, Henri called a halt, declaring that they had done enough if they wanted to be fresh when they marched out in the morning. Leaving the men to their ease, Hortense headed back towards the château and was surprised when Raoul fell into step beside her.

She could not resist glancing up at him, and his eyes narrowed as he studied her. 'I hope you aren't hoping to put your new skills to work.'

'You mean the volley?' she asked innocently, thinking that he was a great deal too astute. When he nodded she admitted, 'No, I don't intend to fight in any battles.'

He wondered why that didn't reassure him. Maybe it was because he was coming to know her too well. 'You won't be going anywhere near the fighting. Henri says you are to remain here as company for Marie.'

'Marie and I have other ideas,' she replied smugly, thinking back to a conversation she'd had with her cousin's wife the previous evening. 'She thinks you need someone to organise the care of the wounded. I admit I didn't relish being left behind, but it was her idea, not mine. She is already gathering together some things she thinks we might need.'

'I don't want you to come,' he declared.

His directness both surprised and disappointed her.

'Why?' she demanded, bracing herself to contest the issue. Henri, she knew, she could easily persuade, but Raoul was an entirely different proposition.

'To answer that I would have to show you the horrors of the battlefield strewn with dead and mutilated bodies,' he replied tightly. 'There are sights to turn the stomach of even the most hardened. You would be better off staying here. You've done your part by bringing Henri the jewels. Leave the nursing to the peasant girls.'

'Because some accident of birth has placed me in a privileged position?' she replied with a sniff of derision. 'Be careful, Raoul; the influence of your illustrious ancestors is showing.'

As she turned to walk away he caught hold of her arm, swinging her back to face him. A flush of anger stained his cheeks and his eyes were as hot and blue as a summer sky. 'Has anyone ever told you that you're too determined for your own good? You've no idea what you're getting into!'

'I have to do something to help,' she snapped. 'Staying at home and wondering what was happening would surely drive me mad. As for Marie, she wants to know that there will be someone to look after Henri if he is hurt. She would be going herself, only this baby is too precious to both of them.'

'I think Henri's a fool if he lets you come with us, and I shall tell him so!'

Hortense glanced pointedly at his hand still curled around her arm and immediately he released her. 'Henri won't stop me,' she informed him coldly. 'He knows that if I don't ride with you then I shall only join another unit.'

Raoul knew when he was beaten and, sighing, shook his head. Looking up into his handsome face, Hortense realised that he was genuinely concerned for her, and almost instantly her anger melted away, to be replaced by a pleasing warmth. Henri had always treated her rather as a brother, and her father had been too vague and scholarly to notice what she was doing, so that it was a novel experience to have someone being protective towards her.

She took special pains dressing for dinner that evening, knowing that Raoul would be there. Marie had generously laid out an assortment of dresses for her to choose from, and she finally settled on an elegant gown of dark blue silk. She brushed her short curls until they shone and, in an uncharacteristic moment of vanity, regretted cutting them. She told herself that the short style would be easier to look after, but that practicality didn't really help. Tonight she wanted to look beautiful, to be as feminine and lovely as Marie, and she wished she were more practised in the art of flirtation. She had never set out to impress a man before, but she desperately wanted Raoul to be attracted to her. She knew he was begining to regard her as a friend, but she wanted so much more from him than that.

After fastening a short string of pearls around her throat she surveyed herself critically in the long mirror. Fortunately she looked a great deal more sophisticated than she felt. Her eyes sparkled with a mixture of satisfaction and anticipation, and, with her pulse a little unsteady, she made her way downstairs.

Raoul and Henri were standing in front of the drawing-room window when she joined them, and her cousin made a noise of approval.

'Quite the little lady,' he teased, raising the glass he was holding to toast her. 'I wonder how long it will last.'

Raoul said nothing, but he smiled engagingly and his blue eyes were full of warmth. When they went into the dining-room it was he who held out her chair for her, and from time to time during the meal she felt him watching her.

He was looking exceptionally handsome in a uniform coat of fine blue wool that complemented the startling colour of his eyes. Like Henri's coat, it had a heart and cross sewn on to the pocket, and when Hortense commented on this he admitted that the coat had once belonged to Philippe.

Marie was surprised by its colour and said as much, for she had expected all officers to wear green, like her husband.

Henri laughed. 'I'm afraid we're not that organised, my sweet. General Bonchamps has tried to put us into uniform—green for the officers and brown for the men— but the other generals are not so concerned about dress. I have seen officers in blue and also black. Roche-Jacquelein even turned up wearing bandanas. Personally I don't think it matters what we wear.'

'There are those who think putting men into uniform is more likely to make them act like soldiers,' Raoul commented. 'Bonchamps may have a point.'

'Mostly it's a question of finance,' Henri replied seriously. 'There just isn't the money to supply provisions and uniforms.'

Hortense certainly wasn't going to let him get away with that. 'Papa's money could help supply both,' she replied tartly.

'You've already persuaded me to take half of it,' Henri snapped, 'and that's against my better judgement. For heaven's sake, Hortense, you're going to need some money yourself!'

Marie, sensing a confrontation, glanced appealingly at Raoul, who deftly changed the subject, asking his friend what he thought of his general's plans. Henri's face glowed with enthusiasm as he detailed what he thought would happen. By comparison, Hortense thought Raoul looked sceptical, and rather sad. The candle-light seemed to accentuate the planes and hollows of his face and his eyes appeared dark and troubled. He ventured no opinion of his own and, once again, she realised that his heart was not really in the coming fight.

Finally, tired of war-talk, Marie introduced another topic and for a while they were all transported back to the time before the conflict. For a soldier Raoul proved to be surprisingly knowledgeable on literature and music, exhibiting a sensitivity that both surprised and intrigued Hortense.

In fact he was enjoying himself, finding his companions intelligent and surprisingly open-minded, considering their station in life. When Henri asked his opinion on Payne's *The Rights of Man*, however, he was once more aware of how important it was for him to stay on his guard. That book, along with Voltaire's novels and his *Lettres Philosophiques*, had been partly responsible for converting him to the Republican cause and, although it might have been wise, he could not bring himself to speak against it.

Surprisingly Henri too expressed a certain amount of sympathy for the ideal of equality. At one time Hortense would probably have agreed with him, for it was a subject her father had often championed, but she had come to loathe anything that smacked of Republicanism. She watched the two men as they talked and was pleased by the obvious friendship growing between them. When Henri reiterated his belief that landowners were responsible for their peasants she nodded approvingly, thinking that if all aristocrats had thought like that then there would have been no Revolution.

Raoul also expressed his agreement, but went on to say that he felt landowners and employers should have a legal obligation to treat their peasants well.

'You sound remarkably Republican when you say that,' she commented sharply.

It was as if a shutter came down behind his eyes; then he smiled and she felt sure she must have imagined it.

'I just don't think the quality of a man's life should be governed by whether he is fortunate enough to be born on Claviere land or on that of another, less fair-minded landlord.'

For some reason his attitude annoyed Hortense, perhaps because he sounded so like her father. 'You mean like the Duchambrays?' some devil prompted her to ask.

Immediately his mouth tightened. 'Yes, like the Duchambrays! I am quite aware of my family's reputation.'

'But you are not at all like them,' Marie told him, flashing Hortense a look of reproach.

Raoul shrugged and smiled bleakly. 'But then, I am

not really a Duchambray. . .and over the years I have come to be thankful for it.'

Once again Hortense was surprised by the rush of protectiveness she felt towards him. She wanted to ask him if he had ever found out whose name he should have carried, but the question was just too intimate. No outsider seemed to know and if the Duchambray family did then they had kept the secret well.

'The men like and respect you,' Henri commented, 'even that giant, Letouc. Did you know that he'd had a run-in with your cousin? Letouc used to be a farrier and loves horses. Apparently he was over at Ramboulard, shoeing a horse, when he saw Philippe take a whip to that black stallion he had. I don't know exactly what happened, but Philippe ended up on his aristocratic backside and Letouc has never been allowed back on Duchambray land.'

Raoul smiled warmly at that, and was just muttering something about having to congratulate the peasant when they were disturbed by a commotion in the hallway. They all turned towards the door as old René, the only manservant remaining at the château, entered in obvious agitation. Behind him came two dusty and extremely impatient peasants.

Before René could speak, one of them, a husky, self-confident fellow with a shock of wheat-coloured hair, pushed past him and asked, 'Is Duchambray here?'

Henri rose from the table, scowling, obviously angered by this show of bad manners, but the peasant looked right past him and at Raoul.

'You must come at once, *monsieur*!' he exclaimed. 'The Republicans are attacking the area around St Fulgent. They have already burned a number of farms and are marching towards Ramboulard.'

The colour drained from Raoul's face and the stem of

the wine glass he was holding snapped under the convulsive pressure of his fingers. Shaken herself, Hortense reached out to ease it from his hand as he froze like a man in a trance.

'Dear God!' he muttered after what seemed like an eternity, climbing to his feet and swaying slightly.

Frowning with concern, Henri reached out a hand to steady him. 'How many men have the Republicans got?'

The peasant shrugged and his older companion admitted, 'We do not know, *monsieur*. Perhaps not that many, but we have no defence. Most of our able-bodied men are either here with you or away with the Army of the Centre and General Royrand. I beg of you, come with us now. There is no time to waste!'

Raoul struggled to gain control over his churning emotions. It was like a nightmare with the added horror of knowing he wasn't going to wake up. Fear, anger and remorse all boiled inside him and he felt physically sickened. Hortense was as stunned by his reaction as she was by the news. She had never seen a man look so stricken.

'I'll get my men,' he finally managed to say, and moved somewhat unsteadily towards the door.

'What about you, *monsieur*?' the young peasant demanded of Henri.

Claviere chewed thoughtfully on his lip; he was in something of a dilemma. Although he was committed to a rendezvous with Bonchamps, every instinct urged him to follow his friend.

'Surely you're not going to let Raoul go without you?' Hortense exclaimed. By now she, too, was on her feet.

'It's not as simple as that, Hortense.' He sighed, then swore an oath he had never before used in the presence of ladies. 'All right,' he told the peasants. 'I'll come, but I must write a letter to General Bonchamps first.'

'You'd better hurry, then,' Hortense snapped, moving towards the door.

Before she had really thought things through she was in her bedroom and changing into her boy's clothes. If Raoul was riding out then she was going with him. If he knew he would obviously protest, but in the darkness it was unlikely that he'd notice her. She was ready in less than five minutes and, after collecting a small package of medical supplies from Marie's bedroom, almost flew down the back stairs.

There was chaos in the courtyard as a number of men appeared, leading their horses. Hortense noticed Raoul in conversation with the two peasants and, giving them a wide berth, slipped off to the stables. By the time she had saddled her horse her cousin too was on the scene, giving orders to the foot soldiers who were to follow later. Hortense waited quietly in the background and a few minutes later, when he and Raoul spurred out of the château grounds, followed by some fifty men, she quietly tagged along behind them.

It was a cool night for September and the moon was almost full, creating silver patterns between the rustling trees. The horses' hoofs pounded along the uneven track. Leather creaked and harnesses jingled as the small contingent moved rapidly through the darkness like spirits of the night.

Hortense was full of a heady excitement and, even after an hour or more of riding, felt not the least bit tired. Coming to a crossroads, Henri called a halt, and she could see him in urgent conversation with Raoul and the two peasants. After a moment they continued on, bearing to the left, but now there was a discernible feeling of tension in the air. About a mile further on, where the road swung down into a shallow valley and across a stone bridge, they halted again, and Henri held up his hand for silence. For a moment they could hear

nothing but the wind gusting and sighing through the
trees, the snuffle and stamp of the horses, and the ripple
of the stream as it curled its way between the stones.
Somewhere in the distance a night bird called, and then,
carried faintly on the wind, came the distant crackle of
musket fire.

Cantering over the narrow bridge, they climbed
slightly then paused again on the low hill-top. Below
them, isolated fires pierced the darkness of the night.
Once more the leaders held a hurried conversation and
then the party divided, Henri turning south with the
peasants and most of his men while Raoul led the
remainder westwards towards Ramboulard. For a
moment Hortense hesitated, but when the two men next
to her joined the Duchambray contingent she did so too.

Leaving the roadway, they continued along a soft,
leaf-strewn track that bordered the woodland. Ten minutes later Raoul again signalled for his men to stop and
in a tense voice told them to load their muskets. Hortense
noticed he wasn't carrying one himself, but he checked
his pistol and then, returning it to his saddle holster,
withdrew his sword. She too primed her pistol and to
her horror found that her hands were trembling. When
the man next to her, unaware of her identity, made a
crude joke, she forced herself to laugh, but it had a
distinctly hollow sound. In fact she wasn't feeling the
least bit humorous and was beginning to wonder if
tagging along had been a terrible mistake.

The woods on their right thinned and then petered
out as they reached the unmarked boundary of the
Duchambray domain. Hortense thought she could see
the château ahead and to her right, but, before she could
be really sure, the leaders had spotted the enemy and
they were all charging forward to engage them.

Jumping or pushing through a sparse hedge, they hit
the unsuspecting Republicans obliquely. Musket fire

rattled, horses whinnied, and through the chaos the girl glimpsed Raoul, charging into the blue-coated infantry, sabre-swinging. Then she too was in the fight. She discharged her pistol and saw her target fall. When another man tried to drag her from her horse she hit out frantically with the empty weapon and felt the sickening thud of metal against bone. The fellow cried out in pain but it was the Vendean next to her who finished him off, running him through with a hand-held bayonet.

Sickened, Hortense closed her eyes and allowed her horse to have its head and carry her out of the conflict. A hoarse cheer went up from the Vendeans as the Republicans turned to flee, and more were ruthlessly cut down from behind. Undoubtedly the Vendeans would have finished off every last man, only Raoul halted them. As he called them together more musket fire sounded in the distance, and their protests died on their lips.

'They're attacking the château!' someone shouted.

Raoul turned his horse and spurred across the bracken and down on to the narrow road that bordered the château grounds, his men and Hortense strung out behind him. They galloped madly along beside the high wall, but by the time they turned in at the entrance to the stables the flickering of fire could be seen through the trees.

When more Republicans appeared in front of them Raoul ruthlessly charged them down, laying about him with his sabre like one demented. Hortense found herself being carried along with the rest of the men. Panicking, the Republicans, who were surprisingly few in number, tried to retreat towards the main gates of the château, only to be met by an advancing Henri Claviere and his men. Unbelievably no quarter was given and none was asked.

By this time the lower floor of the château was an inferno. Raoul and some of his men dismounted and raced towards the main doorway, but a solid wall of flame drove them back.

'Paul?' Raoul demanded, his eyes frantic. 'Has anyone seen my cousin?'

'We think he's still inside,' an ancient footman offered.

Raoul glanced towards the main door again, then started off at a run for the side of the building, Henri Claviere and the giant Letouc close on his heels. Hortense followed on horseback, her heart racing. Looking up, she could see yellow tongues of flame racing through the upper storey and, behind the flames, thick, billowing smoke.

Inside the great house the conflagration was devastating all in its path, furniture collapsed into piles of charred wood and ornate silver melted. As they reached the side-door one of the upstairs windows shattered beneath the pressure of expanding air, and glass showered down around them. The girl's horse reared up in panic and she was forced to draw back from the ever-increasing heat. Dismounting, she tethered the beast to a convenient tree and stood watching the blaze with horrified fascination.

Raoul rushed in at the side-door and was met by a blast of hot air. By now the fire seemed to be everywhere, crackling and sucking and devouring everything in its path. Heat seared his cheek and he lifted his arm to protect his face as he moved towards the already disintegrating stairs. All around him was scarlet and yellow, and it was almost impossible to breathe.

Before he had reached the first step Henri and Letouc had hold of him and were dragging him back towards the door. Part of the elaborate plastered ceiling collapsed, and still he tried to pull away from them. He only knew that Paul was upstairs and that somehow he had to reach him. It's your fault, his mind kept screaming; your fault!

Hortense breathed a sigh of relief when she saw the struggling figures emerge from the burning building.

She saw Raoul roughly push Henri aside before a
frustrated Letouc cuffed him savagely across the head
and he crumpled like a sack of flour. Together the other
two men dragged him back to where she was waiting.
They were both breathing heavily and their faces were
streaked with soot. Henri was surprised to see her there
but, although his eyes flashed angrily, he made no
comment.

'He was determined to get himself killed,' he complained, kneeling beside Raoul. 'There was no reasoning
with him!'

He loosened his friend's cravat and, having assured
himself that he was going to be all right, looked back
towards the fire. Tongues of flame were billowing out of
the upstairs windows and sending ripples of red across
the slate roof. More windows shattered, and even from
fifty yards away they could feel the intense heat. By now
the great flames had turned the night sky a dusty pink
and the ornamental lake was a great shimmering pool of
reflected red and yellow light.

There was so much destruction, and tears ran
unchecked down the girl's cheeks. She felt Raoul stir
beside her and saw Henri reach out a comforting hand
to clasp his shoulder as he sat up to stare at the burning
château. Until the day she died she didn't think she
would ever forget the haunted look on his face, and in
the dancing light of the flames she saw that he was crying
too. Scrambling to his feet, he staggered away from them
and into the concealing trees. Every instinct urged
Hortense to follow him, to give him what comfort she
could, yet she knew he needed this time alone.

In fact, it was guilt as much as grief that devastated
Raoul, for he knew it was his advice to Saurin that had
brought the soldiers there. He ached with it, and felt so
consumed and bowed down that at that moment he
didn't want to live. Death would be easy, he thought. It

would free him from this soul-wrenching conflict of loyalties. . .and yet that was the coward's way out and, whatever else he was, Raoul Duchambray was no coward.

Drawing in a ragged breath, he stared up at the rose-tinted sky. His throat still burned and his stomach was churning. Purgatory could be no worse, he thought, and he was certainly condemned to that. He was responsible for the death of his cousin and later he would betray his friends. Far better that he had gone to the guillotine; there was at least some honour in that. With an animal-like groan he smashed his fist against the nearest tree. He bruised his knuckles badly and yet he did not feel the pain; it was nothing when compared to the agony in his mind or the grief in his heart.

'Does the destruction of the ancestral home upset you?' asked a butter-soft voice behind him. 'You always maintained that you hated the place.'

Raoul turned to face the speaker, who was standing in the deepest shadow. He could scarcely make him out but he didn't need to see Michel Saurin to know that he was smiling. He could hear it in his voice.

Suddenly hatred rose up inside him, so intense that it almost choked him. He took a step forward, ready to kill, but was halted by the sound of a pistol hammer being drawn back.

'I saw you leave the others and thought I would take the opportunity to pass on further orders,' Saurin continued tightly, keeping the pistol trained on Raoul's chest. 'Carrier is now with General Westermann, and any information you can gather is to be sent to him there. How you manage it is your own affair. Personally I don't think you'll find out anything worthwhile, and I still don't trust you. You are too much like the rest of your relatives.'

'Damn you! You directed the soldiers here!' Raoul accused.

Saurin shrugged. 'I merely suggested the St Fulgent area. Ramboulard was the obvious target. If you're as Republican as you profess you'll be glad to see the end of the place and all it stands for.'

'Paul was trapped in there!' Raoul grated, his body trembling with the force of his emotions. Ignoring the other man's pistol, he made another threatening move forward.

'Don't press your luck, Duchambray,' Saurin snapped. 'I'd like nothing more than to shoot you. You're only alive now because Carrier thinks you might be useful. As far as your cousin is concerned, there's one degenerate the less.'

Raoul ached to get his fingers around the Republican's neck and squeeze until he had choked the life from him. He didn't care whose side he was on. He only knew that he was hurting and that he needed vengeance to assuage his pain.

'You shall pay, Michel,' he promised. 'When this war is over I shall find you and kill you.'

'You'll be welcome to try,' Saurin replied coldly, 'but be warned; I shall not play by your rules. Chivalry means nothing to me and I have no intention of giving you the advantage of a fair fight. . .and, if you're thinking of setting your friends on me now, just remember; I'll be only too pleased to denounce you.'

Watching the Republican walk away was one of the hardest things that Raoul had ever done. Hatred boiled inside him and he was filled with a bitter self-disgust. He had never wanted so much to kill a man and, in letting Saurin live, felt he had sunk as low as any man could. It was small consolation to realise that there had been no alternative.

Hortense did not see Raoul again until it was dawn. A

red glow still hung in the air over the sad shell of the château, and in the increasing grey light the scene looked like something from hell. Perhaps most poignant of all was the sight of the rose garden, its bushes turned brown and twisted by the intense heat. The air was heavy with smoke and the watchers' faces were streaked with it as they surveyed what was left of the Duchambray home with stinging red-rimmed eyes.

Having slept for an hour wrapped up in her cloak, Hortense awoke feeling stiff and cold. Henri was dozing at her side, and instinctively she looked for Raoul. She saw him sitting alone with his back to a tree trunk. He was so still that at first she thought he was asleep; then she noticed that his eyes were open. He looked dreadful, the streaks of soot on his face only serving to emphasise his pallor, but it was the emptiness and pain she saw in his eyes that shocked her the most. Without thinking, she got up and went to sit beside him.

'I'm so sorry,' she whispered, slipping her arm through his and hugging him. 'I wish there was something I could do to ease what you are feeling.'

'Don't!' he spat with surprising vehemence, turning his head away from her. 'I don't deserve your sympathy. I don't want it! You haven't the faintest idea what I'm feeling.'

His attitude stunned her, but before she could reply Henri came over to join them. He glanced at Raoul and there was no mistaking the concern in his eyes.

'I've been considering our next move,' he said. 'As soon as the rest of my men arrive I'm marching on to St Fulgent. I would like Hortense to return to Château Claviere, taking with her any of your servants who will not be able to find shelter around here. I think you should go with her. You're in no state to fight.'

'If there is to be more fighting then my place is with you,' Raoul replied bleakly. 'I'm still capable of doing my job. I just don't feel much like conversation,' and, climbing to his feet, he walked away from them.

Hortense was dismayed. He had acted as if he hated her, when all she had wanted to do was offer him some small measure of comfort.

'Don't take it to heart,' Henri advised with a sigh. 'He needs to be alone. The best thing you can do is to go back home. You should never have come with us in the first place. Quite honestly I've got enough to worry about without considering your safety.'

She opened her mouth to argue with him, then relented when she realised how desperately tired he was. She had no wish to add to his burden and suddenly wanted to be as far away from Raoul Duchambray as possible.

During the next hour more Vendeans arrived from Château Claviere, and together soldiers and peasants worked to salvage what they could. Fortunately the stables had not been burned and, although the Republicans had attempted to steal the horses, most had pulled free in the fighting and were easily rounded up to be taken to Château Claviere along with the spare tackle and grain.

Hortense spent the time administering to those who were hurt. In fact, the Vendeans had got off very lightly, with only five dead and a handful of wounded, none of them seriously. Several people had nasty burns, however, and she did her best to alleviate their discomfort with one of Marie's salves.

She had just finished applying cream to a scorch mark on one young man's neck when Raoul came over for her help. He had removed his coat and the sleeve of his shirt was rolled up to reveal a nasty burn.

'I don't know what you are using,' he commented, unsmilingly holding out his arm. 'I only hope it works.

This is smarting like the devil. I don't know why I didn't notice it before.'

Hortense frowned at him in concern. His skin looked waxen and his eyes were suspiciously bright, as if he was still struggling with tears. She had seen the scorch mark on his sleeve but he had given no indication that it was more than that.

'You should have come to me sooner,' she chastised as she examined the wound, then began to smooth on the salve, being careful not to puncture the blisters.

'You were busy with more severe cases.' He didn't add that he would not have come to her at all if it had not been so painful. He couldn't stand the sympathy he saw in her eyes. If only she knew, he thought; how would she look at him then?

As soon as she had finished he thanked her coldly and drew away. He saw the hurt in her eyes but forced himself to ignore it. For her sake as well as his own he had to distance himself from her. In view of what he was involved in, what he had done, he had no alternative.

Hortense watched him walk away and battled with anger of her own. She knew he was hurting but she still resented his rejection. In spite of the way she was attracted to him, she had been offering him friendship, nothing more, and he had thrown it back in her face. He could, she decided, be quite hateful at times, every bit as aloof and insensitive as his aristocratic relatives.

Over by the main gateway something seemed to be happening, and for a moment she feared the arrival of more Republicans. As she moved forward the Vendeans let out a ragged cheer to greet the entry of more of their men. Into the trampled grounds they marched, accompanied by pipe and drum and continuing cries of welcome. Their leader, mounted on a sleek chestnut horse, lifted his high-crowned hat with its dashing white cockade and waved it in acknowledgement, revealing dark hair covered by a red and white kerchief. Hortense had never seen him before but guessed him to be none other than François Charette, the renowned leader of the Army of the Marais.

The general's eyes narrowed as he took in the blackened shell of the château. After gently lowering the young drummer he had taken up before him he dropped lithely to the ground.

'It seems we were both too late,' he commented, adjusting the white sash he was wearing over his green jacket and walking forward to embrace Henri, who afterwards introduced Raoul.

'Then this was your home,' Charette commented sympathetically. 'I hope your family got out.'

'My cousin was killed,' Raoul replied flatly.

For a moment the general studied him, finally nodding as if coming to a decision. 'Then you'll be wanting revenge. You are both welcome to ride with me. With luck we'll catch up with the Republicans before dark.'

Henri nodded. 'We've already decided on that course. We intend to march just as soon as my cousin leaves with the servants for Château Claviere.'

'Does your cousin not wish to fight too?' the general asked.

Henri laughed and reached out a hand to draw Hortense into the conversation. All around them men were cheering and shouting. 'She has every wish to. It is I who forbid it. She will serve us best by seeing Raoul's people safely to our home.'

Charette's eyes sparkled and he smiled appreciateively at Hortense, exhibiting the accomplished charm that had captured more than one female heart. Although not handsome in a conventional way, he was lithe and humorous, and Hortense found the roguish smile above the rather prominent chin definitely appealing.

'She makes an exceptionally pretty soldier,' he

informed Henri teasinsgly. 'I would be delighted to have her march with us, but as she's your cousin I can quite see your point.' He bowed elaborately over her hand and carried to it his lips. 'I shall look forward to seeing you again, *mademoiselle*.'

'Perhaps you should introduce her to your wife,' Raoul replied drily.

Instead of taking offence the general laughed good-naturedly. 'Am I trespassing on your territory, Duchambray? I'm sorry, but I can never resist a pretty face!'

Hortense was a little taken aback by both the general's interest and by Raoul's remark. For just a moment she debated asking Charette to take her with him, then decided that to bow to her cousin's wishes on this occasion might make it easier to have her way another time.

The preparations to leave Ramboulard continued in earnest, and in less than half an hour the two parties were ready to leave; Hortense to head east with the servants and salvaged supplies, and the soldiers to continue on into St Fulgent. As she watched the men march away the girl stood up in her stirrups and waved until her arm ached. Then, feeling strangely empty and depressed, she led the way home.

# CHAPTER FOUR

A WEAK sun shone through the half-covered trees, its dappled light making intricate patterns on the browning leaves underfoot. Hortense leant her shoulders back against the gnarled trunk of an ancient oak tree and smothered a sigh. It was somehow ironic that, in such a peaceful little village as Beaupréau, everyone's thoughts should be of warfare and death.

At the far end of the clearing the Vendean leaders, the flower of the Vendean nobility, were gathered to discuss their next move. Only two important leaders were missing; the Marquis de Lescure, who had been badly wounded in the fighting the previous day, and the ebullient Charette.

The chief marachin's angry return to Legé had particularly distressed Henri, who had come to like and respect him, but, as Raoul had said, who could blame the man? For while he had been fighting in St Fulgent the other generals had distributed the captured booty without a thought for him or his men. It seemed that his victories at Montaigu and St Fulgent or his bravery at Torfou counted as nought, and instead they blamed him for failing to support Bonchamps and thus making it impossible for the Vendeans to completely rout the Mayençais troops. In that respect the Republican's diversionary attack had proved more successful than they could have hoped, not only saving one of their armies but in completing the split between the Army of the Marias and the other Royalists.

Henri too had received a reprimand for missing the rendezvous, but his friendship with Bonchamps and the cry for help he had received from the peasants had been in his favour and, besides, no one was jealous of him. Nevertheless he was becoming increasingly disillusioned with the conduct of the war. All too often the leaders failed to agree among themselves, and the peasants no longer responded to the call to arms with their previous alacrity.

Yesterday, after frightened Royalist civilians had exiled the town, the Republican general, Kleber, had occupied Cholet, and now the Royalist generals were deciding whether to try to take it back. Henri was over at the far end of the clearing, listening to what was going on, whereas Raoul, who more and more seemed to be keeping his own counsel, had gone off to join his men.

In the three weeks since they had been with Bonchamps, Hortense had seen very little of him, and she wondered if he was actually avoiding her. In fact he had been moody and a little distant since his return from St Fulgent, despite the victory they had achieved there. He had scarcely spoken on the ride from Château Claviere to join the Grand Army and that seemed to have set the pattern for the days that followed. It was as if he was censoring his words and feelings, suppressing his pain and hurt and bottling everything up inside him so that no one should know how he really felt. More puzzling yet, she sensed that he was wrestling with something that bothered him greatly.

Last night, after the fierce fighting in which Bonchamps and therefore he and Henri had been involved, she had discovered him sitting alone, looking particularly drained. This did not unduly surprise her, for he had been in the thick of the fighting, and Bonchamps had personally praised his courage, yet when she had commented on it he had nearly bitten her head off. She had chalked his outburst up to the disillusionment and depression they were all feeling, but on reflection she wasn't so sure.

She felt he needed to talk, and yet she no longer felt comfortable enough with him to press him. Not only did he seem to be avoiding her, but he didn't seem to want to touch her any more. In the past he had been willing to accept a hug or a touch of hands, but lately he shied away from her as if she burned. Perhaps he just didn't like her any more. Yet there were times when she caught him watching her, when he thought she was not aware of him, that she had an altogether different impression. She felt hurt and bewildered, and was at a loss to understand the change in him. Obviously the burning of Ramboulard and his cousin's death were partly to blame, but she couldn't help feeling that there was more to it than that.

She was just beginning to think of returning to the cottage where she and some of the other girls were nursing Château Claviere's wounded when she saw Raoul approaching through the trees. He entered the clearing quite close to her, and for a moment she thought he was going to ignore her completely. She called out a greeting, and after hesitating he came over and sat down at her side. Like everyone else, he was looking tired.

'Having a rest?' he asked quietly, his mouth lifting in that heart-wrenching half-smile she had come to know so well.

She nodded. 'I needed some fesh air. Pierre Reauseau died this morning and I'm afraid Lallange won't last the night. . .'

Suddenly she was overcome with hopelessness. The Vendeans had done so well, defeating some of the Republic's best troops, and yet it was not enough. The Republicans only seemed to find more soldiers and better generals to send against them.

'Where's it all going to end?' she asked tiredly.

Raoul shrugged, and wished he could say something to comfort her. His admiration for her had increased immensely over the last couple of weeks. She had worked hard and selflessly, taking care of Château Claviere's wounded, and he had never once heard her complain. In fact, with her bright hair and cheerful personality, the men had nicknamed her la Petite Lumière—the Little Light.

He had been trying to keep his distance from her for weeks, and it was driving him crazy. He told himself that she was bound to end up hating him, that it would be foolish to get involved with her now; yet, no matter how he reasoned, it didn't stop his body's response to her. All he could do was try and stay out of her way.

'The Grand Army and the Army of the Centre are still forces to be reckoned with, not to mention Charette,' he told her.

Her face brightened, and immediately he regretted his comment. 'Then you think we still have a chance of winning this war?'

He hadn't the heart to disillusion her. 'If we fight Kleber tomorrow the battle could go either way.'

'Particularly as he won't be expecting a counter-attack so soon,' Henri added, coming to join them.

He was looking rather pleased with himself, and Raoul feared the worse. 'So they've decided to attack the town.'

Henri nodded. 'Yes! Actually, Bonchamps was against it. He was all for crossing the Loire and making for the Normandy coast, where we would be able to get help from England, but d'Elbee and young Jacquelein carried the issue.' He grinned. 'The one drawback is the size and number of the enemy's ordnance, and I've volunteered to try and do something about that. If we can locate Kleber's guns a small party might be able to sneak in under cover of darkness and disable some of them. Are you game to come with me?'

Raoul had never felt so frustrated and helpless in his life. Events were carrying him along and demanding responses from him that he really didn't want to make. He knew how much the Vendeans were counting on the element of surprise, and yet it was up to him to warn the Republican general.

'Well? Will you be coming or not?' Henri demanded, and Raoul was conscious of the girl's eyes upon him.

'I think you were a fool to volunteer,' he grumbled, rising to his feet, 'but, for what it's worth, I'll come with you.'

'Now what's got in to him?' demanded Henri crossly as they watched him walk away. 'If I didn't know better I'd say he was afraid. You know, I don't think his heart has been in this fight since the very beginning. He's with us because he feels a sense of obligation, but he doesn't really believe in what we are doing. Not that it matters, I suppose. He has fought extremely well, and if he comes with me tonight then I know I can rely on him. Which is more than I can say for a number who are most vociferous in support of our cause.'

'I wish you weren't going,' Hortense confided.

Smiling, he patted her hand in what she considered an annoyingly condescending manner. 'We shall be careful. There is no need for you to sit around and worry.'

'Oh, I shan't,' she replied with conviction. She didn't add that if they were going on this hare-brained mission then so was she!

During the afternoon she heard that the Republican artillery had been spotted on the plain to the north-east of the town. Preparations began for the night attack, and Bonchamps himself came to wish the men good luck. The Vendean leaders might have been sceptical of Henri's success, but they were more than willing to let him try.

Just before midnight about a dozen men gathered in

front of one of the cottages, and Henri carefully
explained what they were going to try to do. Absolute
silence was going to be essential, he told them, and
because of that they were only going to ride part of the
way. Nothing that jingled or rattled could be taken, and
they were to wear nothing white. Sashes and arm-bands
were to be left behind, and their faces were to be smeared
with mud to prevent them showing up in the moonlight.
As before, Hortense, dressed once more in breeches,
found it quite easy to mix with the men and accompany
them when they rode out.

The night was virtually moonless, and because of this
they proceeded with care. At times it was almost impossible for them to see their way, and the hedgerows loomed
on either side of them like formless monsters. There was
not a light showing in the whole deserted countryside,
not a cottage or a farmhouse remaining occupied as the
people fled before the dreaded Republican menace.

At the roadside lay the occasional Republican corpse,
stark evidence of the Vendeans' rapid flight. They hadn't
been able to take all their prisoners with them and some
had been murdered without a thought. Such brutality
had inflamed both Henri and Raoul, but the peasants
had insisted that it was no worse than the atrocities
perpetrated by the Republican general, Westermann. It
all seemed so savage and unnatural, and Hortense felt a
momentary chill of superstitious fear. Surely in such acts
lay the road to damnation?

They covered about five miles without incident, and
then Henri called a halt. Dismounting at the entrance to
a little-used cart track, they tethered their horses and
then proceeded stealthily on foot, using trees and bushes
for cover whenever possible. Like grey wraiths, they
slipped across a meadow and then dropped down in the
shelter of a hedge.

Hortense, still wary of discovery, had kept a little to

the right of the others, and it was this that was her undoing. One minute she was on level ground and the next she was tumbling and sliding down into a deep ditch. She scraped her knees and banged her hip quite badly, but somehow she managed not to call out. For a moment she lay stunned, hardly daring to breathe. Her face was buried in a pile of fallen leaves, and the dank earthy smell of them tickled her nostrils and made her want to sneeze. Swiftly she covered her nose with her hand, and the sneeze came out as a muffled snort.

The leaves rustled as someone dropped down beside her, and a low voice asked her if she was all right. She knew it was Raoul, and while she was deciding whether she should risk a reply his hands began to move over her, searching for the place where she was hurt. When he reached her thigh she felt him stiffen, and he swore harshly under his breath.

'Please don't give me away,' she whispered.

'Not give you away!' he spat. 'God, woman, have you any idea how dangerous this mission is? I wouldn't be on it myself if I weren't concerned for Henri.' That was at least partly true. He was also hoping that he would somehow be able to make contact with a Republican, and through him warn Kleber, but obviously he couldn't tell her that.

'If you send me back I shall only follow along behind you,' she told him. 'If you want me to I'll promise to stay well away from any fighting, but please don't tell Henri.'

'Shut up; just shut up!' he hissed. He was worried and furious and all too aware of her slender body stretched out beside him. 'You're too damned used to having your own way!'

She could feel the tension in him, feel his anger and frustration in the hard pressure of his fingers biting into her shoulders. Instead of arguing with her he gave her a rough shake, and then, to her consternation, did what he had been aching to do for weeks. Taking her upturned mouth, he kissed her as if his life depended on it.

She resisted at first, struggling to maintain her anger and independence, but she couldn't deny herself the pleasure of holding him in her arms, no matter how untimely. Her mouth opened beneath his, and her whole body softened. Almost of their own volition her arms crept up to encircle his neck and cradle his head in her hands. Gradually his mouth began to gentle on hers, tasting and savouring and coaxing her to respond. When she began to kiss him back Raoul felt as if he was drowning in the sweetness and solace her lips offered.

From the very beginning he had been drawn to her, drawn to her courage and warmth like a freezing man to a fire. It was as if only with her was he completely whole. Almost fiercely he moulded her soft body to his. It was madness! He heard her appreciative groan, and that small sound brought him back to reality with an unpleasant jolt.

Hortense reeled beneath the raw hunger in his lips, and need, hot and unrestrained, surged through her until she thought she would explode. When Raoul suddenly pulled back, breaking the contact, it was all she could do not to cry out in dismay.

'Hortense, I. . .' Desperately he struggled for the words to explain his behaviour, but somehow they just wouldn't come.

'Don't,' she whispered, laying a hand against his cheek. 'Don't say anything.' If he was going to apologise she didn't think she could bear it, not when she had enjoyed it so.

A sigh escaped him and he swore savagely beneath his breath. He had to be insane! He didn't want the girl's tenderness. He couldn't afford to let her get too close. When the battle was over he would have to find himself another woman. Perhaps that would ease the sexual tension that had been building inside him and threatening to blow him apart.

'Raoul?' Henri's concerned voice floated down to him, but it was a second or two before he could answer.

'It's all right,' he called softly. 'No one is hurt.' Sitting up, he brushed the leaves from his coat and peered into the darkness. 'This ditch seems to be leading in our direction. I'll scout ahead.'

'No, we'll both go.' Henri slid down to join him. He was very close, but still failed to recognise Hortense, and surprisingly Raoul did not give her away; he thought Henri had enough on his mind as it was.

Together the two men disappeared into the darkness, leaving her to wait alone. The minutes dragged interminably, and it felt as if the coldness of the earth were rising in a solid wave to cut into her bones. Above her she could hear the rest of the men shuffling and sighing as they too endured the enforced inactivity.

Lifting a hand to her swollen lips, she smiled in spite of her discomfort. Surely Raoul had to feel something for her to kiss her like that, even if it was only lust? He might have begun it in anger, but it had ended with such sweetness and longing, such unexpected tenderness. What a strange man he was, so full of contradictions and suppressed passion.

Ten minutes later Raoul and Henri returned, both elated.

'It's perfect,' Raoul whispered as Henri climbed to fetch his men. 'This ditch leads right up to the Republican guns. They can't have been aware of it. It's not even guarded and, as far as I can see, there is only one picket between us and their emplacement.' Pausing consideringly, he added, 'If you come with us then you must promise to stay close to me.'

'I promise,' she replied, and she smiled as he protectively took her hand. His touch was both stimulating and reassuring, and she curled her fingers trustingly around his.

Swiftly and silently they proceeded along the shallow cutting, the rest of the men strung out behind them. It continued, without interruption, for perhaps a quarter of a mile before running out in a tangle of matted vegetation and stones. Raoul halted her with gentle pressure on her arm, and they both clambered up to peer across the surrounding countryside. Here the land was quite flat, mostly grassland interspersed with occasional small copses. Less than ten yards away and slightly to their right was a Republican picket. Obviously he was not expecting trouble, for he had dropped his musket and was leaning lazily against a tree, smoking his pipe. Henri climbed up beside them and motioned to one of the men. With the skill of a cat the young peasant edged silently forward, and within seconds the sentry was dead, a knife slipped up and under his ribs.

Hortense winced and gritted her teeth against a sudden moment of nausea as the rest of the men moved forward.

'You'd best wait here,' Raoul hissed before following them. 'This isn't going to be pleasant.'

As Hortense watched them moving silently towards the gun emplacement her heart raced with fear for them. Moonlight glinted on cruel bare steel, and once more her stomach turned over at the thought of what they were going to do.

The Republican gunners were sleeping beside their weapon, but its might was powerless to save them now. Like avenging spirits, the Vendeans fell upon them and ruthlessly slit their throats. Raoul hung back, unable to kill in cold blood men he still considered his comrades. He experienced an almost overwhelming desire to call out a warning, but he knew it would mean certain death for Henri and Hortense. It was war, he reminded himself, and would have happened with or without his presence.

Henri glanced around quickly to make sure they had missed no one, then gestured to the nearest gun. It was a massive eight-pounder and, in his eyes, the damage it could have done to the Vendeans more than justified his actions. One of the men drew a metal spike from his pocket and, climbing on to the gun barrel, pushed it into the touch hole. Covering the spike with some cloth to deaden the sound, he began hammering it in with a wooden mallet.

Raoul moved on to the next gun and, after helping a young peasant to mount its giant barrel, handed him another spike and mallet. There were four cannons in that particular battery, and in less then five minutes all had been disabled. Elated with his success, Henri ordered the men on to the next emplacement. Raoul thought he was pushing his luck, and said as much, but his friend was quite determined.

As they crept through the small copse that separated the emplacements Raoul was uncomfortably aware of his heart hammering against his ribs and the coldness of perspiration on his forehead. His hand curled around the letter in his pocket. It was a warning for Kleber, and he hoped he would get a chance to pass it across. Desperately he sought for some way to end the silent slaughter, but could think of nothing that would not involve the death of his friends. In his heart he knew he was right not to give them away, and yet he realised the night's work would haunt his dreams for years to come.

Studying the sleeping forms around the next emplacement, he had the distinct feeling that something was wrong. The men were ready to go, but some sixth sense made him hold them back, his heart beating even faster as he tried to find a concrete reason for his fear. When he scanned the sleeping figures again he realised that there were less of them. Desperately his eyes probed the darkness. His nerves were at breaking-point and something like panic welled up inside him, making it difficult for him to breathe. At last he picked out the back of an artillery man standing by some trees.

Letting his breath escape in a pent-up sigh, he reached out to grasp Henri's shoulder and pointed. 'Let's leave it,' he advised.

Henri slanted him a look that was suspiciously like contempt, and declared that they would wait a little longer. For a moment Raoul debated telling him that Hortense was waiting back at the drainage ditch, and that she was in as much danger as the rest of them, but he didn't think even that would influence his friend. Frustration gnawed at him, and he ached to shake some sense into the man at his side. The fool had no right to be risking his life when he had a beautiful pregnant wife at home. He didn't want to admit that in Henri's position he would be doing exactly the same.

The Republican seemed to take an eternity to return to the proximity of the gun; in reality it was only a couple of minutes. Still he did not settle and, standing beside his blankets, looked nervously around. In that whole dark panorama nothing moved, and there was only the wind moaning in the trees and the hoot of the occasional night bird to disturb the silence.

Drawing his sword, Henri Claviere slipped silently forward. Some sixth sense seemed to warn the Republican and he turned, surprise and fear apparent in his face as he made a desperate run for the muskets that were stacked up beside the dying fire. He was obviously no novice, and, snatching up a weapon, cocked it and levelled it at Henri in one smooth movement. As he fired Raoul cannoned into him and the shot went wide.

Then all hell seemed to break loose as the other

soldiers struggled from sleep and the Vendeans sprang upon them, ruthlessly cutting them down. Someone screamed horribly and the alarm was sounded further down the Republican line. There was nothing to do but retreat, and the Vendeans hurtled back the way they had come as other half-dressed Republicans came at them through the trees.

Back in the cover of the ditch, Hortense heard the musket fire and her stomach turned over. Common sense told her she should flee, but somehow she just could not bring herself to, at least not until she knew what was happening. When she saw the first retreating Vendeans running towards her she still hesitated, her eyes searching the darkness for Henri and Raoul. She saw her cousin spin around and knew he had been hit, then watched, horrified, as the Republican who was responsible closed the distance and lifted his musket to administer the *coup de grâce* with his bayonet. Henri tried to roll out of the way, but he was still stunned and would not have been quick enough had Raoul not charged into the fellow and sent him sprawling. Taking advantage, the big Letouc grabbed Henri by the arm and half dragged him towards the ditch.

Falling across the Republican, Raoul frantically pushed the letter for Kleber into his hand.

'I'm on your side,' he hissed. 'Give this to your general. . .' Then suddenly his head seemed to explode in a blaze of pain as another Republican clubbed him ruthlessly across the head with a musket butt.

Hortense saw it all happening like some horrid slow-motion nightmare. Her mind told her that it was real, and yet she could hardly believe it. For a moment shock kept her rooted to the spot, then Letouc jumped down beside her, and shoving her violently in the back, yelled at her to run. Partly supporting Henri, he followed close on her heels while a handful of Vendeans who still had muskets hung back to cover their retreat.

She ran with a speed born of panic until her lungs seemed ready to burst. The blood was pounding in her ears. Her throat stung and her chest was tight with the sustained effort, and still the big Vendean shouted at her to hurry. When she nearly stumbled on the uneven ground he reached out to steady her, and then they were on the last lap, racing across the meadow towards the track where their horses waited.

Blood was pouring down Henri's arm, but he insisted he could ride and climbed into the saddle unaided. He was, however, in no condition to remonstrate with Hortense, and accepted her presence without comment. Without being ordered, Letouc took a couple of horses and rode back to collect the rest of their men. Tragically only four of them made it.

'Duchambray?' Henri asked, and the big peasant shook his head.

Hortense felt devastated. She thought Raoul was dead, and the realisation that she would never see him again was almost impossible to bear. To think that less than an hour ago he had felt so warm and alive in her arms. Suddenly it was as if all the colour had gone out of her life, all the meaning and warmth; after her father's death she had never wanted to feel such emptiness again.

Henri's wound was not serious, a pistol ball having lodged in his arm, and, once back at the cottage, he bore its removal stoically. He was tired, though, and thoroughly dispirited, and his depression did not lift even when Bonchamps assured him that the partial success of his mission had been well worth the cost.

'I don't think you'll be fit to fight tomorrow,' Hortense told him as she draped a blanket around his shaking shoulders and settled him back on the bed. 'The men will have to manage without you.'

In spite of everything, he smiled. 'I'll be fine after I've had a sleep.'

Suddenly she'd had quite enough of his masculine bravado, quite enough of his risking his life when it was not expected of him, and her protest tumbled out in a torrent of angry words. He should be thinking of Marie, she told him. He too could have been killed that night. How could anyone think the mission had been worth the appalling cost?

'Those guns would have killed a lot more than the men we lost,' he replied quietly. 'I'm only sorry one of them had to be Raoul.'

'Oh, Henri,' she protested, 'I never thought war would be as bad as this!' And the next moment she was in his arms, sobbing as if her heart would break.

He held her trembling body to him and buried his face in her wind-blown hair. At that moment he would have done anything in his power to bring his friend back.


Raoul struggled back to consciousness through waves of pain. Sickness clawed at his stomach, and his vision was so blurred that he could not make out the face banding over him.

'I think he's coming round.' The voice was familiar, yet filled with an unusual element of concern.

When they lifted his head so he could drink he nearly blacked out again. Raw spirit burned his throat, and gradually his vision cleared. His natural father was bending over him, and Raoul didn't think he'd ever seen him look so relieved.

'You were involved in some bloody work tonight, Duchambray.' The young dark-moustached face that swam into his view looked decidedly hostile. 'If it were up to me I'd shoot you out of hand!'

'Can you stand?' Beaulieu asked, his expression once

again so inscrutable that Raoul thought he had imagined
his earlier concern.

He nodded, but when he tried to do so his legs
buckled under him, and he would have fallen had not
the two men on either side of him supported him and
almost dragged him to a chair.

'What are you doing here?' he asked after a moment,
when the world had righted itself and he felt that he
could speak without throwing up.

'Your—er—father is one of our representatives on
this mission,' a highly accented voice supplied, and Jean
Baptiste Kleber moved forward into the lamplight.

He was a stocky man, probably no older than forty,
with a round, strong-featured face and full, rather sen-
suous lips. Raoul was surprised that he should know of
their relationship, for it was something that Beaulieu
rarely admitted. It was too much of an embarrassment
for him, having a son who was an aristo, no matter how
liberal.

Another wave of dizziness assailed Raoul, and he
closed his eyes. His head was aching quite abominably,
and the pain was threatening to plunge him back into
the darkness from which he had just come.

'Get him another drink,' Kleber advised.

Having downed another brandy, he felt a little better
and was able to take stock of his surroundings. He was
in an extremely comfortable house and he guessed that it
was where the general had billeted himself.

'This doesn't tell me an awful lot,' Kleber grumbled,
holding up the letter. 'In spite of what my commanders
thought, I was half expecting an attack tomorrow. . .
I'm not sure it's enough to exonerate you from what was
done to my guns.'

'That would have happened had I not been present,'
Raoul replied, thinking quickly and lying through his
teeth. 'In truth I debated giving the alarm, but, had one

Vendean escaped, then I would no longer have been of use to you. As it was, I didn't think you'd miss four cannons.'

'And my men?' snapped the dark young officer, curling angry fingers into the front of Raoul's coat. 'What about the men who were butchered, good Republicans all of them?'

'That's enough, Marceau.' Kleber laid a restraining hand on the younger man's arm. 'However, I don't like wasteful death, Monsieur Duchambray. You should bear that in mind. War is horrific enough without our acting like animals. This time there has been no looting or wholesale slaughter in Cholet.'

It was ironic, Raoul thought, but here was a general he would have enjoyed serving under, a general who was worthy of respect, unlike Westermann, whose barbaric ways had earned him the title Butcher of the Vendée. In men like Kleber rested the region's salvation, and knowing he would be magnanimous in victory made it easier for Raoul to disclose what he knew of the Vendeans' plans. In fact, he doubted it would be enough to affect the outcome of the battle. The two sides were evenly matched and equally determined, so the conflict was likely to be bloody and long.

When he had finished Kleber not only seemed satisfied with him, but he also seemed to sense something of the self-loathing he felt.

Turning to Beaulieu, who had remained silent and inscrutable through the entire proceedings, he said, 'I think your son has done well. It is not easy for a man of honour to play the spy. What you are doing is necessary,' he told Raoul; 'rest assured of that. For the sake of the peasants the conflict here must be resolved, and that can only be achieved with a decisive Republican victory. Like you, I suspect, I have every respect for my Vendean adversaries. They are good and able men, but their loyalty is misplaced. A swift end will be a kindness.'

He glanced again at Beaulieu and a silent commitment seemed to pass between the two men. 'I promise you, the more humane of us will do our best to keep fanatical representatives like Carrier in check. Now I'll give you a few minutes alone with your father.'

Giving Raoul's shoulder an encouraging squeeze, he motioned for the other officer to follow him, and they both left the cosy drawing-room.

As he studied his son Thomas Beaulieu felt a surge of affection that quite surprised him. The boy was sick and dispirited, yet hiding it well. Suddenly he wished it were possible to relieve him of his dangerous and distasteful mission, but what he was doing was just too valuable to the Republican cause.

'You have to go back; you know that, don't you, Raoul? he said quietly and with obvious regret. 'You may rest for a couple of hours, and then we must see about returning you to the Vendean fold. It shouldn't be too difficult. You've obviously been injured, and you need only say that we left you for dead. With a little acting you may even be able to use your head-wound to keep you out of the fighting tomorrow.'

Raoul nodded tiredly, the sick feeling in his stomach due to more than the blow on his head. At that moment he would have given anything to be able to ride off and leave the Vendée far behind him, or he would have done had it not been for a beautiful rebel girl.

'Did you capture anyone else?' he asked, praying he would get the answer he wanted.

'The Vendeans lost half a dozen men, I believe, but none of them were taken alive. There will be no one to dispute what you say, if that is what you're worried about.'

Beaulieu had not mentioned a woman, and relief flooded through Raoul; Hortense must have escaped. In spite of everything he felt a pleasurable anticipation at the thought of seeing her again.

# CHAPTER FIVE

THE grey light of dawn was filtering through the unshuttered window when Hortense rolled, fully clothed, from her pallet. As soon as she was awake despair was tugging at her, pulling her down into a deep, dark abyss from which she felt she would never escape. Stretching to remove the stiffness from her limbs, she walked shakily across to the nearby bed to look at her cousin.

Henri tossed restlessly in his sleep, and when she reached out to touch his forehead he felt hot and dry. The fever was not unexpected and she felt a certain amount of satisfaction. He certainly wasn't going to be able to take part in the fighting that day. In fact she had every intention of persuading him to return to Château Claviere with the other less seriously wounded.

'He has a slight fever,' a young peasant girl told her from the doorway. 'I checked on him while you were asleep. He'll feel miserable when he wakes up, but I'm sure he'll be all right.'

'What about the others?' Hortense asked.

'Young Lallange died a couple of hours ago, but the rest are all improving. We should be able to move them to make room for today's casualties. Why don't you go back to bed? Everything's in hand, and you look terrible.'

Hortense decided that she felt as bad as she looked, but she was still determined to do her share. 'No, I'll be all right,' she sighed. 'In any case, I don't think I could sleep now. God! I shall be glad when this next battle is over and we know how things stand.'

'You could always drive the wagon to Château Claviere,' the girl suggested.

For a moment she was tempted to agree. Oh, how she longed to leave the suffering and uncertainty behind her and return to the tranquillity of her home. Maybe then the stomach-wrenching pain she was suffering would ease and she would be able to come to terms with losing Raoul, but it would be running away, and pride would not let her accept the offer.

'No, I'll stay,' she replied flatly. 'Old Denis can drive. He's too old for all this and really ought to go home.'

She walked through to the next room with its half a dozen makeshift beds and out into the cold morning. Drawing some water from the well at the side of the cottage, she washed her hands and face, and tidied her hair with her fingers. Slowly the sun came up, edging the light cloud with pink, and the birds began their morning song.

She felt sick and shaky with tiredness, and the chill that was seeping into her bones was much more than physical. It was a new day, and yet for some men, she knew, it would be their last. She had never felt so cold and empty, so utterly depressed, in her life, and for a moment she felt close to tears. Forcing the pain away, she filled the bucket again and carried it inside so that the men could be washed.

One of the peasant girls had already begun to heat up some broth for breakfast, and Hortense went over to help her. Between them they fed the men, and then they began getting them ready for the journey home. Hortense was just easing a young peasant into his jacket when her cousin walked into the big room. Somehow he had managed to dress himself, even down to his uniform jacket, and his flushed face bore a look of determination.

Leaving her patient, Hortense turned in exasperation

to confront him. 'You are not taking part in the battle today, Henri. I won't let you. You're not up to it!'

'Don't make things more difficult for me,' he replied irritably as he walked unsteadily across the room and slumped down in a chair. 'Someone has to lead our men.'

'You're not fit! Think of Marie,' she snapped. 'Risking your life is one thing, but you've no right to throw it away!'

'She's right and you know it.' They froze at the sound of that familiar well-modulated voice from behind them, and the girl's heart accelerated to an alarming rate.

Hardly daring to breathe, she turned to find Raoul standing in the open doorway. He was looking pale and a trifle haggard, but he was marvellously solid and alive. For a moment she could only stand and stare; then she was in his arms, clinging to him as if she would never let him go. Tears of relief trickled down her cheeks and she squeezed him to make sure that he was real.

For a moment Raoul held her, indulging himself in the feel of her lovely body so close to his own. She was comfort and caring, friendship and sensuality, all that he wanted in a woman, and holding her close was more than he could refuse.

'That's quite a welcome,' he told her, his sigh a warm whisper across her hair as he reluctantly drew away from her.

'We thought you were dead,' she muttered huskily. Dabbing at her wet cheek, she turned away to hide her embarrassment. She hadn't meant to betray her feelings quite so completely.

Smiling wearily, Raoul glanced at Henri. 'I nearly was. I must have been deeply unconscious because the Republicans left me for dead. I managed to creep away and walked for hours before coming across a stray horse.'

'You were hurt. Let me see,' Hortense insisted, guiding him to a chair across from her cousin.

Reluctantly he bowed his head, and she winced when she saw the cut and swelling behind his ear. Fetching a cloth and some water she gently bathed the wound while he explained in more detail how he had managed to get back to Beaupréau.

'Are you sure you're all right?' she demanded once she had finished. 'A blow like that could have killed you.'

Raoul felt his guilt expanding under her gentle care and spoke more sharply than he'd intended. 'I'm fine. Don't fuss! I have a headache, that's all!'

Hortense fought down the hurt, telling herself that he had every right to be short-tempered. She knew he found it difficult to accept attention and care. Even so, when she looked into his eyes she was stunned by the anger she saw there. He just wasn't the same man she had met only a few short weeks ago. The war was changing him, making him harder and even less communicative.

For a moment his eyes silently challenged her; then, turning to Henri, he asked, 'How's the arm?'

'Sore, but I'll manage.'

Raoul frowned, and Hortense could see that he was not at all fooled by her cousin's bravado.

'You're an idiot if you ride out today,' he grated. 'Think of your wife, for God's sake!'

'The men need me,' Henri insisted miserably. 'You know how inexperienced they are.'

'I know you'll be of little to use to them in your present condition. I'll be surprised if you can even stay on your horse.'

Henri still seemed determined, and Raoul knew that there was only one thing that would change his mind. Suddenly he was furiously angry, feeling trapped by circumstances and honour, and by the reluctant affection he felt for the man sitting across from him. His friend had everything to live for and yet seemed determined to throw his life away. When he thought how worthless his own existence was in comparison he wanted to lash out in frustration.

'Damn you, Henri!' he snapped. 'Damn your stiff-necked pride and your sense of obligation. I'll lead your men!'

'But you can't!' Hortense protested, her emotions vacillating between relief and horror. 'You're not really fit either. After a blow like that no one would think any the less of you for remaining here.'

'I've told you, I'm fine except for a headache!' He stood up abruptly, still simmering with anger. 'All I need is some sleep.'

'I can't let you do it for me,' Henri protested. 'Hortense is right, and you look like hell.'

'My friend, you can't stop me,' Raoul replied heatedly, glaring at him and heading towards the door. 'In any case, I'm not doing it for you. I'm doing it for Marie and your unborn child!'

Hortense was stunned by his angry outburst, and, after a questioning glance at Henri, followed him. She caught up with him just as he was entering the trees, but he did not slow his pace.

'I'm not going to discuss it,' he growled, sensing her presence behind him.

'I wish you wouldn't go,' she blurted out, laying a restraining hand on his arm. 'Why do it? You don't even believe in our cause—at least not as fervently as some of the others.'

When he turned sharply to look at her his expression was hostile, his eyes diamond-bright. At the time when she really wanted to be close to him, when fear for him was tearing at her, he seemed once more to have retreated behind an emotional wall.

'I don't need to believe in anything,' he replied nastily. 'I'm a soldier. I'll just do what I was trained for.'

'And the reason behind it means nothing to you?'

'No!' he snapped angrily. 'If you're looking for a hero with a cause then you've got the wrong man. I'm a realist, Hortense, and at the moment I wish I'd never returned to the accursed Vendée. Amateur soldiers with their enthusiasm and high ideals make me sick!'

Hortense was shocked by the force of his anger and was at a loss to understand what had brought it about. She had already guessed that he was not totally committed to their cause, but the depth of his resentment appalled her.

Raoul saw the disappointment and confusion in her eyes, and somehow that only served to anger him further. Taking her quite by surprise, he pushed her back against the nearest tree and pinned her there with his body, his hands resting on either side of her head. A flush stained his cheeks and his eyes smouldered with blue fire.

'I'm sick of trying to be something I'm not!' he hissed.

She couldn't follow his reasoning, and she stopped trying to as he kissed her with an anger and passion that took her breath away. There was nothing tender in his kiss, nothing coaxing or cajoling; in fact he was quite brutal. She tried to push him away and, after a moment, he let her, lingering just long enough to establish his superiority.

Her eyes searched his face as she struggled to understand his behaviour. For a moment she thought he looked a little shocked by what he had done. He was hurting, she was sure of it, and her expression softened.

'Don't make excuses for me,' he snapped, wishing he didn't have to look at her. Her small chin was tilted defiantly, and she was too attractive by far. 'You don't really know me. I'm no saint, and your provocative little body has been driving me mad! I'm not in the market for a wife, so do yourself a favour and stay away from me!'

Hortense could hardly believe what he was saying. 'Why, you conceited beast!' she hissed, letting rage block out the pain. 'You're as arrogant and unfeeling as the rest of your family!'

'That's right.' His eyes challenged her. 'And I'm not even going to apologise for it. Go back to Henri, for God's sake. I'm too tired to debate the merits of the Vendean cause. I need some sleep before we continue with this futile war.'

Hortense stared mutely after him as he stalked off through the trees, anger and compassion warring within her as she studied his stiff back. He had acted like a stranger, and an intolerant, unlikeable one at that. She knew she had seen the Duchambray arrogance at its worst, and had longed to slap his handsome face. Damn him! He had almost accused her of chasing him! Well, he needn't worry; now she knew how he felt she would willingly stay out of his way.

He's not worth crying over, she told herself, kicking at the fallen leaves. She wanted to hate him, and yet some softer part of her prevented it. She had the strangest feeling that his anger had been only a smoke-screen to conceal his vulnerability, and wondered if, perhaps, she was getting too close. Obviously he wanted her to draw back from him, and after his angry words her pride would permit nothing else, no matter how she might wish it otherwise.

Returning disconsolately to the cottage, she continued helping the wounded get ready for the journey home. Henri glanced at her curiously, but did not ask her what was wrong and after a while fell asleep in his chair. She woke him when it was time for him to get into the wagon, and he did not protest, but leant heavily on her as she helped him outside.

Sitting with his back propped against the side of the vehicle, he smiled weakly and asked, 'I don't suppose you'll come with us?'

She shook her head. 'No, I'm needed here.' Then, to make him feel easier, added, 'Raoul will keep an eye on me.'

Reaching out his good arm, he gave her hand a reassuring squeeze. 'I don't know what's going on between you two, but I do know I can rely on him to take care of you.'

She leant over to kiss his cheek. 'Give my love to Marie.'

She felt incredibly lonely as she watched the wagon drive away, but she was also relieved. At least Henri would be safe, and if Marie had any sense she would try to keep him at home. She smiled wryly to herself, thinking how her attitude had changed. Her horizons were drawing in, and she was beginning to care more about her family than the cause. Raoul was right. There was no glory in war, only squalor, pain and grief. In fact it was incredible what people could endure. She only hoped that her own strength would not be tested to the full.

Not long after that the Vendean army, once more restored in morale, set off for Cholet, and Hortense, together with the two peasant girls, walked down to the narrow main street to watch them march out. They were a motley crew, the only item of clothing they had in common being their wide felt hats. Their armament varied from expensive muskets to peat-cutters, and their ages from beardless boys to grandfathers, but they were all willing to lay down their lives for their religion and their king.

Most of the principal leaders were there, the handsome Maurice d'Elbee, nominal Commander-in-Chief, Bonchamps, Roche-Jacquelein, Stofflet, and the grey-haired Royrand. The scene was one of organised chaos as the men formed up behind their commanders, talking and joking and waving at the women who had come to see them off.

Hortense searched for Raoul, and finally caught sight of him in conversation with the big Letouc. He was standing by the head of his grey horse, and when the beast whinnied and sidled away from a passing cannon he soothingly petted it nose. Their conversation finished, Letouc rejoined the foot soldiers, and, swinging into the saddle, Raoul rode to the head of Château Claviere's mounted contingent. He glanced around and, catching sight of the girl, hesitated a moment before riding over to her. He still looked tired, but he had taken the time to shave and his face bore a look of grim determination.

'You should have gone home with your cousin,' he grumbled. 'This is no place for a woman alone.'

'You don't need to feel responsible for me, if that is what's worrying you,' she replied tartly.

Instead of snapping back at her he smiled wryly. 'I don't need to, but I do. Promise me that, if things go badly, you'll ride back to Château Claviere. If I can I'll meet you there.' And it was a big 'if', he thought, for he, more than anyone, realised how bloody the battle was going to be.

Hortense knew what he was thinking, and her stomach contracted with fear for him. Nodding, she told him to take care.

Raoul looked down into her tense upturned face, and struggled not to drag her into his arms and kiss her. There could never be anything between them, he reminded himself, and it was kindest not to encourage her.

'I always take care,' he lied, before turning his horse and cantering back to his men.

Hortense forced a smile and waved as they went by,

swallowing hard against the lump forming in her throat. Inevitably there were faces she would not see again and, come the evening, there would be many grieving wives and mothers. Silently the women watched until the cavalcade was out of sight, then, glancing at each other with haunted, knowing eyes, moved off to prepare for the influx of wounded.

Around midday the first rumble of gunfire echoed across the countryside, signalling that the battle had been joined in earnest. Everyone was tense, and, unable to relax, Hortense prowled about among the trees. Please God, keep him safe, she prayed, glancing up at the clearing sky. Even if I can't have him then I must know that he's safe.

Around two o'clock in the afternoon the first wounded started coming in, and with them they brought news of the battle. It seemed that the Vendeans had already broken through to the town. They had even managed to capture some Republican artillery and turn it against their enemies. Hortense was jubilant, thinking that the battle would soon be won, but this hope died as the number of casualties increased. Kleber had brought up another battalion and, advancing in almost parade order, had forced the Vendeans to retreat, leaving behind them the captured guns.

For the next few hours she toiled as never before, finding herself confronted with sights so dreadfully gory that, had it not been for her natural compassion, she would have turned and fled. Gradually she became inured to the blood and the vomit, aware only of the need to clean, comfort and bind. There were so many mutilated and shaken men, most no older then herself, and all of them so pitifully grateful for her incompetent care.

The frailty of the human body was brought home to her with a frightening clarity, the frailty of spirit too;

many young farm boys were unable to stand up to the
deadly thunder of the guns and remain sane. Some broke
down and cried, others retreated into a shell and sat
staring at the world through empty, pain-filled eyes. And
I encouraged them, she thought bitterly, encouraged
them to march out bravely and be blown to pieces.

More wagons arrived, bearing dirty dispirited men,
their faces pale beneath the grime, their clothes smelling
of the same acrid smoke, and each time she scanned
their faces apprehensively, searching for Raoul. Darkness began to fall, and still the Republican cannon
thundered, spitting death and destruction into the Royalist ranks. Hortense bent to remove some wooden
splinters from the shoulder of a young peasant and cried
as he told her how his friends had been cut down.

'Did you see Monsieur Duchambray?' she asked.

'He was alive when I left the field,' the young man
replied between gasps of pain.

'I've just heard that General d'Elbee has been brought
in,' the peasant girl, Nicole, added from the doorway.
She too looked tired and her face was the colour of baked
clay. 'They say he has a bad chest-wound. Worse still,
one of the men thinks he saw General Bonchamps fall.'

'Dear God!' Hortense muttered, dabbing at her tears.
She genuinely liked Henri's friend and general. He was
a kind and sensitive man, and her cousin was devoted to
him.

The fighting continued on into the darkness. News
came that the Vendeans had been routed and that only
young Roche-Jacquelein and a few well-trained men were
holding to cover the retreat. At nine o'clock the Marquis
de Bonchamps was brought into the village and taken to
the house of Madame de Bonnay. He had been hit in the
stomach by grape shot and it was obvious he was going
to die, something he faced with courage and equanimity.

A young peasant arrived with another wagonload of

wounded, and helped the women to carry them inside. Among them was Charles Letouc, who had suffered a musket ball in the thigh. He confirmed what Hortense had already begun to fear—that Raoul and the mounted men had stayed behind with Roche-Jacquelein.

'It's every man for himself now,' the young peasant declared. 'I'm going home to collect my family. When the Republicans break through, God knows what will happen. Our only chance is to fall back and cross the Loire.'

'What about the wounded who remain at Cholet?' Hortense demanded.

The young man shrugged. 'I'm afraid they'll just have to take their chances with the Republicans.'

When he stepped towards the empty wagon she halted him with a touch on his arm. 'Go home if you wish,' she snapped in disgust, 'but the wagon stays here. It belongs to my cousin and I'll find someone else to drive it.'

For a moment she thought he was going to argue with her, even push her out of the way and take the vehicle anyway. Fortunately the tradition of discipline and respect was too strong in him, and after giving her a look of intense dislike he hurried away.

'You won't find anyone else to go,' Nicole told her, standing in the doorway and wiping her bloody hands on her apron. 'The men may have fought well, but now they are running like sheep.'

'Then I'll do it myself,' she declared determinedly. 'You and Lucille can manage here. Just one last run. I can't stand the thought of our men lying wounded and waiting for the Republicans to take them.' Not, she added silently, when one of them might be Raoul.

Her heart was pounding in her breast and she was shaking with tension and suppressed fear as she guided the wagon down the narrow, rutted road. It was almost dark now and a mist was beginning to rise, curling in wispy tendrils above the surrounding fields. Now and then she passed groups of retreating soldiers. They looked at her curiously, and one man even called out that she was going the wrong way, but no one tried to stop her.

The sound of musket fire grew louder, punctuated by the base rumble of heavy artillery. In the distance she saw the glow of a fire. Across quite a wide area the broom was burning, and by its light she saw the Vendean army in full retreat. It was like a scene from Dante's *Inferno*, all fire and smoke and running silhouettes.

Leaving the road, she headed towards the conflagration. A smell of cordite hung heavily in the air, mingling with wood-smoke and powder-smoke and making her eyes stream. The noise was horrendous—cannon fire, musket fire, men screaming in agony or blood-lust, and the steady pounding of horses' hoofs across the trampled ground. Men streamed past her, some on horseback, others on foot, most ignoring her in their panic. Finally one young officer stopped and yelled for her to turn back.

'But there must be some wounded I can take with me,' she insisted. 'It won't take a minute to load them up.'

Sighing, he pointed across the plain to a small hill topped with trees. 'Roche-Jacquelein is making a stand on that rise. I believe he does have some wounded with him, bad cases all of them.' He gestured wearily to a soldier being held in the saddle by another. 'If they weren't we'd have brought them with us, but you must hurry. Soon he'll be falling back too.'

Giving the horses their heads, Hortense sped forward, the wagon bouncing bone-jarringly across the uneven ground. She had covered half the distance, and the retreating troops were nearly a mile behind her, when a score of riders came charging down from the hill-top.

Other cavalry came out of the trees and, with swords drawn, charged after them. It was too dark and the smoke was too thick for her to be able to see the colour of their uniforms, but she knew instinctively that they were Republicans.

Swinging the wagon around in a wide arc, she hurtled back the way she had come. Men from the retreating rear guard drew level with her and some even passed her. Looking over her shoulder, she saw the advancing Republicans drawing closer, and, lifting the whip from the seat beside her, used it ruthlessly on her horses. Her speed was reckless, considering the state of the ground, and ultimately she paid the price. One of its wheels collided with a small boulder, and with a sickening lurch the wagon crashed over on to its side. Hortense was thrown clear as the vehicle was dragged on by the frightened horses.

For a moment she could only lie stunned and sickened. She knew the Republicans were approaching her, but, for the life of her, couldn't move. Then someone was pulling at her and hauling her roughly to her feet. She felt herself lifted, and the next moment she was being swung across a horse. Reacting instinctively, she managed to right herself in the saddle as her rescuer swung expertly up behind her.

'For God's sake, hang on!' Raoul hissed, reaching around her to catch the reins and kicking the horse into a gallop.

Glancing anxiously over his shoulder, he changed direction slightly and headed towards a nearby wood. He knew he was veering away from the rest of the retreating Vendeans but considered that all to the good. Miraculously they made it to the shelter of the trees, and, looking back, saw that the Republicans had neglected to follow them.

'Are you all right?' Raoul asked as he slowed his horse

and allowed it to find its own path. There was little light beneath the high branches and it was necessary for them to proceed with care.

'I'm fine,' Hortense replied shakily. 'Do you think they'll follow us?'

'I doubt it.' He sighed and she could feel the movement of his chest against her back. 'But we'd better keep moving. . .west for a while and then south, if I'm to get you back to Château Claviere.'

'But the main body of the army is making for St Florent and the Loire,' she protested.

'I don't care about the army,' he told her, and she thought he sounded exhausted. 'I'm taking you home.'

For another hour they continued slowly, moving out of the wood and towards the river. The horse was tired after its gallop with a double load, and Raoul did not push it. Above them the moon was only a sliver but the stars were bright, and, once out of the trees, it was easier for them to see their way. Hortense began to shiver with reaction and cold, and Raoul pulled her closer against him in an effort to keep her warm. After a while he seemed to doze, and his head dropped forward against her shoulder. Worried lest he fall off, Hortense gently shook him awake. He apologised thickly and made an effort to sit up, but from time to time she could still feel him leaning against her. Lack of sleep was telling on him, but he refused to stop and rest.

They crossed the road south of Torfou and, on reaching the river, followed it west. It was taking them away from their destination, but they were not sure how far the Republicans had advanced. The water below them looked inky and uninviting as it flowed sluggishly between the crumbling banks. It was over a mile before they found a suitable place to cross, and then Raoul dismounted to lead the horse between jagged rocks and stones.

When they reached the other bank he paused for a moment, letting his head rest against the horse's flank. Hortense was swamped with compassion, and reached down to touch his face. She thought it a measure of his exhaustion that he did not pull away.

'We ought to stop,' she said.

He merely shook his head and, summoning the remainder of his strength, swung stiffly into the saddle. After another couple of miles he again began to lean heavily against her and, regardless of what he might want, she decided to halt. Guiding the horse into another band of trees, she eased Raoul away from her and slipped from the saddle. Deprived of her support, he weaved unsteadily.

After leading the horse into the shelter of a large oak she turned to help him dismount.

'No. . .' he muttered thickly, leaning forward over the horse's neck. 'I'll never get on. . .again. . .'

The horrible truth was just beginning to dawn on her when he half rolled, half fell from the saddle and sprawled at her feet. He groaned softly, and when she knelt beside him she heard him swear.

'You're hurt, Raoul; where?' she demanded, trying to keep the panic from her voice.

'Back of my shoulder,' he muttered.

He was trying to rise and, slipping her arms around him, she helped him to sit up. Her stomach turned over when she felt the warm wetness beneath her palm. She was terrified for him. Dear God! He must have been bleeding for hours. His head was resting against her breast and he gave a deep sigh.

'Go home. . .Hortense,' he said quietly. 'You have to go home. . .'

Before she could even answer him his eyes had closed and he had slipped away in a dead faint.

# CHAPTER SIX

A SUFFOCATING panic welled up inside Hortense. Raoul was a dead weight against her, and, almost sobbing, she carefully eased him down until he was stretched out on the damp grass. Desperately she chafed his hands and rubbed his face. He made no response, and after a moment she struggled to roll him on to his side. Somehow she managed to free one arm from his jacket and, dreading what she might find, ran her hand under it and across his back.

'Oh, God!' she gasped, feeling the ugly, sticky hole beneath the thin fabric of his shirt. Tugging off his cravat, she folded it and pressed it against the wound, then slipped his jacket back on to hold it in place. Turning him on to his back, she ran her hands across his chest and shoulders. There was definitely no exit-hole, which meant the ball was still in him. In one way that was good because it meant less bleeding, although eventually there would be the problem of getting it out. Without bandages, equipment or light there was nothing she could do for him, and tears of anguish and frustration streamed down her face.

Warmth! she thought desperately. Somehow she had to keep him warm. Her senses swam with relief when she remembered the blanket rolled up behind the saddle, and on trembling legs she walked over to retrieve it. She removed her cloak and, after spreading it out on the damp grass, eased Raoul on to it, using the blanket to cover them both. Then, drawing him against her, she held him with his head pillowed against her shoulder. He was going to survive, she vowed and, without being aware of it, began whispering words of comfort and encouragement he couldn't possibly hear.

The night dragged interminably as she lay trembling with reaction and cold, listening to the ragged breathing of the man at her side and expecting it to cease at any moment. High above her the trees hissed and rustled and, looking up through their thinning branches, she could see the star-studded sky. Then she prayed as she had never done before, bartering promises and pledging all manner of selfless deeds in return for Raoul's survival. She could not, dared not, sleep for fear that he slip away from her in the night, for she had already seen men die of less serious wounds.

Her stomach was in knots and her limbs cramped from lying too long in one position, when gradually, almost imperceptibly, the sky began to lighten and the stars faded one by one, to be replaced by a dull, uniform grey. Drawing her arm from around Raoul, she rubbed it to restore the circulation, wincing at the fierce throb of returning feeling. When the pain had eased she bent over him and gently touched his face. It was like ice beneath her fingers, and in the early light he looked frighteningly pale. Touching her fingers to his lips, she felt the reassuring warmth of his breath, and tears of relief stung her eyes.

It was then that she heard it—the rumble and creak of an approaching wagon, and peering through the early-morning mist, she caught sight of the vehicle through the trees. It was moving slowly along a narrow track some fifty yards away from her, pulled by two stout oxen. With beasts like that the driver had to be a Vendean. Scrambling to her feet, she began shouting and waving her arms wildly, then raced through the trees towards it.

'Oh, please!' she shouted breathlessly, hurtling into

the road just in front of the vehicle. 'You have to help me, please!'

The middle-aged man driving pulled up and for a moment studied her intently. His eyes were shadowed by a large flat-brimmed hat, and most of his face was concealed behind a dark beard so that it was impossible for her to tell what he was thinking.

'Please!' she said again, this time addressing her plea to the plump, homely-looking woman sitting beside him. 'My friend was wounded in the battle at Cholet. He has fallen from his horse, and there is nothing I can do to help him.'

With an almost imperceptible nod the man handed the reins to his wife and climbed from the wagon. Without further ado Hortense hurried back through the trees, turning only once to make sure that he followed.

'Is he badly hurt?' he asked dispassionately when they reached Raoul.

'I don't really know.' Hortense resented his apparent callousness and felt a strong impulse to shake him. 'He passed out last night and I haven't been able to either talk to or examine him. If you would only take us to les Herbiérs, to Château Claviere, then my cousin would reward you handsomely.'

'We're not going that way,' he replied so definitely that she knew she would not be able to change his mind. 'But we'll take you with us to Lége. Now our village is in danger of being overrun we're going to stay with my wife's sister.'

It was not at all what she had wanted, but better than nothing, she supposed. At least she would be able to find Raoul shelter and a doctor to take care of him. He really was looking terrible, and even when the burly peasant lifted him he did not stir, his arms and head hanging limply like a well-worn rag-doll.

By the time they reached the wagon the woman had

already cleared a space in the back among the various
household items, and the injured man was carefully laid
down. Hortense tied their horse to the back of the
vehicle and then, climbing in, carefully covered Raoul
with the blanket.

'Here!' the woman said, smiling gently and passing
her a thick quilt. 'Use this too.'

When Hortense thanked her the woman shrugged,
and her eyes filled with pain. 'My older son died of
wounds earlier this year. I'd like to think someone was
kind to him too. My other son rides with General
Royrand.'

'We haven't heard from him in weeks, have we,
Louise?' her husband complained. 'We don't even know
if he's alive or dead!'

And you're afraid he's dead, Hortense thought, suddenly understanding. That's why you appear so distant
and cold. She had already learned that people handled
grief in different ways, but to lose both sons. . . Reaching down, she picked up Raoul's hand and, although he
could not feel it, squeezed it encouragingly. She had
ceased to wonder why she loved him and now merely
accepted it as she did the colour of her hair or her need
for food. He did not return her feelings, but that made
little difference.

As the wagon continued along the rugged track the
sun rose higher in the sky and the early-morning mist
began to clear. Hortense felt the warmth of the sun
seeping into her tired and cramped limbs and, in spite of
her anxiety, began to doze. When the wagon lurched
into a particularly deep rut she was partially shaken from
sleep. She felt Raoul's fingers tighten around hers and
heard his soft groan. Instantly she was fully awake, and
looked down to find him watching her with eyes that
were slitted and cloudy with pain.

'How are you feeling?' she asked, gently touching his

pale cheek. He was shivering, she noticed, in spite of the fact that he was warmly covered.

'Like hell,' he replied, gritting his teeth as the wagon lurched again. 'My shoulder's on fire and my leg hurts too. I don't think I could move, even if my life depended. . .on. . .it.'

'You won't have to.' She squeezed his hand reassuringly. It felt unnaturally clammy. 'If you can just hang on, we should reach Lége in another couple of hours.'

'Why Lége?' he asked fretfully. 'Hortense. . .you should be going home.'

'All in good time,' she answered, seeking to soothe him as she would a child. 'First we have to find a doctor to take care of you.'

When the wagon hit another rough patch Raoul closed his eyes and swore weakly beneath his breath. He made no complaint but Hortense could tell that he was suffering greatly. She was swamped with compassion and at that moment would have done almost anything to ease his pain.

'See if he will take some of this,' the peasant women said, turning and offering her a flask. 'It's good cognac. It may help a little.'

Mercifully she managed to get him to swallow several mouthfuls of the potent spirit, and then he slept with his head pillowed against her thigh. Tentatively she ran her fingers through his dark hair, then down across his stubbled jaw. Even wounded and dirty, he stirred her as no other man had. It was not just because he was handsome; there was far more to it than that. His appearance attracted her, yet for some reason she suspected that she would have loved him had he been the ugliest man on earth.

They reached Lége in the late afternoon, when the sun was sinking and an autumn chill again filled the air. It was a typical market town, consisting of small terraced cottages set around a great grey church. They circled this imposing edifice and then turned down a step lane, pulling up after perhaps a quarter of a mile in front of a small one-storey farmhouse.

Raoul woke up then, but passed out again when the peasant and his brother-in-law carried him inside. He was taken to the only spare bedroom, and while the two men carefully removed his soiled clothes a doctor was summoned. In due course, the man arrived and spent almost an hour removing the ball from Raoul's shoulder and stitching up the gash on his thigh.

For the next day the patient remained flat on his back, sleeping most of the time and too weak even to lift a cup to his lips. Hortense spent all her time with him, and the two peasant women helped when they could, washing his clothes and soiled linen and even lending Hortense a dress while her own skirt and blouse were laundered. However, the work on the farm had to continue and Hortense was very conscious of being in the way. Not only were she and Raoul occupying what had been the only spare bedroom, but they were eating food and using up linen for which they could not pay.

There was only one bed, and at night Hortense shared it with Raoul, stripping down to her chemise and keeping as far away from him as possible, not only so as not to disturb him but because his naked proximity was a temptation almost impossible to resist. She had seen more of his lean, well-muscled body than was good for her and, ill as he was, still ached to hold him in her arms.

On the second morning when she awoke it was to find him watching her. She got the impression that he had been doing so for some time.

'You look like a child when you're asleep,' he told her, his expression oddly serious. 'You could be twelve rather than twenty-two.'

It was the last thing she wanted to hear from him, only reinforcing her fear that he thought of her merely as a sister or a friend. 'And how do you know how old I am?' she snapped.

He shrugged, wincing as the movement hurt his shoulder. 'Henri told me.' Then, eyes sparkling with pure mischief, he asked. 'Is this the first night you've spent in my bed?'

Hot colour flooded her face. 'As a matter of fact, it's the second, only you've been too ill to notice it. This is the only spare bed! As it is, Louise and Jean have been sleeping on the floor.' She was furious with him for making her feel so embarrassed. 'I'm getting up,' she snapped waspishly. 'Turn around.'

'Why?' Again his eyes sparkled. 'I know you're not naked beneath the covers.'

'Raoul Duchambray, you looked!' she choked, nearly speechless with indignation, then, calming down, slyly added, 'But I should be careful what you say if I were you. One flick of the covers and I shall be able to see exactly what you're made of!'

He laughed then, and she was sorry that she had made him because it obviously caused him pain.

'Hortense, you are no lady,' he commented between clenched teeth, although he was obviously still amused.

'Then we are well suited,' she snapped, climbing from the bed and reaching for her clothes, 'because you, sir, are no gentleman!'

He sighed then and his light-hearted mood seemed suddenly to leave him, making Hortense regret her quick retort. It had been such a long time since she had seen any sign of his boyish good humour, and she wished she had encouraged it, even at her own expense. Whatever he was thinking saddened him, and she was struck again by the realisation that there was more than the war on his mind.

Although he remained subdued, Raoul managed to eat some breakfast, and, when a Vendean officer arrived at the farm later that morning, insisted that he was well enough to speak with him. Hortense did her best to dissuade him and finally scolded him roundly, but he was not to be put off.

'Duchambray!' the fair-haired young man exclaimed as she reluctantly showed him into the bedroom. 'I'd heard there was a wounded officer here but I had no idea it was you. . . Perhaps you do not remember me—Jacques Martin? We met once at Thierry's.' His smile was full of warmth and youthful enthusiasm. 'I'm Jeanne Raveneau's brother. I cannot thank you enough for getting my sister and her children out of Paris.'

'How is she?' Raoul asked a little awkwardly. 'I thought she was in England.'

'Oh, she is,' Martin replied, turning to smile appreciatively at Hortense. 'She's with my parents in London.'

He couldn't have been more than twenty, she thought. In fact he didn't even look as if he needed to shave, but he carried with him an easy air of authority—and she found what he had to say intensely interesting.

'She writes to me when she can,' Martin continued. 'She explained how much you risked in helping her. . . Is this beautiful lady your wife?'

Raoul's lips twitched in amusement, and Hortense coloured to the roots of her hair. 'No, we just happen to be travelling together, but I agree—she is beautiful. . . Her name is Hortense Claviere. You may have met her cousin Henri.'

Mindful of his manners, young Martin then took the girl's hand, lifting it to his lips with exaggerated courtesy. 'I came to offer you both safe conduct with me to Noirmoutier. I have orders from Charette for his commander there.' He glanced questioningly at Raoul. 'There are several wounded in our party so we shall be

travelling slowly, and I wasn't sure how comfortable—
or, indeed, safe—you'd be here. My family have a house
on the island and, now the place is back under our
control, it would give me great pleasure to offer you
hospitality.'

'It's very kind of you,' Hortense replied quickly, 'but
I'm not sure Raoul is up to the journey.'

'That has got nothing to do with it,' Raoul grumbled.
'I had hoped to return Hortense safely to Château
Claviere.'

'I wouldn't recommend it.' Young Martin looked
serious as he settled himself on the edge of the bed. 'Our
intelligence reports large numbers of Republicans
advancing from that area. Not that you are much safer
here. It wouldn't be the first time Charette has had to
evacuate the town.'

'In that case,' Raoul conceded, 'we'd better go with
you.'

Hortense thought he was being very foolish and told
him so, continuing to debate the issue long after arrangements had been made and Martin had gone.

'I don't want to hear any more about it!' he finally
snapped irritably. 'I can manage the journey. It will be a
lot safer for us to travel with Jacques.'

'For me, you mean!' Suddenly she understood why he
was being so determined, and she was furious with him.
'I can rough it if I have to; you know that. I don't want
you feeling responsible for me, I told you that at Cholet.'

'But I do feel responsible. I can't help it,' he hissed,
reaching out and catching hold of her hand, surprising
her with his strength as he pulled her down on the bed.
'Don't you feel a certain obligation towards me? We're
friends, aren't we? Friendship brings with it a certain
commitment!'

'Yes, we're friends,' she replied, looking into his

blazing eyes, but it was so much more than that keeping her at his side.

'Then let's hear no more about it. You said yourself you feel we're in the way here. Jacques's offer is too good to refuse.'

He continued to stare into her face and, for a moment, she thought he was going to kiss her. It crossed her mind to goad him further; when he had kissed her before it had been because some incident had pushed him beyond control. Then the anger seemed to fade from his eyes, to be replaced by a sadness she could not understand.

'I'm tired,' he said flatly, settling back against the pillows. 'I need to sleep.'

For a long time that night Hortense lay awake, trying to make sense of their relationship. Was Raoul friend or enemy, lover or comrade? She wasn't even sure if he liked her or whether she irritated him beyond measure. He had told Jacques she was beautiful, and that surprised her. He also thought she looked like a twelve-year-old! He seemed to care enough about her to place her welfare above his own, but he would do that anyway, she realised. There was an innate chivalry in him when dealing with the young or the weak, and somehow she knew he could be really ruthless in their defence.

Turning her head on the pillow, she glanced at his shadowed profile and felt that familiar ache. It's madness, this feeling I have, she thought; almost like being bewitched. Perhaps it was the war, but she was feeling things so much more intensely.

The following morning Raoul insisted on dressing for the journey, even managing to do so alone. By the time he had finished, however, he looked decidedly wrung out and could only lie quietly on top of the bed, waiting for Martin to arrive. Finally, when they heard the sound of horses outside, Hortense helped him on with his blue

coat, leaving the right sleeve hanging free to accommo-
date his sling. He thanked her politely as she slid her
shoulder under his right arm to support him, even
though she knew he hated to be dependent on her.

Outside Martin dismounted and came to greet them.
Beaming proudly, he gestured towards a coach that had
definitely seen better days. Hortense could have hugged
him, knowing it would prove more comfortable than any
wagon. Jean brought the horse from the barn and tied it
behind the coach. Raoul waited until he had finished,
then, leaning heavily against the side of the vehicle, held
out his hand.

'Thank you,' he said simply as the peasant grasped it.
'I suspect I owe you my life.'

Hortense saw him reach into his pocket and, retrieving
his watch, press it into the peasant's hand. Before the
man could protest he climbed into the coach, looking a
little embarrassed when he realised that she had noticed
what he had done.

The journey took the best part of the day and Raoul
paid dearly for it. By mid-morning he had given up any
pretence of not being in pain and had stretched out full-
length on one of the seats, looking decidedly pale and
strained.

He hissed in pain when they hit a particularly bad
stretch of road. 'I think the driver is going through every
damned pot-hole just to torment me!'

As the day wore on the girl's concern for him increased
a hundred-fold. He developed a fever, and freely admitted that his shoulder was killing him. It had to be bad,
she knew, because he even let her hold him to protect
him from the worst of the bumping.

When they reached the coast the tide was mercifully
out and they were able to cross the causeway to the
island without delay. The sun was low in the sky as they
traversed the sand and mussel beds, and the distant sea

was very blue. At any other time Hortense would have appreciated the beauty of the scene—the pink-tinged clouds, the sparkling rockpools, the seagulls banking and swirling above guinea-gold sand. She noticed none of it; she was too concerned for the man whose head lay pillowed in her lap. He seemed to have lapsed into something between a sleep and a swoon, his eyes tightly closed and his breathing rapid and unsteady.

Darkness had fallen by the time they had reached Jacques's house, and Hortense, too, ached from the continuous jolting. It was a two-storey, rather unpretentious manor-house set just outside of Noirmoutier town. There were five bedrooms and Raoul did not stir as they carried him up to one of them. Because he was seldom at home Jacques kept no servants, and the place was cold. With surprising competence he set about lighting a fire in the bedroom hearth and then, as the room began to warm, helped Hortense to undress Raoul.

A doctor was summoned, but his diagnosis was not encouraging. There was little to be done, he told them dispassionately. Raoul's wounds had become infected and his body would either succeed in fighting the infection or not. All they could hope to do was to reduce his fever by regularly sponging him down.

Over the next few days Hortense learned what real tiredness was as Raoul tossed and turned in delirium, needing almost constant care. Jacques found a woman from the town, a Madame Rother, to help with the nursing, and at times even sat with the patient himself. Nevertheless the brunt of the nursing fell on Hortense, not that she would have had it otherwise.

Sometimes, when Raoul tossed and turned upon the bed, she was sure he was reliving the fire as he called out for Paul and muttered fretfully about things being his fault. She did her best to soothe him, but it was obvious that his memories were causing him considerable distress.

'If he doesn't improve over the next twenty-four hours,' the doctor finally told them, 'then I think you should call a priest.'

All through that night Hortense sat with Raoul, bathing his fevered brow and willing him to live. She would not let him die, she vowed, not when they had been through so much together. Then, towards morning, it seemed as if her prayers had been answered. His temperature began to drop. His mutterings became less, and he fell into a deep, natural sleep. Even then she refused to leave him but took what rest she could, curled up in a bedside chair.

She was still there when he finally regained consciousness, and her throat tightened as she looked down into his puzzled eyes, eyes that looked impossibly blue against the dark hair and rapidly thickening beard. Even as she watched he blinked, struggling to bring her face into focus.

'I feel as weak as a kitten,' he complained in a voice so huskily low that she had to strain to catch his words.

'That's to be expected.' She gently placed the back of her hand against his cheek then over his forehead. Having assured herself that all trace of his fever had disappeared, she persuaded him to take a drink, lifting his head so that the cool water could trickle down his throat.

'Thanks, that's much better,' he muttered as she laid him back down. For a moment he was silent, then, frowning, asked, 'How long have we been here? Somehow I seem to have lost track of time.'

'Almost a week,' she replied thickly. 'You've been out of your mind for almost a week. Oh, Raoul, you nearly died!'

Suddenly it was all too much for her and, worn down

by tiredness, she could no longer keep her emotions under control. Tears streamed down her face and she hiccuped loudly in an attempt to restrain her sobs.

'Don't. . .' he protested weakly, reaching out for her hand. 'Don't cry, Hortense. Please, *chérie*. . .I can't stand to see you cry.'

Dabbing at her wet cheeks, she finally managed to control herself.

'That's better,' he told her, closing his eyes with a weary sigh. 'I love. . .you, you know. . . It hurts to. . .see you. . .cry.'

By the time his words registered he was sound asleep, and she was left wondering if he was even aware of what he had said. Dared she believe him? She desperately wanted to, and yet common sense warned her not to take to heart words spoken at such a time. For ages afterwards she just sat there, unable to drag her eyes away from his still, pale face and feeling the love expand inside her until it was almost an ache. Then, very gently, she bent to plant a kiss on his lips. It was a liberty she felt he owed her and she was pleasantly surprised by his small, instinctive response.

October gave way to November, and slowly Raoul began to recover. He did not speak again of love, although often when she was in his room she would find him watching her, a strange, soft look in his eyes. Was it gratitude, she wondered, or was it something more? As the days passed she became more and more optimistic about his feelings towards her, but, although he had every opportunity to declare himself, something seemed to be holding him back.

When Jacques left to rejoin Charette, Raoul and Hortense had the big house to themselves. At one time such an arrangement would have been considered unseemly, but the war had changed all that. Raoul was still a semi-invalid and Hortense needed to be on hand to look after him. Since their arrival she had occupied the room adjacent to his and, even when they were alone, saw no reason to change the arrangement. Madame Rother still popped in from time to time to help with the washing and cleaning but, on the whole, Hortense enjoyed running the house.

Jacques had generously made funds available for clothing and food. Raoul had staked Jeanne and paid for her passage to England, he insisted, and he was merely repaying the debt. When Hortense curiously questioned Raoul on the matter he was not very forthcoming, although she gathered from Jacques that he had only managed to save Madame Raveneau at considerable personal risk.

The time they spent together was precious, and as Raoul's strength increased they spent several companionable evenings sitting together beside a roaring fire. It was a time of discovery, of learning intimate little things about each other and, out of friendship, seeking to please. The girl's love deepened and expanded to something far beyond the physical, and yet she remained acutely aware of Raoul as a man. At times his closeness was pure agony and she literally ached for his embrace. Often she would lie sleepless in her bed, feeling empty and imcomplete, and then she would hear him tossing and turning too.

At last he took his first stroll outside, walking the halfmile or so down to the harbour. Hortense was hurt when he did not ask her to accompany him, yet respected his need to be alone. He was gone for nearly two hours, far longer than was good for him, and returned looking tired and drawn. Resisting the urge to fuss, she made him a cup of hot chocolate and, after drinking it, he went upstairs to lie down. For almost half an hour she managed to occupy herself, dusting shelves that did not need it and wandering aimlessly from room to room.

Finally, unable to restrain herself any longer, she went up and knocked on his door.

'I came to see if you were all right,' she blurted, entering as soon as he answered. 'I was afraid you'd overdone it.'

He had removed his boots and jacket and was sprawled out on the bed, looking incredibly masculine and appealing. A book was tossed face-down on the covers, but she got the impression that he had long since given up reading it.

'You don't need to fuss over me,' he grumbled. 'I'm not a child.'

Hortense struggled to conceal her hurt. She deserved his curtness, she told herself. After all, he had made it quite clear that he wanted to be alone.

'I'm sorry,' she confessed. 'I shouldn't have intruded. It's just that I suddenly seem to have too much time on my hands. . .'

Raoul sighed and closed his eyes wearily. 'I'm sorry too. I didn't mean to be short with you. . .and you're right, I did overdo it. My shoulder is stiff and aching like the devil.'

'Oh, so that's it,' she replied, feeling happier now she knew just what she was dealing with. 'Perhaps I'd better take a look.'

'No!' he snapped, wondering why fate had decided to torment him so. Then, in the face of her confusion, he relented. 'Oh, all right, but I don't think there's any real damage.'

As she had done many times before, she helped him with his shirt then leant around him to loosen the light bandage he still wore. Pulling away, he untied the knot himself and began to unwind it, his mouth tight with irritation. When the healing wound was revealed she breathed a sigh of relief.

'It seems perfectly all right. In fact, you could probably dispense with the bandage as long as you don't do anything too drastic.' Her fingers probed gently at the ridge of muscle across his shoulder. 'I'm not surprised you're hurting; you're much too tense.'

'Hortense!' he grated, grasping her hand and holding it away from him. 'Don't you know you're killing me with kindness?'

He did not release her wrist but continued to stare at her, his blue eyes glittering with sudden, unmistakable passion. At that moment she could not have spoken had her life depended on it. Nor could she drag her eyes away from his, but knelt there on his bed, feeling his intense, hungry stare with every fibre of her being. With a soft groan she reached out to touch the curly black down on his chest. It was the only encouragement he needed. When he hungrily took her mouth she was ready for him and poured all her love and longing into the kiss.

'Oh, God!' he groaned against her neck as he eased her down beside him on the bed. 'Woman, you've been driving me crazy, touching me, always touching, and never in the way I wanted! It wasn't so bad when I was really ill, but lately every time you've changed my bandage has been a torture.'

Just once more, he promised himself, struggling to control his passion. I'll kiss her just once more and then I'll try to put some distance between us, but even as his lips touched hers he knew it was not going to be enough. Her hands were running over him in an unconsciously provocative way, and he was literally burning up with need for her. It's lust, he tried to tell himself, not love, but it was impossible to tell where the one ended and the other began. When she groaned into his mouth and he felt her hand curl into the muscles at his waist he knew that he was lost. She wasn't going to stop him and he just hadn't the will-power to draw back.

Desire, hot and molten, surged through Hortense,

and with characteristic honesty she made no attempt to
conceal it. Although she had never before made love, she
moaned appreciatively when Raoul caressed her breast
and did not demur when he unfastened her blouse and
then her chemise. It just seemed so natural, so right, and
by now she knew his body as well as her own.

I love you. I love you! The words burned like fire
inside her and yet, somehow, she managed to hold them
back. His body was like a furnace. She had never known
such heat! He had bewitched her, and now, at last, she
had succumbed. Feverishly his hands stole over her skin,
caressing, possessing, tender in spite of his need, and
she responded mindlessly with the age-old instinct of
womankind.

He is so beautiful, she thought, glancing up into his
taut face bathed in the last rays of the winter sun as it
spilled through the bedroom window; as beautiful as a
Grecian hero or pagan god, yet oh, so warm and alive,
so marvellously, thankfully alive! For a short while, at
least, he was hers, utterly and completely, and she
surrendered to him gladly, trading her virginity for a
moment she knew she would never forget.

# CHAPTER SEVEN

WHEN Hortense awoke morning sunlight was streaming across the bed in a golden waterfall. She stretched languorously, aware that the morning warmth held a new texture, a new excitement. Raoul's arm was draped across her body and she could feel one of his hair-roughened legs touching her thigh.

Some time during the night they had both stirred sufficiently to pull the bedclothes up around them, but they had been too tired, too overwhelmed by what had happened between them to talk. Raoul had gathered her close, and she had fallen asleep with her head pillowed on his chest, lulled by the steady beating of his heart.

For a while Hortense just lay there, staring up at the sun-speckled ceiling and savouring the feelings of peace and contentment that enfolded her. She had no worries, no regrets, but felt only a sense of completeness and belonging. Having Raoul for a lover just seemed so right.

Easing away from him, she turned her head to watch him sleep. He had most of the pillow, and against its whiteness his face was deeply tanned, shadowed by the stubble that grew on his jaw. He looked younger with his hair tousled, and more relaxed than she had ever seen him.

What drives you? she wondered fondly. What makes you so solitary and afraid to let me close? She had shared her body with him and she wanted to share her emotions too. Last night he had been so fired by passion, so oddly vulnerable, and yet he had shown tenderness and consideration too. Holding himself back, he had comforted and encouraged until she had shared his pleasure and his

release, her body exploding with sensations she had
never dreamed of. Remote and arrogant he might be,
but there was a gentleness in him and a warmth just
waiting to be explored.

It was the change in the level of his breathing that told
her that he was beginning to wake. The arm draped
possessively across her waist tightened and he gave a
sleepy groan.

'Good morning,' he murmured after a moment, his
incredibly blue eyes heavy-lidded and full of warmth.

'Good morning.' Hortense found herself unable to
hold his gaze. Nothing in her previously celibate life had
prepared her for how she should act now. She was
embarrassed and, moreover, concerned in case he should
think she expected some sort of commitment from him.

'You're not sorry, are you?' he asked quietly. 'I should
hate it if you regretted what we've done.'

The concern in his voice brought forth a tender smile
and she shook her head. 'I don't regret it. . .I was just a
little afraid that you might.'

'It was special, Hortense. You're special, only. . .'

'I don't expect any commitment from you,' she told
him a little too brightly, swinging her legs over the side
of the bed and reaching for the quilt to cover her
nakedness. 'The pleasure was mutual, I assure you.'

'Hortense?' The word was both a question and a plea.
'Hortense, we have to talk!'

'No, we don't,' she replied, standing and wrapping
the coverlet around herself, her expression almost regal.
'You don't owe me anything, and I don't want expla-
nations or excuses.'

Feelings of tenderness and possession welled up inside
Raoul and he ached to draw her back into the comfort of
his arms. More than anything he wanted to be free so
that he could love her and take care of her as she
deserved. She was the best thing that had ever happened

to him, and the worst. He loved her, damn it, in spite of her politics and her independent ways, and yet he had spilled his seed into her without thought of the consequences. Making love had never been like that for him before.

Memory flooded his senses and, once again, he felt his body tighten in need, making him long to pull her down and take her again there and then. Fiercely he reminded himself that she was no camp-follower. He wanted to do what was right for her, only he wasn't at all sure what that was. He was her enemy, for God's sake, a man without principles or honour. He knew she would be better off without him, but he didn't think he had the strength to let her go. . . What if she was already carrying his child?

'I think we should get married,' he blurted as she moved towards the door, the quilt trailing untidily behind her. 'You could be pregnant.'

When she turned back to face him she was blazingly angry. Damn him, she thought, for taking something so breathtakingly beautiful and tarnishing it with his cold practicality. 'I told you, you owe me nothing!' she snapped. 'I won't be wed out of feelings of guilt! What I did I did freely. You need feel no responsibility towards me whatsoever!'

Raoul was too stunned by her outburst to reply, too stunned and too unsure. She was right, and he knew he ought not to press the issue but rather look on it as a reprieve, yet he found he couldn't face the idea of her walking out of his life. There could be no simple friendship between them now, no easy companionship; last night had put an end to that. The only way he was going to be able to keep her with him was to marry her. Take the chance, he told himself as he stared at the door that had just slammed behind her. Take the chance or

you will always regret what could have been. In a month
or two you could even be dead.

Having dressed quickly, Hortense hurried downstairs.
She had intended to prepare breakfast but the thought
of food sickened her. Her feelings were in turmoil and
she desperately needed time to think things through.
Even being in the house with Raoul was a distraction
and, collecting her cloak, she went out in search of the
solitude she needed.

Hurrying through the secluded garden, she passed
under a wide gateway and out into a narrow lane. Instead
of heading towards the town with its harbour and
fortified château she turned right, looking for the narrow
sandy pathway that led down to the nearest beach. It
was a beautiful, clear morning and a stiff breeze tugged
at the couch-grass and sprayed sand across her ankles as
she walked down the track towards the sea. Settling
down in the shelter of some rocks, she stared out across
the cold blue water and distant salt-beds, trying to come
to terms with what she must do. She loved Raoul quite
desperately, yet knew she could not trade on his honour
and marry him, not when he so obviously didn't return
her feelings. Her pride had already taken enough of a
beating and, unless he could persuade her otherwise, she
intended to move into the village. He was well enough
to take care of himself now, and had been for some time.
In fact, he was incredibly self-sufficient and didn't really
need anyone.

In spite of the sunshine, the morning was chilly, yet
Hortense failed to notice it. The wind tugged at her hair
and crept under her cloak but she remained unaware of
any discomfort, continuing to stare sightlessly across the
white-tipped waves.

She had been sitting there for nearly an hour when
Raoul joined her. He had noted her direction from his
bedroom window but it had still taken him a while to

find her. She did not look up at his approach and, in fact, was not even aware of him until he sat down beside her, his hands resting easily across his bent knees.

'I asked you to marry me because I love you,' he said without looking at her. 'If I seemed unsure it was because of circumstances, not because I don't care enough about you.'

Hortense turned her head to look at him, drinking in the sight of his handsome profile, aching for the strain she saw in his face. The wind had tousled his hair into boyish disarray. He had not taken the time to shave, and beneath his blue coat the neck of his shirt hung open.

'I love you,' he repeated, meeting her eyes, 'more than I would have thought possible.'

Hope swelled inside her as she searched his face, wanting to be sure he was not lying to her out of pity. She saw pain and sadness there but, above all, she saw the same tenderness and yearning she was experiencing herself.

Raoul looked down at her fiery head shimmering with curls. Her lashes were glistening with unshed tears and her small nose was red with the cold.

Reaching out, he cupped her face with his hand. 'I know I'm being selfish, but I can't fight what is between us any longer. I want you to be my wife.'

His hand slipped behind her neck and he urged her forward for a kiss. For Hortense nothing else existed in that sun-coloured moment but the warmth and softness of his mouth against hers. It was as if they were both in some sort of limbo. Time and place were no more, and she felt only love and a sensation of caring so intense that it hurt. Even after he had finished kissing her he continued to hold her, her head pressed tightly against his chest. She slipped her arms around his waist and sighed possessively as a slow tingling relaxation swept over her and a feeling of such happiness that she felt she would burst.

'Will you marry me?' he asked huskily.

She laughed and glanced shyly up into his face. 'Whenever you like.'

'As soon as possible,' he replied, conscious that their time together might be short. Then he kissed her again with a hunger and desperation that surprised her.

Hortense was moved by his apparent insecurity, and if possible loved him even more because of it. A fierce sense of protectiveness rose up inside her. There was such passion behind his controlled façade; such passion and such endearing need. Nothing, she thought in her naïveté, could ever change the love she felt for him.

They were married three days later in the impressive church in the centre of Noirmoutier town. Raoul looked particularly handsome in his new dark green uniform coat, and Hortense was glad he had persuaded her to purchase her own gown of ivory silk. They had both expected it to be a quiet affair, and were surprised by the number of people who turned up to wish them well. Afterwards, on the orders of General d'Elbee, who was also on the island, recovering from the wounds he had received at Cholet, they were taken to the Château and wined and dined in fine style.

After the meal d'Elbee himself joined them, although he was still in considerable pain, and so weak and breathless that he was unable to remain on his feet for more than a minute or two. De Tinguy, Charette's commander on the island, was also there, and Raoul spent some time in conversation with him, leaving Hortense sitting beside the fire with the ailing d'Elbee. She did not know the general well and had previously considered him rather surly and aloof but, on further acquaintance, was surprised by how much she liked him. He was shy rather than arrogant, she discovered, and, with his dark, brooding looks and pleasantly husky voice, was extremely attracitve. Not that she had eyes for anyone but Raoul, something the general actually commented on, causing her colour to rise and those around her to laugh.

It was getting dark by the time they left the château, and purple-tinted storm-clouds were gathering threateningly above the setting sun. Raoul heaved a sigh of relief as he slipped his arm around her shoulders and began walking with her through the narrow streets of the town. D'Elbee had offered them the use of his carriage but they had politely declined, neither of them wanting to linger while the vehicle was got ready.

'You really don't mind walking?' Raoul asked again, and she shook her head. 'It was nice of everyone to go to so much trouble, but watching you and being unable to make love to you has been driving me insane.'

'You were the one who insisted on not touching me again until after we were married,' she reminded him with a gentle smile.

'I know,' he groaned, pausing to kiss her hand. Then, eyes alight with rare laughter, he added, 'Tonight I'm going to make up for it!'

On reaching Jacques's house they found that Madame Rother had been there before them. A cheerful fire burned in the hearth, and a basket of marzipan and sweetmeats stood upon the sideboard. Raoul removed the girl's cloak and, after tossing it carelessly across a chair, drew her into his arms.

'I love you,' he whispered, 'more than my life. Whatever happens, I want you to remember that.'

There was something in his voice that disturbed her, some element of desperation and warning, yet she ceased to wonder about it the moment his lips met hers. Her senses were filled with him, and at that moment nothing else seemed to matter.

Raoul held her close, feeling the sweet warmth of her mouth so responsive under his, and found it easy to push his misgivings aside. His nostrils were full of the fragrance of her hair and the subtle perfume of her skin. He had been wanting her all afternoon but until that moment he hadn't realised just how much. She was like a fever in him, a fire that burned and boiled in his blood, and he knew he would never be able to get enough of her.

Swinging her into his arms, he carried her up the stairs and into the bedroom, where another fire glowed welcomingly in the hearth. None too gently he placed her upon the bed, and while he began undressing her her hands worked feverishly on the buttons of his shirt. Naked and clinging, pressing close in the circle of his arms, Hortense responded once again to that slow, secret awakening she had experienced only once before.

There, in that firelit room with storm-clouds gathering threateningly outside, they made love with a fervour that stunned them both. Then afterwards, their passion spent, he held her tenderly, her cheek nestled against his neck. His body felt boneless, his energy spent, and yet his mind still teemed with plans and possibilities.

'I've offered my services to de Tinguy,' he told her after several moments of silence. 'I think we should stay on the island for a while, and I want to earn my keep. He was more than happy to take me up on it. It will involve some picket duty and maybe the odd reconnaissance trip to the mainland, but I shall still be able to spend a lot of time with you.'

'I thought we would be going home,' she protested, both disturbed and disappointed because he had not thought to discuss the matter with her.

'We don't know what is happening between here and les Herbiérs,' he replied reasonably. 'I know you're worried about Henri and Marie, but I don't think we should risk returning just yet. We should at least wait until we have news from either Jacques or Charette. For all we know, the entire Vendée may have fallen to the Republicans by now.' And if that was the case, he thought optimistically, then he might even be able to persuade her to leave France—then she would never need to know of his deception. It was too much to hope for, and he sighed tiredly.

Immediately she was all concern, mentally berating herself for forgetting how recently he had been ill. Swallowing the protest she had been going to make, she planted a kiss on the line of his jaw. He was, after all, only doing his best to take care of her.

'Whatever you decide,' she told him with unprecedented docility, 'as long as we're together I really don't mind.'

She found the days that followed some of the most blissful of her life. Raoul proved an ideal husband, humorous and loving, and appreciative of anything she did for him. For her part, she enjoyed playing house. The lack of servants did not bother her, and she began to enjoy preparing simple meals. On occasion, when he was not on duty at the castle, Raoul would help, proving quite a competent cook—a result, he admitted, of living off the land when he was on campaign.

Evenings they spent reading and talking and making love. Hortense got so that she could tell when Raoul wanted her, and a certain look in his eyes would be enough to set her tingling in anticipation. She didn't think she would ever have enough of his lovemaking and, as the days passed, found herself wanting him even more. Their relationship flourished, and Hortense felt closer to him than she had to anyone.

Only in her more introspective moments would she acknowledge that he was no more open and ready to share his thoughts than he had been at the beginning of their relationship. There were still times when he seemed preoccupied and the look in his eyes would shut her out. Always he would deny that there was anything bothering him and would throw himself into some domestic or romantic pursuit as if trying to prove that there was nothing wrong.

Halfway through December their blissful domestic idyll was curtailed when de Tinguy asked for volunteers to go into Nantes. Rumours of the most horrendous slaughter were coming out of the town, now occupied by the Republicans, and he was anxious to find out exactly what was going on. They hadn't heard from Charette for several days and there were fears that the Republicans on the mainland had finally bested him.

Hortense was furious when Raoul agreed to accompany another man into the enemy-held town. He was still not fully recovered, she insisted, and no one would have expected him to go. When he refused to change his mind it sparked off the first real argument of their marriage.

Raoul remained adamant. Not only would he be helping de Tinguy, he told her, but he knew a banker in Nantes and rather thought he would be able to borrow some money aginst the small inheritance his grandmother had left him. He didn't add that for his own peace of mind he needed to know exactly what was happening in the town. The tales of Republican atrocities had been bothering him. He thought they had been exaggerated, but he felt he had to know for sure. It would also be an opportunity for him to contact his Republican masters, although he found himself increasingly reluctant to do so.

Hortense tried every tactic to make him change his mind, and the night before his departure lay stiff and uncooperative in his bed. However, she found she could not let him leave with her still angry with him, and, when he woke her at dawn the following morning, went willingly into his arms. He had already shaved and dressed in his peasant's disguise, and she choked back a sob as she burrowed against the coarse material of his coat.

'I still wish you weren't going,' she told him. 'I'm sure it's dangerous.'

He kissed her and squeezed her hard. She smelled of soap and sleep, and leaving her was one of the hardest things he had ever had to do.

'I'll take care,' he promised. 'In fact, now I wish I hadn't agreed to go. I'd much rather climb back into bed with you.'

Surprisingly she believed him; in the early-morning light he looked strained and serious, and a sad smile tugged at the corners of his mouth.

'I love you,' she blurted.

It was the first time she had said the words outside the heat of passion and, in the midst of his fears and misgivings, Raoul felt a surge of happiness. He wanted to kiss her again, but he didn't dare. He knew too much tenderness would only weaken him and make it impossible for him to leave at all.

Hortense had to fight a childish urge to cling on to him, to hold him back by sheer force. Not only did she fear for his safety, but she somehow knew that when he returned things just would not be the same. The demands of war had once more intruded on the feelings they had for each other, and she was afraid they would never be able to recapture the intimacy of the last few days.

'I'd better go,' he sighed, and then, because he could not stand to prolong the moment, hugged her briefly and left.

With a sigh Hortense rolled over and buried her face in the soft pillow where, only a short while ago, his head

. had lain. The smell of him was strangely reassuring, and she promised herself that she would not change the linen until he had returned.

She found the next few days even emptier and more lonely than she had expected. Time dragged, and she wondered constantly what Raoul was doing. Was he missing her too or was he completely wrapped up in the machinations of war? Evenings were the worst, and on more than one occasion she went early to bed, only to toss and turn restlessly. In the short time she had spent with Raoul she had become so used to the comfort of his body lying next to hers, and without him her bed seemed cold and empty.

He returned on the evening of the fourth day, and as soon as she saw him riding up the lane she felt as if a great weight had been lifted from her. Both horse and rider looked exhausted as they passed under the arched gateway. Raoul glanced up at the bedroom window and, catching sight of her, smiled and waved. Pausing only to return the gesture, she hurtled downstairs, out of the kitchen door and into the small stable-yard.

Raoul had just dismounted, and before he could even loosen his saddle girth she was in his arms. The urgency of his embrace surprised her, and when she finally drew back to look at him she was appalled by how haggard he appeared. Not only were his eyes red-rimmed with tiredness, but there was a haunted look in them, and his face was pale beneath his sprouting beard. He did not seem to want to talk as they unsaddled and stabled his horse, and she resisted the urge to press him. He was obviously exhausted and she sensed that now was not the time.

Later as, washed and shaved, he sat across the table from her, eating a specially prepared meal, she again thought how strained he looked. He smiled from time to time at things she said, but the light never reached his eyes. Having finished her own meal, she watched in concern as he pushed the food around on his plate. He was not usually a pernickety eater and she took it as another indication of how tired he was.

'You don't have to finish it,' she told him, 'if you're not hungry or you're too tired; I shan't be offended.'

Smiling ruefully, he laid down his knife and fork and stood up. 'I'm sorry. I'll help you clear away.'

'There's no need,' she replied, slipping her arm through his and hugging him. 'Madame Rother is coming in to clean in the morning. Let's go and sit by the fire.'

She led him into the drawing-room and across to the hearth, and, after stirring the smouldering logs to life, went to join him on the chintz-covered sofa. He had rested his head back against the cushions and his eyes were closed.

'I'm all right,' he lied, reaching out and drawing her into the circle of his arm. In fact he felt sick and had done since he had witnessed the happenings in Nantes. While he had been in the town the guillotine had not ceased in its bloody work, and then there were the drownings. He had actually spoken to a boy who had seen his mother and father herded into a barge that was then taken out into the river and sunk. The description had been too vivid to be a fabrication, the lad's distress too acute. The rumours had proved all too true and he was finding it hard to live with his compatriots' barbarity.

It was Carrier who was at the root of the killings, and it was Carrier he was supposed to serve. In the end he had never made his intended report to the fanatical commissioner, even though he had managed to give his Vendean companion the slip. Revolution involved bloodshed, he knew, but the wholesale murder of innocent peasants was more than he could stomach. He felt disillusioned, empty and somehow cheated by what he considered a despoiling of the Republican cause. For the first time, as it seemed to him, he truly understood how foul this world was.

'Was it very bad in Nantes?' Hortense asked quietly.

'Yes,' he admitted flatly. 'The rumours were true, every one of them. Anyone even remotely connected to the uprising is being slaughtered, women and children as well as men. . .and it's all so pointless; all they are doing is creating martyrs.'

'All Republicans are barbarians,' Hortense snapped. 'They won't have the intelligence or sensibility to appreciate that. Killing is all that they understand; murder and vandalism and theft. Oh, God, Raoul! I feel so angry and so helpless. . .and it must have been so much worse for you. . .being there and not being able to do anything.'

You have no idea, Raoul thought bleakly, no concept of how I feel. A shudder ran through him, and, seeking to comfort him, the girl snuggled closer still.

'Make love to me,' she whispered. 'Make love to me now.'

Without speaking, almost without thinking, he bent his head to take her lips, seeking to lose himself in her softness, to smother his pain in the healing warmth of her love. She clung to him, her fingers digging into his shoulders, even through the coarse material of his jacket, and her body trembled with relief and joy to feel his arms around her once more. He was everything to her, the centre of her entire world, and she was offering him a comfort far beyond words.

Later, their passion spent, they lay half-naked in front of the flickering fire. Raoul had propped his back against the sofa, and Hortense rested her head against his bare chest. His hand caressed her shoulder as he stared unseeingly into the flames and Hortense knew he was again thinking of the horrors he had seen.

'Let's leave France,' he said suddenly, taking her by surprise. 'Let's go down to La Rochelle and find a ship to take us to America. I have some money now, enough to get us started.'

'You mean run away,' she said after a while, 'when the war is not yet lost.' She was disappointed in him, and it showed in her voice as she added, 'After you've witnessed the Republicans' savagery at first hand I don't know how you can think of giving up! If everyone felt like you then we might as well surrender and be done with it. They are evil, Raoul, and somebody has to stop them.'

His hand ceased its comforting caress and he turned his head to look at her. His expression could have been carved in stone. He looked suddenly hard and unapproachable, and yet there was a hint of uncertainty in his eyes.

'I don't want anything more to do with this war,' he said quietly. 'You are my wife. If you love me you'll do as I ask.'

Hortense was stunned by his words, and the regret she felt was almost a physical pain.

'I'd do anything for you,' she answered hesitantly, 'anything but leave France. The Vendée is my home and I love it.'

'You're being stupidly sentimental,' he snapped irritably, pulling away from her and sitting up. 'The Vendée isn't really your home. You spent most of your life in Paris, for God's sake!'

'I won't run away,' she replied hotly.

'And if I do?'

Her stomach twisted and she felt suddenly sickened. 'Raoul, are you offering me an ultimatum?'

For a moment he glared at her, then, climbing stiffly

to his feet, reached for his shirt. 'No,' he replied tightly, 'I'm afraid I haven't the courage to do that,' and, without uttering another word, he went up to bed.

For a little longer Hortense sat huddled in front of the fire, feeling both guilty and confused. She was annoyed with Raoul for springing the request upon her, and bitterly disappointed in him. In spite of her love for him, she had no intention of going along with his wishes—at least, not yet; not while her friends fought on. To do so would be disloyal, and little better than cowardice.

He's tired, she told herself, and upset by what he has seen. In the morning he'll view things differently; in the morning everything will be all right.

In fact, the atmosphere between them remained a little strained for days. Much to her relief, Raoul did not mention leaving France again, but quite clearly he was brooding on her refusal. He remained affectionate and polite, and yet she had the disconcerting feeling that he was distancing himself from her once more. Hortense felt guilty, as if she had let him down, and tried in every other way to assure him of her love.

Christmas and the new year were approaching, and she determined to make the time really special for him. She brought pine boughs in to decorate the house and, while he was out, worked on a pair of felt slippers she intended giving him for his New Year's gift.

The morning before Noel he went off to the castle as usual. Hortense had expected him to be gone all day and was therefore surprised when he returned after only an hour. The expression on his face told her immediately that something was wrong.

'Get anything you really need,' he said grimly. 'You will be safer at the castle. The Republicans are just across the water. They want to take the island, and de Tinguy is going to make a fight of it.'

While he was talking he opened the bureau in the

corner of the room and, removing the gold he had brought back from Nantes, risked burning his hand to place it on a ledge inside the chimney.

'You'll know where to find it,' he said seriously, 'if anything happens to me.'

# CHAPTER EIGHT

HORTENSE gazed anxiously out of the château window, over the high curtain wall and straggling roof-tops to the harbour and patchwork of salt-beds beyond. Storm-clouds were gathering threateningly over the mainland, and the ocean appeared an uninviting gun-metal-grey.

Behind her in the large room with its bare flagged floor a fire flamed and sizzled in the enormous hearth. A wind had got up, and from time to time a down-draught sent wood-smoke from the still green logs billowing out into the room. One of the other three women waiting there complained vociferously but Hortense hardly noticed it as she brooded on what might be happening outside.

The fighting had been going on intermittently for several days as the Royalists spiritedly defended the island against vastly superior odds. The situation was becoming desperate, she knew, but if they could last out a little longer then they would at least have some respite. The tide was coming in, and by nightfall the causeway and mudflats would be covered and the island completely cut off. A message had already been sent informing Charette of their plight, and they were all praying that he would return to the island in time.

She had not seen Raoul since the onset of the fighting, and for the hundredth time wondered where he was and how he was faring. After taking her to the castle he had gone off almost immediately with a fellow officer and a party of peasants. De Tinguy had given him a list of the most vulnerable points on the mainland side of the island and he had orders to check that they were properly

140

defended. There had been some fierce fighting, that much she knew from the reports being sent to the injured d'Elbee, but she had no idea how much Raoul had been involved.

As the first drops of rain splashed like dried corn husks against the window the straggling pine trees beside the nearby church bowed and rustled in the quickening wind. The daylight began to fade, and a peasant woman came into the room to light the candles that were set in sconces on the wall. Feeling suddenly chilly, Hortense moved across to join another woman seated on the wooden settle in front of the fire. Madame Rougane, the wife of one of the older officers, reached across and patted her hand.

'Don't worry, my dear,' she said with a reassuring smile. 'I'm sure your husband will be all right.'

Hortense could only smile weakly, and, when the other two ladies came over, found it difficult to take an interest in their rather trivial conversation. Almost an hour later, when de Tinguy arrived with two other officers, she breathed a sigh of relief, thinking that she would have news at last.

'Your husband is all right,' the commander told her, squeezing her shoulder reassuringly as he walked behind the settle and over to a table where refreshments had been laid out.

Hortense was nearly bursting with curiosity but somehow managed to contain it as she watched him pour a glass of wine and then help himself to a chicken leg. He was looking tired and drained, she thought, but otherwise gave no indication as to how things stood.

'Well?' Madame Rougane demanded of the portly grey-haired captain who was her husband. 'Tell us what is happening!'

Rougane glanced questioningly at de Tinguy and,

when the latter nodded, admitted, 'We've been talking about surrender.'

For a moment there was a stunned silence.

'Is there no hope at all?' Hortense finally asked.

'There is always hope,' de Tinguy replied tiredly, 'but I'm a realist, Hortense. It is highly unlikely that Charette will return in time. We could hold out a little longer, but at what cost? I will not sacrifice life fruitlessly. As the Republicans are going to occupy the island whatever we do I'd much rather they were well disposed towards us. I have the peasants to think of as well as our soldiers, and I would do anything to prevent reprisals such as occurred in Nantes.'

'But will General Haxo agree?' Hortense asked worriedly.

Since the Republicans had first arrived she had been filled with a disconcerting sense of foreboding. It was as if the events were all taking place in a dream that she knew was shortly going to turn into a nightmare.

'Your husband seems to think so,' de Tinguy replied indulgently. 'He knows something of the man's reputation from his days in the army. Apparently Haxo is too good a soldier to want to waste his men. He is a hard man but known to be fair, and he does not have a reputation for being vindictive. Raoul seems to think that if we lay down our arms then he will be willing enough to grant us our lives.'

'I only hope he is right,' Rougane commented.

Hortense hoped so too. Privately she thought her husband held too rosy a view of the Republicans, and she wanted to warn de Tinguy to place no trust in them at all.

'Duchambray's opinion aside, we have no choice but to rely on Haxo's honour,' de Tinguy continued. 'Tomorrow I will send a deputation to him, stating the terms on which we are prepared to surrender. We shall not demean ourselves, but it is pointless to continue with a fight we can only lose.'

Everyone in the room expressed agreement in some way, and yet they all felt badly about it, as if they were giving in too easily and somehow failing to keep faith with the Vendean cause.

'There is also another factor to be considered,' de Tinguy told them, his tone deadened by despair. 'Just yesterday I received word of a terrible Vendean defeat at Sauvenay. After weeks of campaigning across the Loire Henri de la Roche-Jacquelein was trying to bring his army home. I don't know yet if he escaped with his life, but to all intents and purposes the Royal Vendean Army is no more. Charette is now our only hope, the only worthwhile champion of God and the King.'

A shocked silence greeted his announcement as those around him assessed the effect the news would have on their lives and aspirations. For the first time Hortense acknowledged that they might well be fighting for a lost cause and that determination and a sense of right did not necessarily mean success. Suddenly leaving for America with Raoul didn't seem quite so terrible. If they got off the island, she vowed, then she would give his suggestion some serious thought. After all, it didn't really matter where she lived as long as she was with him. Most important of all was keeping him alive.

She spent that night in a cold, sparsely furnished bed-chamber on the first floor of the château, and she slept hardly at all. The following morning was a hiatus as everyone waited for the terms of the surrender to be finalised. Hortense was all for returning to Jacques's house, but de Tinguy would have none of it. She was to remain at the castle with the other ladies, he insisted. Now was certainly not the time for a young lady to be on her own and, besides, Raoul had specifically asked him to keep an eye on her.

Hortense had never felt so helpless and frustrated in her life. De Tinguy and the other officers left the castle at first light and, like the other wives, she had no idea how the negotiations were progressing. She even went to visit d'Elbee in the hope that he might have a better idea of what was going on, but, having approved of the surrender, the general was as much in the dark as she. He was pleased by her visit but even half an hour of conversation seemed to tire her. She realised that his condition had not improved at all since the day of her wedding, and visiting him made her feel even more despondent.

Around noon the first Republicans arrived, and Hortense seethed as she watched them from her usual vantage point, marching arrogantly and in tight formation to take up a position in front of the church. Their hated blue uniforms were in surprisingly good condition and struck a discordant note beside the peasants' drab browns and greens. With solemn ceremony de Tinguy's soldiers and peasants began laying down their arms, then, after some minutes of discussion, allowed the Republicans to herd them into the church. Heads bent, they walked like tired old men who had lost their energy and their pride.

Fruitlessly she searched for Raoul, and her stomach twisted in anxiety when she failed to catch sight of him.

'Do you think they are all there?' she demanded of Madame Rougane, who had come to stand beside her.

'Those from the more remote beaches will still be coming in,' the older woman assured her. 'Don't worry yourself. There has been little fighting since de Tinguy last saw your husband.'

They were still watching, hating what they were seeing and yet unable to draw their eyes away, when, a few minutes later, booted footsteps sounded on the stone stairs. The door swung open and a handful of Republican soldiers entered the room. Captain Rougane was with them, his expression anxious and a little unsure.

'You ladies are to join the rest of us in the church,' he told them apologetically. 'I'm afraid the Republicans want the officers' wives to be confined with their men. They are emptying the château and intend to make it their own headquarters.'

'But what of General d'Elbee?' his wife asked. 'He can't possibly manage the walk to the church.'

'We are aware of that, *madame*, and we shall question him here,' a quiet voice interrupted from the doorway.

Hortense glanced at the two soberly dressed civilians following in the wake of the soldiers, and her heart turned over. They were commissioners of the convention, and she knew only too well what that would mean. Whatever terms de Tinguy and Haxo had agreed upon, these men would still have their way. Eyes as cold and lifeless as blue glass met her own as the slighter of the two commissioners stepped forward. Hortense shuddered. She had never before been in the presence of real evil, and the experience chilled her to the bone.

'You will accompany the soldiers without fuss,' he told them. 'We shall remain here to speak with the wounded generalissimo.'

Hortense felt sick. The slight emphasis on the word 'speak' implied that there was more than conversation on the man's mind. Much to her annoyance she found that her legs were trembling as she preceded the soldiers down the stairs and out into the courtyard. More people were gathered there, and they all stood around for ten minutes, waiting for the Republicans to search the rest of the castle. The ladies had not been given time to fetch their cloaks, and by the time they were moved off Hortense was frozen.

Inside the church the heavy pews were already three

quarters full of anxious Royalists. Pale faces turned towards the new arrivals, and Hortense managed a sad, reassuring smile. Even among so many people, she felt lonely. She ached for Raoul's companionship, yet at the same time prayed he would not appear. She had a nasty feeling about what was going to happen to them and, reason how she might, she could not suppress it.

In fact, it was almost dark before the last of the prisoners arrived, Raoul among them. With his neck-cloth askew and his jacket smeared with mud, he was looking grubby and dishevelled, his expression showing the same resigned anxiety as the rest of the men. Tired though he obviously was, he still carried himself with his habitual easy assurance, and when a Republican hurried him forward with a hefty push in the back the look he gave the man would have frozen a stone.

His eyes surveyed the church and, catching sight of Hortense, he smiled. As she hurried towards him he opened his arms and pulled her into a comforting embrace. For a moment he held her so tightly that she could hardly breathe, then, kissing her briefly on the mouth, he drew her against his side and led her towards a vacant pew.

'What's going to happen?' she asked as she snuggled against him like a child. 'What are the Republicans going to do with us?'

'I spoke to one of their officers,' he told her flatly, his sigh gusting across her hair. 'There are commissioners here. Haxo is not his own master, and what happens to us is going to depend on them.'

'I saw them.' As she recounted what had happened at the château, she was unable to suppress a shudder.

'You're cold,' he said in concern, noticing that she was clad only in her blouse and skirt.

Before she could even reply he had slipped out of his jacket and wrapped it around her. She started to protest that now he would be cold, but he silenced her with a quick kiss. In spite of their situation, Hortense had never felt so protected and cherished, and in that moment she had never loved him more. His coat was warm around her, smelling faintly of salt and of him, and his arms cradled her closely against his side.

The church was almost dark now, and someone began lighting the candles on the altar and set into embrasures in the walls. The conversation around them became muted, as if by some strange magic the soft light compelled people to speak in whispers. Wrapped in the security of her husband's arms, Hortense drifted off to sleep.

Raoul, like many others, was not as fortunate, but it was not only physical discomfort that kept him awake. He ached with feelings of inadequacy and foreboding; having visited Nantes, he had a good idea what the morning would bring. Part of him wanted to deny it, to believe that his fellow Republicans couldn't be that brutal, that false, but it was patently obvious that they had no intention of adhering to the terms of the surrender.

Glancing down at the sleeping woman in his arms, he felt his heart contract with love for her. The light from the flickering candles picked out the delicate curve of her jaw and glinted on her tumbled curls. Such fiery innocence, he thought, resisting the impulse to kiss her slightly parted lips. He would sell his soul to protect her.

When he could stand the discomfort of remaining in one position no longer he eased his numbed arm from around her and lowered her carefully down on to the hard seat. Madame Rougane, who had been sitting in front of them, smiled and offered her shawl.

'Go on, take it,' she told him on seeing him hesitate. 'With or without it, I shall not be able to sleep.'

Hortense still did not stir, even when Raoul tucked

the folded garment beneath her head, but muttered a sleepy groan. His stomach tightened with ill-timed desire as memories of her softness and passion returned to him in an intoxicating rush. Smiling wryly to himself, he stood up and stretched, wincing as the feeling returned to his arm.

'The sleep of the innocent,' Captain Rougane commented, smiling indulgently at the sleeping girl.

Raoul nodded and, after stretching again and finding that it gave little relief to his cramped muscles, declared that he needed to walk.

'I'll join you,' the older man told him, and together they edged out of the pews and walked down the aisle towards the nave.

Around them people slept in uncomfortable positions or sat gritty-eyed and insomniant. The flickering candles gave the building an eerie, unearthly air, their shimmering patches of ochre light surrounded by endless black shadow.

'Have you thought about trying to escape from here?' Raoul asked.

The older man stiffened. 'Then you think matters are that desperate?'

Raoul merely nodded.

'I haven't seen de Tinguy since he was taken away shortly after we were brought here, but he seemed to believe this confinement merely a precaution on the Republicans' part. You said yourself that Haxo is an honourable man.'

'Haxo is straightforward enough, but you know as well as I do that things become less predictable when there are commissioners from Paris involved!'

Rougane shrugged. 'In any case, the church is too well guarded. All we can do now is pray.' He looked up at the wooden icon strikingly picked out in the uneven light, and his smile was a little wry. 'Are you a religious man, Duchambray?'

'I used to believe,' Raoul answered, thinking that it seemed a lifetime ago. 'Now I am not so sure.'

Eventually dawn came, pale and wind-torn, with the moon set tardily in a cloud-streaked sky. One by one the candles in the church were snuffed as the Royalists dragged themselves from uncomfortable sleep and prepared to face whatever horrors the day might hold. No food was brought to them, although they were offered water and in small groups allowed a necessary trip outside.

Then, when the wintry sun was scarcely over the rooftops, a hard-faced captain arrived. He stood in the church doorway, surrounded by a silent escort of about a dozen soldiers, and dispassionately counted out thirty of the Vendean men. At the uneasy stirring from the other Royalists he smiled bleakly.

'Just a few questions,' he told the gathering in general, 'and then they'll be released.'

The closing of the heavy church door rang unnaturally loud in the sudden stillness as people fretted over what they dared not put into words. No one wanted to say it—they dared not even think it—but dread was closing around them in an ever-thickening cloud.

'It's going to be all right,' Rougane said almost too brightly. 'This evening we shall all be able to sleep in our beds.'

Raoul didn't believe a word of it and, glancing at her pale face, saw that neither did Hortense. She said nothing, however, and even managed a weak smile when he drew her close. Outside the wind was rising, sighing and groaning against the ancient church like a woman in torment and mercifully disguising other, more sinister sounds. Raoul felt sick with apprehension and fear, not so much for himself, but for Hortense. He knew he had to do something and, by the time the captain returned an hour later, had determined to speak with him, hoping that by revealing his previous allegiance he would be able to save his wife's life.

'*Monsieur*,' he said quietly, moving forward and holding the man's cold gaze, 'I wish to speak with you. I think you will find what I have to say both interesting and beneficial.'

'We have orders to speak with no one,' the man snapped, motioning his soldiers forward into the church.

'You are making a mistake,' Raoul protested. 'I——' He was cut short as a musket stock crashed into his solar plexus. As he fell to his knees a well-aimed boot thudded into his side.

'There is nothing you can say, pig, that will change things!' the captain snarled. 'All of you men are now going to die, and maybe later even the women!'

There was a general gasp of protest, but when several Vendeans made to move forward a wall of levelled muskets forced them back.

'*Monsieur*, have pity, I beg of you!' Captain Rougane cried. 'If not for us men then for our wives. They have done nothing to harm you!'

'Don't demean yourself by pleading with them,' his wife calmly told him. 'I, for one, would rather share your fate than owe my life to such *canaille*!'

Catching hold of the older woman's hand, Hortense glanced towards Raoul, her expression forbidding him to make any further entreaties. 'I too would rather die than grovel. We are fighting for God and the right; we have nothing to fear!'

Raoul's eyes were like chips of blue glass, and the anger in him was almost palpable as he rose stiffly to his feet and faced the Republicans. They were his enemies now, not only because of circumstances but because of what they had done. He shuddered to think that he had once supported them, once believed in them, and his abhorrence of them was all the more. He knew he was asking for trouble, but somehow he just could not hold the words back. They tumbled from him in an angry torrent, fuelled by his disillusionment and his contempt.

'You'll all be damned for this,' he hissed, 'you and the rest of your kind, though you are no more than the tools of those mad dogs from the convention. Call yourselves soldiers! You are no more than gutter-bred murderers, the lot of you!'

Furiously the nearest soldier again lifted his rifle, only to be halted by a sharp word from his superior. With a coolness that was all the more blood-chilling the latter began picking out more Vendeans, Captain Rougane among them. When he reached twenty-nine he smiled and turned to Raoul.

'And you, *monsieur*,' he informed him, 'with your big mouth and your aristo's arrogance, shall be the thirtieth.'

Raoul turned briefly towards Hortense, his eyes sending her the messages of love and apology he could not put into words. He would have done worse than grovel to save her life but, at the same time, knew he had to respect her courage and pride. She was standing very stiffly, determined to hang on to her self-control, and her expression showed the same love and anguish as his own. He had time for one brief parting smile and then the Republicans were hustling them out into the cool, windswept morning.

Hortense managed to maintain her composure only until the door had closed behind the soldiers, then, moving away from the others to the side of the church, she let the tears fall. His last, lop-sided smile had almost been her undoing; until her dying day she would remember it. She felt a comforting hand on her shoulder and looked up into Madame Rougane's watery blue eyes.

'All we can do now,' the older woman said, 'is to die with courage.'

Raoul found his heart hammering with something he suspected was fear as they were marched between the straggling pine trees and down on to the coarse sandy beach. For a moment he considered making a run for it, but the soldiers' muskets were already primed and he decided he would rather meet death with dignity than be shot down like a dog.

Suddenly he was intensely aware of the beauty that surrounded him, of the dark-feathered green of the trees and the shining, wind-tossed sea. He drew a deep steadying breath, filling his lungs with the salty air, and when he glanced up at the seagulls wheeling below the racing clouds knew they were one of the last sights he would ever see.

'That's far enough,' the captain in charge of them growled.

The guards moved away and a platoon of Republicans, who had been busy reloading their muskets, moved closer. The eyes of the young Vendean standing next to Raoul widened in fear. He looked like a trapped animal, and for a moment Raoul thought that he would bolt. Then Rougane, lined up on his other side, said something to him and the boy lifted his chin.

Raoul attempted to divorce himself from his surroundings and tried to pray. It was a muddled sort of prayer to a god he had often doubted, but it was the only comfort he had. When the firing squad lifted their muskets he stared straight at them, but it was his wife's face that he saw. In that moment she seemed so real, so solid, that he felt he could reach out and touch her, and he was sure he could smell the fragrance of her hair.

Thomas Beaulieu, standing in the shelter of the trees, was surprised how much the shootings had sickened him. A hundred peasants and as many soldiers had already fallen to the firing squads, and the total looked likely to be ten times that. More than once he'd had to bite his tongue to stem the protest, but the three fanatical commissioners in charge had already condemned one loyal Republican for suspected treason. It would be all too easy, Beaulieu knew, to lose not only his position, but his life.

Not for the first time he regretted returning to the Vendée. In Paris he had watched dispassionately while numerous aristos had gone to their deaths, but these peasants were his people, their dress and demeanour resembling too closely the grandparents he had loved. He had been happier with Westermann, but Carrier had wanted someone he trusted to work with the other commissioners, someone who would report back to him and help him maintain a political advantage.

The muskets had spoken again and thirty more peasants had fallen to the ground like puppets whose strings had been suddenly cut. The bodies had been efficiently removed, and now a group of Vendean soldiers stood ready to meet their deaths. Beaulieu had less sympathy for these who had, after all, taken up arms against the glorious Revolution. They were a motley crowd with only the two officers among them wearing full uniform. One of these was a stocky grey-haired man, but the other was young and in spite of his predicament held himself with the pride and stiff dignity of a true aristocrat. Dark hair lifting in the wind, he stared defiantly at the line of muskets.

Beaulieu's gaze swept on, then swung back in surprise to the tall, athletic figure. He uttered an oath as foul as any heard in the gutters of Paris as he wondered what perverse twist of fate had brought his son there. The boy was nothing to him, he told himself, and he had already risked his reputation for him. Yet, surprisingly, he found that seeing his own flesh and blood fall before the rapacious vengeance of the firing squad was more than he could endure. Quickly, but without any appearance of panic, he walked across to the officer who was in charge of the executions, and in less than half a minute two soldiers were marching towards the Vendean prisoners.

When the hail of musket fire failed to materialise Raoul's attention was reluctantly dragged back to the present. Two soldiers marched purposefully forward and, much to his surprise, singled him out. He was given no chance to question or protest, but was bundled roughly across the sand and out of the line of fire.

The muskets spat and he turned his head to see his friends fall. Grief and anger nearly choked him, and in blind fury he lashed out, his fist connecting solidly with a Republican's ear. When they grabbed his hand he brought up his knee. His arm was twisted viciously behind his back and the cold steel of a bayonet was pressed against his throat, and still he struggled to fight them. He was only subdued when the flat edge of a sword was brought sharply against the side of his head and he was mercifully freed from the emotions that tormented him.

# CHAPTER NINE

THE rain beat against the château window in a steady stream, driven by a gale from the Atlantic. Around the building the wind gusted and moaned, finding its way through the cracks and crannies in the ancient windows and brickwork. The château courtyard was almost awash, and rainwater poured in a steady stream down into the once dry moat with its freshly turned graves. Maurice d'Elbee and his entourage had been executed that very morning and now lay in that unmarked resting place.

Thomas Beaulieu, working in one of the offices, tossed his pen down upon the desk and walked over to the window. Outside it was pitch-black with not a star visible in the lowering sky. With a muttered curse he turned to pace back and forth across the worn stone floor. Try as he might, he had found it impossible to concentrate on his report to Carrier; he was too concerned for Raoul.

Commissioner Turillac was with his son now, having taken charge of him almost as soon as he had been removed from the beach, and Beaulieu could only guess at what was going on. He hoped that Raoul was not being foolish and once again letting his heart rule his head. Having made some discreet enquiries, he was aware of his son's marriage and suspected that his allegiance had also undergone a change. The boy could be difficult, he knew, damned difficult, when a matter of principle was involved. He was also acutely aware of his own vulnerability. If Raoul went to the guillotine then a word recognising the relationship between them would bring his father down too.

Beaulieu sighed and continued his pacing, both surprised and irritated to find that his own safety was not his prime concern. He was actually beginning to care for his son, and he didn't like that at all. It was so much safer in such troubled times to have no family, no emotional ties, for they could always be used against you. Damn it, he thought, he was getting soft in his old age! Turning in self-disgust, he went back to his writing, only to be disturbed a few minutes later by the arrival of Commissioner Turillac.

The commissioner, a humourless-looking man with a strong nose and straight, frowning eyebrows, was obviously irritated. Beaulieu immediately feared the worst.

'Duchambray has turned traitor,' Turillac snapped, seating himself in the wooden armchair across from him. 'I have just spent a most unproductive hour with him. You were right; he did at one point work for Carrier, but he now insists he would rather face a firing squad than help us further. In fact he was most abusive. Sergeant Redon was forced to discipline him and I had to remind him that a firing squad was the least he would have to face.' Sighing angrily, he leant forward, bringing his fist down on the desk with a force that made Beaulieu wince. 'When I told him how we deal with traitors he had the gall to tell *me* that we were all traitors to the Republican cause!'

'I suspected as much,' Beaulieu replied quietly, managing to hide his dismay. 'I gather he has just married some rebel bitch and that could well have something to do with his change of heart. It's a pity, though, because he seems to have gained the trust of many of the Vendean leaders. My informant tells me that he is very friendly with one Jacques Martin, a young gentleman who is well thought of by General Charette. It's a great pity he can't be persuaded to return to the cause because he would be in a unique position to help us.'

'He won't change his mind, I'll tell you that,' Turillac snapped, 'although it might be fun working on him. These aristos soon lose their arrogance when submitted to a little pain.'

Beaulieu frowned consideringly, then rose from his seat to pace thoughtfully across the room. His face was turned away from the commissioner as, with a commendable amount of disinterest, he asked, 'But what if he could be brought back to our side? He would be able to reach Charette.'

'He'd never be reliable,' Turillac complained. 'His background has always made him suspect, and now that he has a Vendean wife——'

'That's just it,' Beaulieu interrupted. 'He has a new wife, one he loves very much, from all accounts, and she too is under our control.'

The other man sat up straighter in his chair and a sly speculative look came into his eyes. 'No doubt he would do anything to protect her. . . Do you know her name?'

'Hortense. She is a Claviere, I believe. In any case, she should not be difficult to recognise. My informant tells me she is very beautiful, with an enticing figure and lovely red-brown hair.'

'Then find her,' Turillac ordered. 'As far as I know, Paris has already sent someone to try and deal with the Marais's upstart general, but Duchambray should have a better chance. It would certainly be a feather in our caps. See to it, Beaulieu. Find the girl, and then I'll have another word with our obstinate young friend.'

It was well past midnight when Beaulieu's search led him to the church. The building was very quiet as the remaining prisoners, most of them women, lay stretched out on the pews in uncomfortable attitudes of sleep. As the door opened and the booted feet of the two soldiers accompanying him echoed in the stillness one or two of the prisoners sat up.

Ignoring the muttered protests and questions, Beaulieu lifted the lantern he was carrying and walked slowly between the pews. When he reached Hortense he paused. Unlike most others, she was no longer asleep, and when he looked at her she met his gaze without flinching.

'Stand up,' he ordered, and with a withering look of contempt she obeyed.

He surveyed her from head to foot, noting, not as dispassionately as he would have liked, her slim waist and the enticing roundness of her breasts beneath the soft white blouse. Her face showed the same strain and sadness as the other prisoners, yet somehow she had retained her pride. He held the lantern closer, making a small sound of satisfaction when he saw the glints of red in her hair.

'You are to come with me,' he said quietly.

The middle-aged woman sitting next to her immediately began to protest, and, standing, pushed herself between them.

Beaulieu's mouth tightened in irritation. 'Tell the old crone to mind her own business,' he told Hortense. 'One way or another you are going to accompany me. She can only bring herself harm.'

'He's right,' Hortense told Madame Rougane with a calmness that was almost threatening. 'It will be best if I go without making a scene.'

Like the older woman, she thought she had a good idea what the Republican wanted with her, and she found that she could view it with a surprising amount of dispassion. After all, what did it matter what happened to her now that Raoul was dead? All she had left was vengeance, and if she was adept enough she would at least have the opportunity to make this man pay. If he intended to use her for his pleasure she would wait until he was at his most vulnerable, and then she would incapacitate him for the rest of his life!

He did not take her hand or touch her in any way as they left the church and made their way through the puddles and pouring rain to the château. Not that he needed to; the soldiers with him ensured her compliance. They crossed the drawbridge and, on entering the court-yard, turned left. When they reached the wide wooden door he opened it and, with surprising courtesy, stood back for her to enter before him. They climbed a flight of stone stairs worn smooth by the passage of countless feet, and halted outside what had once been the Rouganes' quarters. After detailing one of his escort to wait outside the door he dimissed the others and ushered Hortense inside.

By this time she was drenched and shivering uncon-trollably. Beaulieu felt a twinge of pity; it changed swiftly to something uncomfortably like desire as he looked at her and became aware of the way the wet material of her blouse faithfully outlined her exquisite figure.

His son certainly had excellent taste, he thought wryly. If she had been married to anyone else then he might have been tempted to try his luck with her. Then again, perhaps not. She was the sort of woman who could get into a man's blood, who would end up claiming his very soul. She could hardly have been at a greater disadvan-tage, and yet she looked him straight in the eye, her expression condemning him to the devil. He felt a reluctant admiration, and in spite of himself his mouth lifted in a wry smile.

'I am not going to assault you, Madame Duchambray,' he told her smoothly. 'However, I suggest you go into the bedroom and change. There must be something there that will fit you. If you stand in front of me like that for much longer then I might forget my good intentions.'

He did not wait for her agreement, but thrust the lantern he was carrying into her hand, then went to light the candles standing on the mantleshelf. Hortense was confused but nevertheless turned to obey. Her mind was racing as she rummaged through Madame Rougane's trunk and, selecting a green velvet gown that must have been at least two sizes too big for her, put it on. She knew she looked ridiculous in it, but it did at least cover her more adequately that the wet blouse, and it was blissfully warm.

When she returned to the small drawing-room Beaulieu was busy pouring wine from a decanter set on a table against the wall. Without even asking if she wanted any, he held out a glass.

After hesitating for a moment Hortense set down the lantern and took the drink, being careful not to let her fingers brush against his. She'd had little to eat during the last thirty-six hours, and, knowing what wine could do on an empty stomach, she sipped it carefully.

'Let's go and sit down,' Beaulieu said.

It was a command rather than a request, and she followed him across to the two chairs that were pulled up in front of the empty hearth. Things were not going at all as she had expected, and she was puzzled as to what kind of man she was dealing with.

As he knelt down and began building a small fire she took the opportunity to study him. He was not bad looking for a man of his age, she thought, although there was an austerity about him and a studied lack of emotion that was not at all appealing. He was tall and still slim, and his dark hair, although liberally streaked with grey, seemed to have retained a tendency to curl. His mouth was thin but firm, the deep lines drawn between it and his nose hinting at sorrow suffered and a lack of humour.

In fact, apart from his courtesy and apparent lack of cruelty, he seemed to her a typical Republican.

Once he was satisfied that the fire he had kindled was going to take hold Beaulieu dusted his hands on his dark-coloured breeches and took a seat across from the girl. For a moment he just looked at her as if making a judgement of his own, and she had the feeling that he missed very little.

'How long have you known your husband?' he finally asked.

He spoke as if Raoul were still alive, but she did not correct him; neither did she answer him. Instead she met his question with two of her own. 'Why do you ask, *monsieur*? What do you know of Raoul?'

He smiled thinly. 'I am the one who is doing the interrogating, *madame*, but, for what it is worth, we have Duchambray and have spent some considerable time questioning him.'

'Then he is alive!' Her heart leapt, only to plummet almost immediately as she realised what being questioned by the Republicans could mean.

'No, he has not been tortured,' Beaulieu snapped, seeing the remaining colour drain from her face. 'We are not all barbarians. However, we would like him to do something for us, and he is proving most stubborn. I do not want to see him killed, but if he continues to defy Commissioner Turillac then I shall not be able to prevent it. It would be better all round if he agreed to help us, and you, my dear, could persuade him.'

A number of emotions boiled inside Hortense. Anger, fear, relief—she experienced them all, but in spite of everything she felt hope. Raoul was alive, and that alone made her feel as if a weight had been lifted from her heart. Perhaps the Republicans weren't asking too much. Perhaps she would be able to bend her loyalty a little.

'What is it you want?' she asked quietly, subduing her feelings of guilt and self-contempt.

Beaulieu smiled coldly. 'We want him to assassinate Charette.'

It was impossible! Unthinkable! Any hope she felt died, and she was filled with an angry despair.

'He won't do it and I won't ask it of him,' she snapped. 'You are monsters to even think of such a thing.'

'I didn't really expect you to agree,' Beaulieu replied calmly, 'but when he realises that your safety depends on his compliance then I think Raoul will. I don't believe he has your strength of loyalty to the Vendean cause.'

'He won't agree to it,' she repeated, and yet she was very much afraid that he might.

Beaulieu, his face inscrutable, merely shrugged.

'Please, *monsieur*, it is unfair to place him in such a position. . . Don't make me responsible for turning him into a traitor, I beg of you.'

'But you are already responsible,' he replied with a spurt of anger, thinking that it was she who had weaned his son away from the Republican cause. 'I didn't expect you to agree. Like the rest of your kind, you are too stiff-necked and intractable. Fortunately it does not matter. It is only necessary for Raoul to know you are in our power.'

Hortense was almost consumed with anger and hatred. 'You Republicans are entirely without feeling or honour. Every time I think I have discovered the worst about you you surprise me with something more! You are truly evil, *monsieur*. You are a devil!'

'This devil, *madame*, is merely trying to keep your husband alive,' Beaulieu replied sharply, struggling to control his own anger. 'If you cared for him you would persuade him to do what we ask. It will be dangerous, I know, but he will at least have a chance of life. We are beginning to win this war, and François Charette is going to die sooner or later; what matter if it's at your husband's hands?'

'It matters to me,' she hissed, 'and it will matter to Raoul. He is no murderer.'

'And he is no saint, thank God!' Beaulieu stood up, sighing in frustration. 'If you are thinking of attacking me,' he said, noting the way the girl's eyes were drawn to the heavy candelabra, 'then I would advise against it. There are guards in the courtyard, so there is no way for you to escape. Also, you would find Commissioner Turillac far more difficult to deal with than me. . .' He smiled in reluctant admiration as he realised what else was going through her mind. 'Neither am I likely to kill such a useful hostage, whatever the provocation!'

Hortense could only glare at him and swallow her threatening tears. In the over-sized gown she reminded Beaulieu of a defiant child with far more courage than sense, and, in spite of himself, his attitude softened.

'You will remain here,' he told her. 'Although the apartment does not lock, there will be a guard on duty outside. You'll be more comfortable here than in the church. I will also have some food brought to you. In the meantime be thankful that you and your husband are still alive! If he takes the assignment and succeeds then you will have the chance of a new life together. I will even find a way to get you both out of the country if that is what you wish.'

'But if he does do such a wicked thing,' she replied brokenly, 'even for my sake, then I don't think I will ever be able to forgive him!'

As soon as Beaulieu had left Hortense got up and began pacing the room; she was too keyed up to sit still. Never had she felt so helpless, such a complete prisoner of fate. Her very presence was going to decide important matters, and yet her actions and opinions counted for naught. When, as Beaulieu had promised, food arrived she found that she had lost her appetite and had to force it down. Irrationally her guilt increased with each mouthful she swallowed. What right had she, she asked herself, to be eating in relative comfort when her friends were starving and cold? And what of Raoul? What privations and agony of mind must he be suffering?

She lay that night in the Rouganes' ancient bed with its dusty plum-coloured canopy, and she felt like an interloper. The older woman's perfume still lingered on the bolster and the captain's shaving tackle was spread out on top of the marble wash-stand. She knew they would not begrudge her the use of their bedroom, but somehow it still didn't seem right. At first she did not think she would be able to sleep at all, but in the early hours of the morning exhaustion finally overcame her and she slipped into a blissful, dreamless oblivion.

Beaulieu was struggling with an unprecedented attack of conscience and self-doubt when, several hours later, he accompanied Turillac into the small first-floor room that served as his son's cell. In the pale dawn light the place looked cheerless and cold.

Raoul was sound asleep on the single narrow bunk. His face looked pale above his dark beard, and there was a small gash across his cheekbone where the point of the sword had bitten into his skin. When the guard shook him awake he sat up groggily. He showed a momentary surprise at seeing his father, but he covered it quickly, and Beaulieu realised with relief that he had no intention of giving their relationship away. Instead his gaze swung to Turillac, his expression one of hatred and contempt.

'Before you insult me again,' the commissioner told him with a sneer, 'I think you should know that we have your wife.'

The remaining colour drained from Raoul's face and his hands curled convulsively around the edge of the mattress, but he made no reply.

'There are all kinds of unpleasant things that could happen to such a beautiful young woman, unless, of course, we felt well disposed towards you; then we might take it upon ourselves to protect her.'

Again Raoul made no reply, but from the level of his breathing Beaulieu could see that he was struggling to remain calm.

'Apparently you have done your job well,' Turillac continued. 'You have gained the confidence of some important Vendeans—even, it seems, General Charette. If you escaped from here you would be welcomed by him. You have friends who are close to him.'

'I've told you that I've finished with the work of a spy. In fact I no longer even support you! I hate what you have done here in the name of the Republic!'

'I know you would rather die than help us,' Turillac replied smoothly, 'but are you ready to sacrifice your wife? She would not die easily, I assure you. Personally I have no taste for Royalist bitches. I would probably give her to Thomas here, and then to the men.'

For a moment Beaulieu thought Raoul was going to be sick. In fact he felt his own stomach churning. There was a short silence.

Then, in a voice that was studiously devoid of all emotion, Raoul asked, 'What is it you want me to do?'

Turillac's smile was almost smug as, with a conspiratorial look at Beaulieu, he replied, 'We want you to kill Charette.'

Whatever Raoul had been expecting it was not that. He rested his head in his hands and rubbed at his throbbing temples as he tried to come to terms with the enormity of what they were asking.

'It's not possible,' he finally replied.

'It's dangerous, almost suicidal, in fact, but it can be done if you are determined enough, and you would be saving your wife's life. As soon as we hear of the general's death she will be released.'

'I don't trust you,' Raoul told him.

Turillac shrugged. 'You have no choice.'

But he did have a choice, Raoul knew. He could tell them to go to the devil. It was what Hortense would want. He would willingly have sacrificed his own life, but not hers. He loved her far too much. He knew he would find it hard to live with himself after doing what they asked, but then it was unlikely he would have to.

'All right,' he answered in resignation. 'I will do it if I can.' He still didn't trust them, but if there was a chance of saving his wife's life then he was going to take it. 'But I want to see her first. I want to know that she is unhurt.'

'That can be arranged,' Turillac replied, now a model of reasonable urbanity. 'You will not be allowed to speak with her, of course.' He smiled nastily. 'We can't have the bitch changing your mind. In the meantime I want you to tell Beaulieu anything you know that might be helpful to our cause. Myself, I have other business to attend to, including the execution of some rather stubborn priests.'

When the door closed behind the commissioner Raoul and his father were left alone.

For a momnent there was silence between them; then Raoul asked heatedly, 'How can you work with him? How can you stand what he does?'

'I have little choice,' Beaulieu replied calmly. 'My own position is not secure enough for me to display a conscience. I am as sickened by what is going on here as you are, but I do not have the luxury of voicing my opinion. However, I can assure you that your wife is all right.'

'Does she know what you want of me?' Raoul asked.

Beaulieu nodded. 'I told her last night.'

Then I've lost her, Raoul thought. She will never

forgive me for what I am going to do. He gave a wry despairing smile. 'I can guess what she said to you.'

'She is a courageous and highly determined young woman. As a matter of fact, I quite liked her. I will do my best to see that we keep our end of the bargain.'

'I think you had better,' Raoul replied coldly, looking his father in the eye and lying quite unashamedly. 'She is carrying your grandchild.'

'You didn't need to tell me that.' Giving a deep sigh, Beaulieu wondered how he had managed to become involved in such a highly charged and emotional situation, he who had come to pride himself on his cool head and cold heart. 'I would have done my best to protect her anyway.'

'I expect more than your best,' Raoul answered bleakly. 'After all, I am more than earning it. I am going to kill a man I happen to like and respect rather a lot.'

'Charette must die,' his father told him, more than a little distressed by the bitterness and despair he could see in Raoul. 'He is all that stands between our complete victory and, therefore, peace. If you want to end this terrible bloodshed then the man must be eliminated. However, it might not actually fall to you to kill him. There is another who has been sent from Paris. Whoever does the deed, your wife will be released as soon as the chief marachin is dead. Turillac would not have wanted me to tell you that, but I thought it might make things easier for you to accept. In the end the death of François Charette is inevitable. . . Now I need a few facts from you—anything that will satisfy our illustrious commissioner.'

Beaulieu's lips twisted in a wry smile. It was a rare attempt at humour, but Raoul was completely unable to respond to it. He felt too drained, too sick at heart. He no longer seemed to have any control over his life. His path was laid out for him. Inevitably he was going to lose Hortense, but then he had known that from the very beginning. Mercifully the pain was beginning to fade and he felt only a blessed numbness. In a way it was as if he were already dead.

In the late afternoon he was allowed one brief glimpse of Hortense. With his hands tied behind his back he was marched into the château courtyard. When the guard with him halted him and pointed he looked up to see her standing in one of the second-floor windows. He was unable to wave to her and could not even manage a smile. Her face was a mask of misery, and there were tears in her eyes as she lifted her hand and, touching her fingertips to her lips, blew him a kiss. She was very much afraid that it would be the last time she would see him alive.

For the love of God, Raoul, she wanted to cry out, don't promise them anything because of me!

It was Beaulieu who, a few minutes later, told her that Raoul had already agreed to the nefarious plan. Then she wept—she could not help herself. She wept for her husband and for herself, for the death of her idealism and her love. Never in her life had she felt such complete and utter despair.

Commissioner Turillac, on the other hand, was in excellent spirits when Beaulieu joined him for supper that evening. As far as he was concerned, everything had gone to plan, and he was optimistic about Raoul's ability to carry out the assassination.

'He'll be able to do it,' he told an unusually quiet Beaulieu. 'I'm sure of it, although he might well die in the attempt.'

Beaulieu nodded and for the umpteenth time that day wondered if what he had done was for the best. At least his son had a chance, he told himself, and the girl and his grandchild would survive.

'Not that it matters,' Turillac continued with an

unpleasant smile, 'because if he returns for his wife then I shall kill him anyway. We can no longer rely on him to serve us faithfully. As for the girl. . . You've done well, Beaulieu. I've seen the way you look at her. You may use her as you will for the next couple of days, then I'll get Sergeant Redon to wring her lovely neck. . . No, you don't need to thank me.' Turillac smiled again and gestured with his knife. A trickle of melted butter ran obscenely down his chin. 'You've earned the pleasure. I always know how to reward those who serve me faithfully.'

To Beaulieu the fish he was eating suddenly tasted like ashes in his mouth. He nearly gagged and, reaching for his wine, finally managed to wash it down, wondering how he could have been such a fool. He felt an insane desire to smash his fist into the commissioner's expectant face, but instead he forced a smile.

'I am very grateful,' he managed to say. At the same time he was thinking that now he would really have to lay his life and his career on the line. Although there was no real love between them, Raoul was his son, the only one that he knew about, and the Vendean girl was carrying his grandchild. To let them die would be tantamount to seeing his own immortality slipping away.

# CHAPTER TEN

HORTENSE lay fully clothed on the Rouganes' ancient bed. She felt sick and aching inside, and her throat was thick with unshed tears. She had been planning and pondering for hours, trying to find some way out of her situation, but all she had achieved was an enormous headache. She wanted to scream and rail against fate, and felt hysteria bubbling up inside her, fuelled by her absolute frustration. Once again she swallowed down her grief, knowing that if she began to cry then she would never be able to stop.

The light began to fade, the shadows in the room changing from grey to purple to deepest black. Soon she could no longer see anything but a square of darkening sky through the unshuttered window. Milky moonlit clouds swirled across it, catching the stars and then releasing them again. The girl gave a ragged sigh and rested her forearm across her burning eyes. It was hard to accept that her life had come to such an impasse.

She must have dozed, because when she again opened her eyes the quality of the darkness was somehow thicker. She knew something had disturbed her, and when she heard someone moving about in the next room she froze. Fear clawed at her and she felt physically sick. Before she could decide whether to scream or hide, the orange glow from a lantern swelled into the room, closely followed by a tall dark-clad figure.

'Madame Duchambray,' Beaulieu called softly, lifting the light so that its amber halo lit up the bed. 'Are you not well? Why are you lying here in the darkness?'

'I was tired,' she replied, hoping he had not witnessed her abject fear. 'What do you want with me now?'

He smiled crookedly and, after placing the lantern at his feet, sat down on the bed.

When she edged away from him he made a sound of disgust. 'Don't worry. I am not going to touch you. We do, however, have to talk.'

'I don't see that we have anything to say to each other,' she answered coldly, drawing her dislike of him around her like a protective cloak.

'I thought it might interest you to know that Turillac has no intention of upholding his bargain with your husband. When he returns to claim you he is to be shot. Your own life expectancy is even shorter. Tonight Turillac has granted me the use of your body; tomorrow you face a firing squad.'

'I'll kill myself before I'll let you touch me,' she hissed, her stomach knotting at his news.

He sighed in exasperation. 'Believe me, I have no designs on your virtue, but for reasons of my own I am willing to help you escape.'

For a moment Hortense thought he was toying with her. 'Why,' she asked, hardly daring to hope. 'Why would you do this for me?'

'I'll leave it to your husband to tell you that,' he informed her brusquely. 'Suffice to say, I feel a certain obligation towards him. As long as it presents no danger to myself, I would like to see you both escape. I have given the guard a flask of best brandy, and although he knows better than to get drunk, he will be less than alert. Later I can dispense with him, making it look like your work. Then we will go together to release your husband. It will be bloodthirsty work. I only hope I can rely on you not to go into hysterics.'

'Over the past months I have developed an exceptionally strong stomach,' she replied, hope and suspicion

warring inside her. Beaulieu's helping her made no
sense, but she knew she had nothing to lose. That
Turillac intended to kill her was all too believable.

The Republican studied her for a moment, then
nodded approvingly as he pulled a pistol wrapped in an
oily cloth from inside his cloak. He glanced around the
room and his eyes alighted on the clothes-trunk standing
against the far wall. With a satisfied smile he went over
to open it, then began dragging out dresses and under-
garments and piling them up on the floor. When the
trunk was nearly empty he tossed the cloth that the gun
had been wrapped in into it.

'I want it to look as if you found the weapon there,' he
said.

Returning to sit on the bed, he took a powder flask
and some pistol balls from his pocket. 'I assume you do
know how to load one of these?'

Hortense nodded but still watched him as he proceeded to load and prime the weapon.

When he had finished Beaulieu looked searchingly at
her, thinking that he had never taken such a chance in
his life. 'I cannot guarantee success. In fact, you could
easily be caught. If that happens I want your promise
that you will not incriminate me in any way. . . I want
you to swear it before I go any further with this.'

It struck her then that what he was doing was completely out of character. Ordinarily he was a man who
would never take a risk but who would plan the course
of his life with exceptional single-mindedness and a lack
of emotion.

'And if I do not?' she asked, wanting to test him. 'It is
a promise I may not be able to keep even if I want to.
You yourself know how persuasive your compatriots can
be.'

To her surprise, he gave a sad, self-deprecating smile.

'Then I suppose I will still help you. . . . I cannot do otherwise.'

Against all reason the girl believed him. 'For what it is worth, you have my word.'

'Come, then.' He got up from the bed and, carrying the lantern with him, walked into the living-room. 'Give me a minute. Wait here and don't make a sound.'

The outer door had scarcely closed behind him before she heard a heavy thump. A few seconds later he reappeared and motioned urgently for her to join him. As she reached him he thrust the pistol into her hand. Outside the guard lay sprawled face-down in the corridor. His hat was missing and the back of his head was smeared with blood.

'He's dead,' Beaulieu coldly informed her. 'I can afford no witnesses.'

It was only then that she became aware of stickiness on the butt of the pistol she was holding. Shuddering, she fought down a wave of nausea and again wondered just how much she could trust her unexpected rescuer. She had the gun, and if they were stopped he was obviously going to say that she had forced him to help her. It was with a feeling of unreality that she followed him down the narrow stairs. Their footsteps echoed hollowly in the empty darkness, and the swaying lantern cast strange shadows on the stone walls. It was the stuff of which nightmares were made, and at any minute she expected an assassin to leap out at her from some deep, unlit corner.

At the bottom of the stairs Beaulieu paused to extinguish his light, then, taking her arm again, led her out into the courtyard. There he paused for a moment, holding her back against the shelter of the wall and staring up at the cloud-tossed sky. When the thin sliver of moon slipped from view he grunted in satisfaction,

and again guided her forward. They crossed the courtyard diagonally to their right, heading towards a tower
in the outer wall. When they reached the low doorway
Beaulieu hustled her inside. It had been difficult enough
to see in the open, but here was as black as pitch.
Cursing beneath his breath, Beaulieu fumbled in his
pocket for a flint and, after several abortive attempts,
managed to relight the lantern.

Hortense saw that they were in an empty rounded
room with another flight of stairs leading steeply upward.

'Raoul is up there,' Beaulieu told the girl. 'You must
wait here. I will deal with the guard and then call for
you.'

Wordlessly she offered him the gun, but he only shook
his head.

'I dare not risk a shot,' he told her in a fierce whisper.
'It will be better if I can take him unawares. I shall
probably be a while.'

He went upstairs, taking the lantern with him and
leaving Hortense to wait in the nerve-straining darkness.
The pistol was her only comfort and it was reassuring to
know that it was really loaded. The minutes dragged as
she strained her ears, listening for any sound of a
conversation or struggle. She thought she heard someone
laugh but she could not be sure, and after that there was
nothing but a heavy, all-encompassing silence.

It must have been at least ten minutes before she
heard the Republican call her name and saw him
descending towards her in order to light her way up the
stairs. When she glanced at him questioningly he gave a
tense nod, then hurried back up in front of her.

On the first floor was some kind of guard-room. A pile
of muskets was stacked up against the concave wall and
rusty bayonets hung from a rack above them. Stretched
out on the floor was a Republican soldier, another
bayonet protruding from his back. Hortense shuddered

at the pool of blood that was spreading around him. Glancing at Beaulieu, she was surprised to see both revulsion and remorse in his face. He masked it quickly and, placing the lantern on the single, scarred table, hurried over to a stout door in what was obviously a partition wall. Dragging a key from his pocket, he unlocked it and pushed it wide, calling urgently for Raoul.

The room behind it was in complete darkness, the only relief from the uniform black being a small high barred window showing a moonlit grey. Someone stirred, and then Raoul was standing in the doorway, looking dishevelled and a trife dazed. Unable to help herself, Hortense flew into his arms, tears of relief streaming down her cheeks. He hugged her hard, at the same time glancing over her head at his father.

'What's happening?' he asked calmly.,

'You'll have time enough to embrace later,' Beaulieu snapped impatiently. 'I've risked a great deal for you, so you can oblige me by getting a move on.' So saying, he turned to one of the windows in the guard-room and, after struggling with the catch, pushed it open. 'There's some rope in that trunk,' he snapped, gesturing behind him.

Raoul extracted a stout piece of hemp and, moving to the open window, glanced around for something to tie it to.

'What has brought on this change of heart?' he asked cynically as he lashed one end of the rope to the bayonet rack and then tossed the other out into the darkness.

'Once you'd agreed to help us Turillac decided to kill your wife,' Beaulieu replied tersely.

Raoul swore and made a succinct comment about the man's parentage, again questioning how his father could work with him.

Beaulieu did not answer but instead gestured for the

girl to join them. 'Can you manage to climb down on your own, or will Raoul have to carry you?'

Momentarily her mind registered the fact that there was some sort of relationship between the two men, undercurrents of both affection and antagonism that she did not understand. That they had known each other before either of them had come to the island was obvious. There was no time to consider the issue, however, before Beaulieu had pulled her to the window and was gesturing down into the moat.

The ground was some twelve feet away, yet in the darkness looked far more, and the rope seemed very thin and frail. A chill, salt-laden wind tugged at it and tossed it nonchalantly against the stonework, making her very conscious of the emptiness and space. It would be all too easy to fall and break her neck.

'I can manage,' pride prompted her to say, although she very much doubted it. Then, before she had a chance to regret her words, Raoul had taken her pistol and she found herself being lowered out into the blustery darkness. Gritting her teeth, she grasped the rope between her hands, then let them take her weight while she struggled to find and grip it with her booted feet.

'I've got it,' she finally gasped, and Beaulieu released the hold he had on her arm.

As she began to descend he turned to Raoul. 'You owe me for this. We may not have your wife, but I still expect you to carry out your assignment. Now, more than ever, you are bound to the cause. You must not weaken again. I know you have some feeling for your Vendean friends but you can not allow that to influence you.'

The wind was whistling around Hortense, making it impossible for her to hear her husband's reply. It was a moment before the implication of Beaulieu's words sank in, and then she was filled with a sick sense of betrayal. Surely Raoul couldn't be a Republican? She didn't want to believe it and yet it would explain so many things, including why he had seemed so uncommitted to the Vendean cause. But this was worse than a lack of commitment. The implication was that he was an enemy, maybe even a spy, and Beaulieu was expecting him to go ahead with the attempt at assassination!

She was scarcely aware of reaching the ground, for her mind was in too great a turmoil. No, she wanted to scream, it can't be true, and yet she knew instinctively that it was. Obviously he'd had some kind of disagreement with his compatriots, but there was no denying that he was a Republican at heart.

Glancing up, she waited for him to join her and was surprised when he did not begin his descent immediately. She decided that he must be talking to Beaulieu, and the thought sickened her. Memories of Raoul's tolerance of Republican ideals and his apparent dislike of needless killing flashed across her mind, and fury welled inside her so great that she would have found it impossible to speak. When he finally dropped down beside her she turned away from him in disgust.

He failed to notice anything amiss and, catching hold of her arm, dragged her down the grassy slope into what had once been the centre of the moat. Still crouching low, they scrambled up the other side, across the sandy track and into the town. Leaning against the side of one of the houses, they paused to catch their breath.

'I think our best bet is to cross to the western side of the island and try to find a boat,' Raoul panted, 'but first I want to go back to Jacques's to see if I can retrieve my gold. We shall need it when we reach the mainland.'

Hortense was not really in favour of this, but she could see that he was not to be dissuaded. It occurred to her then that the fact that he dealt in gold rather than the currency issued by the Vendean rebels was another indication of his pragmatism and lack of commitment to

their cause. He was a traitor, an enemy, and had
undoubtedly been so since the very beginning. How had
she ever let herself be so taken in? she wondered. How
could she have been foolish enough to make such a vast
emotional commitment when on his part there was
nothing but deceit? Numbly she followed along behind
him simply because she did not know what else she
could do.

Swiftly and silently they made their way past whitewashed cottages, out of the small town and up the wide
lane to Jacques's house. Halting in the shadows of the
gateway, they studied the building. With the moonlight
reflecting off the dark void of its windows, it looked
empty and oddly forbidding, not at all like the comfortable home where they had spent the first days of their
marriage.

'I think it's deserted,' Hortense commented.

Raoul replied that he did not think they would be that
lucky; in fact he fully expected it to be occupied by some
of Haxo's officers.

Returning her pistol, he ordered her to wait in the
lane and then made his way swiftly up the unpaved
drive. Shunning the front entrance, he moved silently
around to the rear. Hortense stood alone by the gateway,
cold and unhappy, her arms wrapped tightly around
herself. She waited tensely in the uncomfortable darkness, seeing only the clouds and the swaying trees, and
her thoughts were as unsettled and dark as the night.
Her heart began to race when she sensed movement
further along the lane. A horse clopped, harness creaked
and she thought she heard someone swear. A gleam of
light appeared, flickering weakly in the dark, and two
riders came into view. Faint blurs at first, hardly able to
be seen, they crystallised into two blue-coated offficers.

With her heart pounding the girl retreated beneath the
low branches of a young pine. The long wet grass soaked

through her skirt, and drops of icy water from the tree trickled down her neck, yet she was unaware of any physical discomfort. Clasping the pistol tightly, she concentrated her whole being on remaining still. Panic rose inside her and her heart sank when, rather than continuing on down the lane, the two Republicans turned in at the gateway and rode around the side of the house, in the same direction as Raoul.

In spite of her outrage and hurt at his betrayal, she still felt the need to help him and, after waiting for a moment, followed anxiously behind. From the corner of the house she watched the two men dismount and lead their horses into the small stable. As soon as they were out of sight she dashed for the kitchen door. It opened just as she reached it and it was all she could do to prevent a squeal.

Raoul's fingers momentarily covered her mouth and he frowned warningly. 'I saw them,' he hissed. 'Give me the pistol and go back to the gate. I know how to handle this.'

'Come with me,' she urged.

He shook his head, placing the packet of money into her hands. 'I want their horses and their uniforms. Do as I say!'

There was no time to debate the issue, so she reluctantly retreated as far as the side of the house. There she waited impatiently as Raoul crossed the yard and, after picking up a stout piece of wood, positioned himself outside the stable door. It seemed an eternity before the two Republicans emerged, and then everything seemed to happen at once. Raoul brought his makeshift club down hard on the nearest man's head and then, moving with incredible speed and agility, had the second officer pinned up against the stable wall, the pistol barrel pressed beneath his chin.

'Don't fight me, *monsieur*,' he hissed, 'or you are a

dead man. When I release you we will go together into the stable, where you will saddle me two horses.'

Hortense watched them enter the building and had to fight the urge to follow them. Obviously Raoul was in command of the situation but, in spite of that and the fact that she suspected his loyalty, she still felt concerned for him. It was self-preservation, she told herself, and had nothing to do with loving him.

It seemed an age before he emerged, and for a second her breath caught in her throat. He was dressed in the Republican's uniform, and if she'd had a gun she would probably have shot him. Bending down, he efficiently stripped the coat and breeches from the other officer, then returned to the stable, reappearing almost immediately with the horses. When Hortense hurried to meet him he reached for the pistol tucked into his belt, then swore in relief when he recognised her.

'Damn it, Hortense!' he exclaimed. 'Can't you ever do as you are told!' Swiftly he helped her to mount and then, climbing into the saddle himself, led the way back out on to the lane.

'Where now?' she asked, wondering if he had already made plans.

'We'll forget about getting a boat and head straight for the mainland. The tide will still be out and with a little luck we'll make it across in time. We'll stop in a minute and you can put on the other uniform. Although we have little chance of avoiding the coastal patrols, dressed as Republicans we ought to be able to cross the causeway right under their noses.'

Hortense nodded and followed obediently behind him. She was still seething and knew that sooner or later she was going to confront him with her knowledge of his duplicity. She could hardly contain herself, but now was not the time. First they had to leave the island, and in the meantime she had a chance to consider just how she was going to handle the situation. He deserved to be shot, she told herself, but she would never be able to do it. Moreover, she wasn't sure if she could even bring herself to betray him. Their marriage was over but she still did not want to see him dead. On the other hand, he could not be permitted to work against the Royalist cause.

Half an hour later Raoul pulled off the road into some trees and dismounted. He removed the spare coast and breeches from behind his saddle and held them out to her.

'It will be just like old times,' he told her, smiling easily.

Without speaking, she took the garments and, dismounting herself, moved several yards away from him before taking off her skirt. When she tried to pull on the breeches the skirt of her chemise bunched up awkwardly. Raoul gave a snort of irritation and went across to help her.

'I'm damned if I understand your sudden shyness,' he complained. 'And this thing would be better off!'

'I want to keep on the bodice part,' she snapped, 'and I thought this way would be quicker.'

Impatiently he helped her to tuck it in, his touch brusque and impersonal. Then, while she was buttoning the breeches, he held out the coat. She slipped her arms through the sleeves and turned to face him. Even in the darkness she could see a light of amusement in his eyes.

'Yes, just like old times,' he repeated gently, catching hold of her arm and turning back the dangling sleeves. 'You look a complete hoyden.'

He felt a strong desire to kiss her and, running his hands up her arms, caught hold of her shoulders and drew her close. Once more the thought of his perfidy blossomed inside her, and she knew she dared not let him close. Physically he exerted too much power over

her. She had not yet decided what she must do, but
when it came to dealing with him she knew she could
not afford to be weakened by something that, she told
herself, was no more than lust. When he bent towards
her she unexpectedly pushed against him and turned her
head away.

'I don't want that now,' she snapped, breaking away
from him. 'I just want to get off this God-forsaken
island!'

He frowned, confused by her uncharacteristic
waspishness, and, mounting his horse again, set off
without saying another word. Hortense could tell from
the stiff set of his shoulders that he was angry, maybe
even a little hurt, and she persuaded herself that she did
not care. As they neared the causeway he pulled up and
waited for her to come alongside him. For a moment he
regarded her dispassionately.

'You look a little young, but you'll do,' he commented.
'I expect we'll come across a picket in a moment.
Whatever happens, leave the talking to me.'

She nodded and followed a little behind him as they
headed across the flat and sandy scrubland towards the
sea. After a few minutes the causeway came into view, a
black ribbon stretching out across the ribbed moonlit
sand. Raoul drew rein, and for a moment there was
silence as they looked about them. Seawards the sky was
clear, and they could see the heave and gleam of distant
water. Before them the land sloped gently, sand and
grass giving way to wet round rocks and tangled seaweed,
and the now exposed narrow causeway.

A sentry called out a challenge and, answering that
they were Republican officers, Raoul swung his horse
towards the sound. Hortense followed, trotting apprehensively behind him. When a soldier stepped into view
between the dunes and couch-grass Raoul greeted him
cheerfully and congratulated him on his watchfulness.

They were carrying dispatches to the mainland, he told the man, and he cursed the general's thoughtlessness in sending them off during the night.

Hortense waited tensely, staring silently out across the silvered sand to the mainland. It beckoned to her, promising sanctuary, and it was all she could do not to spur on past. Under his coat Raoul's hand grasped the pistol as he forced himself to indulge the man's wish for conversation. He was playing his part well, Hortense thought bitterly, but then it probably required little acting and he had always had a way with his men.

Finally, when they headed out on to the causeway, she had to fight the urge to gallop. At any moment she expected the alarm to be given, and felt her heart pounding within her chest.

'Don't worry,' Raoul told her, sensing her panic and speaking in the calm, reassuring voice she had often heard him use with young soldiers. 'There is no reason for them to suspect. Just act naturally.'

Is that your secret? she wondered bitterly. Is that how you managed to fool us all so completely? And she had to bite back an angry retort.

By the time they reached the mainland the tide had started to come in and the first white water was streaming and sizzling against the sides of the causeway. Soon the whole thing would be covered. Traversing a band of salt marsh, they headed for firmer ground, away from the splash and gurgle of water. Finally they reached a stand of pine trees where boughs were silver and the shadows pitch. With a feeling of relief they slipped into the concealing dark. It was not until she heard Raoul sigh that Hortense realised how very tense he had been. He had hidden it well, however, and had pulled the whole thing off with a practised aplomb.

They continued on through the hours of darkness, not at all sure where they were heading but anxious to put as much distance as possible between themselves and their erstwhile captors. The girl's mind boiled with questions, and she vowed with bitter determination that soon she would have them answered.

# CHAPTER ELEVEN

DAWN came, grey and misty as the sun tried unsuccessfully to pierce the thickening cloud. Although there had been little rain, the trees dripped with moisture and there was a smell of dank and rotting vegetation hanging heavily in the air. Hortense felt exhausted. Her hair was sodden and she could feel the damp seeping through her coat. She didn't think she had ever felt so uncomfortable and depressed.

Raoul, riding ahead of her, turned and glanced back, his expression full of concern.

'We'll stop soon, *chèrie*,' he promised. 'The horses need a break too.'

She should have been gratified by his consideration, but instead it served to anger her. She didn't want his kindness or his encouragement, not when she was shortly going to take him to task.

'I know you feel badly about leaving the others to their fate,' he continued, thinking this the reason for her silence, 'but there was really nothing we could do.' When she did not respond he shrugged; he was tired himself and not up to coping with her sulking.

They were out of the *marais* now, and the track they were following wound between bare beech trees. Rotting leaves flattened beneath the horses' feet, making the path treacherous as it dipped steeply down towards a river. As they levelled out Raoul's mount fell to its knees, and only his superb horsemanship kept him in the saddle.

He helped the animal right itself, swearing softly, and pointed to a clearing on the riverbank. 'We'd better stop over there. This beast can't go any further.'

They rode across to where soft grass rolled down to a small shingle beach, and there Raoul dismounted. Even though he was exhausted himself, good manners were second nature to him and he turned to help Hortense. She slipped from the saddle into his arms but immediately drew away from him. Unable to meet his gaze, she turned her back and walked over to the water's edge.

'What's wrong?' he asked quietly, although he was very much afraid that he knew. His stomach was churning and yet his mind was filled with a bitter resignation.

Hortense had been brooding on his duplicity for hours, and suddenly her hurt and anger exploded in a torrent of words.

'Traitor!' she spat, her eyes bright with tears. 'You are a pig of a Republican! How could you use us so, pretending to help us when all the time you were working for *them*? I heard what Beaulieu said to you, for God's sake! Go on, deny it if you can!'

He looked at her with eyes of misery, his handsome face as pale as she had ever seen it. 'I can't,' he replied flatly, lowering the hand he had been holding out in protest so that she should not see how it trembled. 'But I swear I have done little to help them. I stopped making contact with them after Cholet.'

'It was bad enough when I thought you were going to help them in order to save my life, but to know you've been working for them willingly, that you only came among us to spy. . .' She choked back another sob, unable to continue.

'Yes, I came to the Vendée to spy,' he replied. His expression could have been carved in stone. Only the muscle tensing beneath his jaw betrayed that he was not as emotionless as he seemed. 'I had little choice. I was released from prison only on condition that I did so. Now I realise that it would have been more honourable for me to die. I won't apologise for my views, Hortense.

I am still a Republican, but I am as sickened by what is happening here as you are. I would have given my life to prevent it!'

When she made a noise of disbelief he revealed anger of his own. 'I wanted to be done with it! I asked you to leave the country with me, damn it! I almost begged you. I didn't want politics to come between us.'

'It's more than politics,' she replied brokenly, 'and you know it. You used me! You lied to me and to my family. I can't trust you any more. I don't for one moment think that you have finished working for the Republicans. How do I even know that you are not going to continue with your mission to assassinate Charette?'

'I'm sorry you think that poorly of me,' Raoul rasped, feeling as if he was slowly dying inside. Only for her would he have sunk so low. He had no intention of harming the general and had, in fact, told his father so, actually defying him to curtail their escape. 'I may be a Republican but I am not like Carrier and his kind. Believe it or not, the Revolution was founded on idealism and should have been all to the good. . . In fact, I think it still can be, but not at the expense of men like Charette. The Republic can win this war honestly.'

'And you call what you did honest!' she scoffed contemptuously, moving back towards her horse.

He had admitted everything, confirming her worst fears, and now she wanted to ride away from him, and never see him again. She could not resist one last glance at him and it was nearly her undoing. He was standing so pale and stiff that she experienced a traitorous urge to wrap her arms around him and tell him that it really didn't matter, only it did! He was her enemy and she was going to have to learn to hate him. Raoul saw her intention, and common sense told him he should let her go, but when had he ever been sensible?

He was damned if he was going to let her ride out of

his life just like that. 'Come with me to Charette. He deserves to be warned. I was not the only one to be given the job of eliminating him.'

With her hand across her saddle Hortense froze. He was going to Charette. Could she believe what he said about warning the general? In her heart she did, but over something so important she could only trust her intellect. He had lied before and he would do so again. She was furious that he should think her so gullible. With her heart pounding she drew the pistol from its holster by her saddle and turned to face him.

'You are not going to him. I won't let you,' she replied desperately. Tiredness had weakened her and she could feel hysteria boiling up inside her. 'I don't trust you, Raoul. I can't afford to. I just can't take the chance.'

'Hortense. . .' he began in protest, taking a step towards her, his hand stretched out imploringly.

She saw the plea for undertanding in his eyes, the hurt and the horror, and she felt so unsure and upset that she began to tremble uncontrollably. Where was her strength, she asked herself, and her determination to serve the Vendean cause? Almost without her being aware of it, her finger tightened on the trigger. The pistol hammer crashed forward; the result was a sharp, condemning click. It was a mercy that the spark had failed to ignite the powder in the pan.

For a moment Raoul just stood there, a look of stunned disbelief on his face that turned swiftly to raw hurt and then anger. With an oath he leapt forward to grasp her by the shoulders and shake her until her teeth rattled.

'So this is all your love is worth,' he snarled. 'How could you?'

Hortense was too stunned by what she had done to protest or fight him. She wanted only to sink down to the soft grass and sob her heart out. He was shouting at her and it was through a haze of dizziness that his words registered.

'I was going to warn the man! My father told me that someone from Paris has also been sent to infiltrate his army and put an end to him. You can bet your sweet life it will be someone far more ruthless and experienced than me!'

'Your father?' she repeated foolishly, staring up into his white, tortured face. 'What do you mean? What about your father?'

He stopped shaking her, although he still retained his grip on her shoulders. Closing his eyes for a moment, he swallowed hard, knowing he was giving her yet another reason to hate him. 'Thomas Beaulieu is my natural father.'

Pushing her away, he turned his back on her. He was breathing heavily and she could tell that he was still struggling for control.

'I didn't think you knew who your father was,' she managed to say.

She felt so sick and shaky that she had to sit down, and, taking a couple of steps, slumped down with her back against a tree. Dear God, but it explained such a lot. Now that she knew she could see a resemblance between the two men in spite of their differing ages and expressions.

It was a moment before Raoul spoke again, doing so without turning around. 'I was given the information in a letter from my mother when I was eighteen. Even then it was some time before I met him.'

'But you're close!' she accused.

'No,' he replied tiredly. 'We are related by an accident of birth, that's all. . . In fact I am an embarrassment to him and he keeps the relationship a secret. . . I really don't want to talk about it.'

'You don't talk about anything,' she replied bitterly.

'Dear God, but you are not at all what I. . .who I thought.'

I am, he wanted to scream. What is between us has nothing to do with politics or who my father was, it's something much more fundamental—but he saw how hopeless it was.

'Rest while you can,' he told her tiredly. 'We will be riding on in about an hour, and together! I have no intention of letting you ride across the countryside unattended.'

'To Charette?' she demanded.

'Yes, damn it!'

'I'll denounce you,' she cried, her anger and mistrust boiling up anew. 'I'll tell them all how false you are. You won't get anywhere near the general.'

'Then you will be signing my death warrant and probably Charette's!'

With a tired sigh he turned away to loosen the horses' saddles, then returned to sit within a yard of her. Trying desperately to ignore him, she closed her eyes and rested her head back, but she was too cold and soul-wrenchingly miserable to sleep. Glancing at him beneath her lashes she saw that, although he was stretched out on the damp grass, his every muscle was tense. Was he still afraid that she would bolt? she wondered. Certainly he was near enough to pounce on her if she attempted it. His expression could have been carved in stone. He looked hard and coldly determined, and she could see not the slightest trace of regret or contrition in his expression. It shouldn't surprise her, she thought. He had to be ruthless and unfeeling to use her so.

In fact, he felt shocked and deeply hurt. She had actually tried to shoot him! His stomach was churning so badly that he wanted to be sick, but he was too proud to let her see the extent of his anguish. Hell and damnation, but she was not the only one who felt betrayed! He should have expected it, he supposed. She was, after all, a true aristocrat, and personalities would mean nothing to her when it came to protecting her cause.

Time dragged, and in order to avoid contact with him Hortense feigned sleep. It was almost an hour before he stirred, and then he walked down to douse his face and hair in the cold river before touching her briefly on the shoulder.

'It's time to move on,' he growled, 'but before we do I think we'd best get out of these uniforms.'

As he spoke he peeled off the blue coat he was wearing and, going over to his saddle-bag, retrieved their own garments.

He frowned consideringly before throwing her skirt at her. 'If you put that on at least you won't look completely like a soldier. You will have to keep the coat, though, or you'll freeze.'

For a moment she only glared at him, not wanting to co-operate with him in any way.

'Do it, Hortense!' he snapped. 'Or, so help me, I'll do it for you!'

She had never seen him so impatient and angry, and realised with surprise that he meant what he said. She decided that she had pushed him far enough, and, walking around to the other side of the tree, hastily complied. When she returned he took the discarded clothes from her and, without saying a word, secreted them under a nearby bush. He went over to tighten their saddles and then called her to him.

She went reluctantly, a look of disdain on her face which made him swear. When he pulled a knife from his belt she could not prevent a gasp. His eyes flashed angrily as he dragged her to him, and some devil made him pause a moment before he savagely sliced the epaulettes and buttons from her coat.

'If I were as ruthless as you think then I would have

slit your pretty throat,' he hissed. 'It's obvious that you intend to make things as difficult for me as you can.'

With an oath of exasperation he pushed her away and swung up into the saddle, then, stopping, collected the reins of her hourse. 'Mount up! I'm going to lead you.' When she glared mutinously at him his eyes flashed, giving her another glimpse of his temper. 'Do it, damn you, or I'll tie you up and toss you across the saddle.'

'Why?' she demanded. 'Why are you forcing me to come with you? There can be nothing between us now!'

'You are my wife and still my responsiblity. Besides, if it comes down to it, I don't trust you either. You'd probably ride off to the nearest peasants and set them upon me.'

That was only part of the truth and he knew it. Keeping her with him was irrational and dangerous, but for the life of him he could not let her go. If she denounced him then so be it. When she climbed into the saaddle he did not show his relief but set off at once at a brisk canter.

They continued on for nearly an hour and Raoul did not say a word. Hortense stared at his stiff back resentfully. She wanted to scream and shout at him, although she knew it would change nothing, but he had distanced himself from her both mentally and physically. When they reached a small crossroads he allowed her horse to come alongisde. His expression was inscrutable, his eyes cold, and yet he was as pale as a corpse. The pointed gash where the sword-point had bitten into his lean cheek stood out sharply above his beard. In all, he looked quite disreputable, every inch a brigand, and Hortense found it difficult to remember how gentle he could be.

No, I don't love him, she told herself. You can't love someone you don't really know, and events had proved that she didn't know Raoul at all. It was a feeling that was reinforced a they continued on through the bleak morning. She felt sick and shaky with tiredness and on occasion began to weave in the saddle.

'We'll stop in the next village,' Raoul told her.

She thought she saw compassion in his eyes, and that more than anything served to stiffen her spine and give her the strength to continue. She didn't want his sympathy. She didn't want him to be nice to her. If it became necessary for her to denounce him then she wanted to be able to do so without feeling as if she were tearing out her heart.

As the morning progressed the weather did not really improve and she began to wonder if she would ever really be warm again. Her teeth had long since ceased to chatter; she was too bone-achingly cold. The wind continually blowing into her face seemed to be sapping her strength, and she began to feel pleasantly sleepy.

'Hortense!' Raoul reached over to shake her awake. 'For pity's sake, don't fall asleep now.'

She wasn't sure whether it was anger or compassion she saw in his face. Well, damn him, she thought. I don't want to keep my eyes open any longer.

She was not aware of him climbing into the saddle behind her to prevent her falling, and even when they reached a small hamlet she did not stir. The place consisted of half a dozen simple farmhouses grouped together around a blacksmith's with a selection of outhouses and barns dotted haphazardly in between.

Leading his own horse, Raoul cautiously made his way up to the door of the nearest dwelling. It was a shabby single-storey building with two small shuttered windows and a single bleached and sagging door. Before he could dismount a bearded peasant emerged to scowl at them suspiciously.

He had no room for travellers, he told Raoul sourly, and it would be the same at the other houses. When

Raoul offered to pay he relented somewhat and finally offered the use of his barn. He was also willing enough to sell them blankets and food. Raoul felt uneasy about the whole affair but their need was desperate. Hortense was a dead weight in his arms and he was really worried about her. It was with immeasurable relief that he dismounted and, carrying her, followed the peasant into the nearest barn.

In fact, the place was not as bad as he had expected. There were no windows to let in the cold and the door was reasonably well fitting. Most encouraging of all, the floor was thickly covered with clean, dry straw. He laid the girl down and, taking a gold piece from his pocket, offered it to the man. The fellow's face lit up at the sight of it and he hurried away, returning a few minutes later with some blankets and food.

Raoul covered Hortense then helped himself to some bread and cheese. He was still not hungry but common sense made him force it down. He was in scarcely better shape than his wife, he realised, and now he was out of the wind his eyelids and limbs felt like lead. He wished he had the energy to stay awake but he knew it was asking the impossible.

Leaning over, he gently touched the girl's face, and was surprised how cold she felt. Telling himself that he was only doing it to warm her, to make sure she didn't escape him, he pulled her into his arms and used the blankets to cover them both. That she would likely scratch his eyes out if she awoke before him was his last conscious thought.

Hortense awoke slowly. She felt relaxed and protected and had snuggled instinctively closer to her husband's comforting warmth. Her memory returned to her with the force of a sledge-hammer and she stiffened. Gently she lifted his arm and inched away from him, scarcely daring to breathe. She had to escape him, otherwise she was very much afraid that she would end up compromising her loyalty and lying to protect him, and she didn't think she could stomach that.

He groaned softly in his sleep but he did not stir and, rolling cautiously away from him, she sat up. It was dawn outside and the barn door stood half open allowing in just enough light for her to see by. Climbing cautiously to her feet, she stretched her cramped limbs and glanced at the man sleeping soundly less than a yard from her. He looked so damned innocent, younger somehow and ridiculously vulnerable. Tears sprang to her eyes but she resolutely blinked them away. There was no way on earth that she was going to be able to denounce him; besides, now she had calmed down she believed him when he swore he wouldn't harm Charette. Whatever else he was, he was no murderer. In her time with him she had seen enough proof of that.

Moving over to the door, she eased it open and slipped outside. Morning sunlight pierced the thinning cloud and somewhere close at hand a cockerel heralded the beginning of yet another day. Hortense was conscious of both hunger and thirst, but her first priority was to get away from Raoul.

Glancing around, she caught sight of their horses tethered beneath the sagging porch of an adjacent barn. They were still saddled and, after checking her horse's girth, she swiftly mounted. There was still no movement from inside the barn and, suppressing feelings of guilt and loss, she cantered out of the farmyard. Lége was not far, she discovered on reaching a signpost, and her spirits rose. She felt sure she would be able to beg food and a night's shelter from the peasants who had helped her before. Then in a day, possibly two, she could be home.

Raoul was both angry and anxious when he awoke to find her gone, and immediately set off in pursuit. He knew he was being foolish and that further contact with

her would only bring him pain, but he didn't want to let
her go. He anticipated her destination in Lége and, had
the fates been kind, would have caught up with her
there, but his horse cast a shoe in the middle of nowhere
and he lost half a day getting it reshod. When he reached
the peasants' house it was to find the girl long gone, and
he was forced to acknowledge that he hadn't a hope of
coming up with her before she reached her home. For a
moment he considered following her there but realised
that Henri Claviere, should he be aware of the facts,
would be likely to shoot him down like a dog.

He felt bowed down by regret and self-contempt and
the disquieting knowledge that he had been supporting
the wrong side. The massacres in Noirmoutier and
Nantes had sickened him. He was still a Republican at
heart but the conflict in the Vendée seemed somehow
separate from what was happening in the rest of France
and his loyalty had been slowly changing. He had
become a Republican because he believed in the rights
of the people, yet here in the Vendée they were the ones
holding out most strongly against the Republican idea.
As for Charette—to hell with ideology. He liked the man
and would do what he could to prevent his death. It was
a way to make amends and in taking it he still didn't
consider himself a traitor to the true Republican cause.

He sat on his horse at the crossroads just outside Lége,
quite unconscious of the bitter wind that tousled his
hair; then, coming to a decision, he turned south in
search of the elusive general.

Hortense reached Château Claviere and was warmly
welcomed by her two cousins. She was exhausted and
desperately sick at heart. Honesty made her admit to her
marriage and, although she was adamant that it was
over, refused to tell Henri and Marie just what had
caused such a bitter rift. As good Catholics they were a
little shocked by her summary rejection of her marriage

vows. However, they could not ignore the state she was in. Reluctantly they respected her wish not to talk about it, and did their best to take her mind off her misery by involving her in the day-to-day running of the estate.

The security and warmth of her home was wrapped around her like a protective blanket and yet it could not lessen the pain she felt. The days dragged, each one as empty as the last. Had Raoul really loved her? Was he really as two-faced and unprincipled as his actions implied? They were questions she often asked herself in the emptiness of the night, an emptiness that seemed to envelop her body and soul. She almost managed to convince herself that she hated him, until she remembered things—his touch, his smile, the way he seemed to understand her every need, and then, in spite of everything, she just missed him. She was hurt and confused and her usual pragmatism deserted her so that she felt like a child alone in the dark. Then she would cry into her pillow, not so much for what was but for what might have been.

Rain poured down Raoul's neck. His legs ached and his shoulder throbbed, but worst of all was the emptiness he felt in the region of his heart. He could not doubt that Hortense hated him. He had always known how it would end but he hadn't expected to feel so soul-wrenchingly, debilitatingly miserable. He told himself that it was for the best that she had left him, that there could be nothing between them now, but that did not make the deep loneliness he was feeling any easier to bear.

After searching for several days he had eventually come up with Charette at the Convent de Val de Moriere near the small village of les Brouzils, where he was recovering from a minor wound. He had been intrigued by Raoul's abridged account of his escape from Noirmoutier and had been happy for him to join his

depleted band. Less than twenty-four hours later they
had been warned that the Republicans were coming and
had fled for their lives.

As Raoul had expected, the last few days had been a
nightmare, testing his endurance beyond anything he
had experienced before. Cold and hungry, Charette and
his small band had run from the Republicans, hiding in
ravines and on desolate moorland, never daring to remain
too long in one place. The cold was bad enough, but
them came the rain. It hammered and bounced against
their hunched shoulders, soaking them completely and
plastering their cloaks to their horses' backs. It doused
any fires they tried to make, pooled in the hollows where
they tried to sleep and turned the powder to gritty sludge
in the musket pans. Often they had to proceed on foot,
leading their horses as they travelled along steep and
slippery pathways or beneath the low branches of trees.
Raoul didn't think he had ever felt so exhausted and
uncomfortable.

Throughout it all Charette remained calm and encouraging, exhibiting the qualities of leadership that had
earned him the undying loyalty of so many of his men.
Raoul too fell under his spell and determined that his
first priority would be to keep the general safe. It was
something he could hang on to, something he knew was
right when all the other issues were grey and confusing.

As he led his horse up the steep moorland track the
beast slithered and fell to its haunches, and Raoul cursed
colourfully as he hauled it upright. Charette, moving
just ahead of him, chuckled and commended his imagin-
ation. There was an easy camaraderie between them and
Raoul decided that he would be proud to call this man
his friend.

# CHAPTER TWELVE

IN THE spring the grounds of Château Claviere were a picture. Lilac and cherry blossom, tulips and honeysuckle erupted into bloom, filling the air with their heady perfume. Sunlight warmed the rustling grasses and played across the mellow stone walls, bringing life where there had only been dampness and cold. Hortense walked regularly in the garden. She found its familiarity and peace deeply soothing, and yet it could not ease the ache in her heart.

Everyone at the château was anxious for news of the war, snatching at any snippet of information and discussing it for hours. Hortense was desperate to take some part in the fighting but Henri refused to let her leave without him, and he had promised Marie that he would remain with her until after their baby was born. Hortense realised that he was as anxious to return to the conflict as she and, because she knew he was finding it difficult enough to keep his promise to his wife, refrained from making this more difficult for him.

On more than one occasion she thought of riding off on her own, but the various Vendean bands were continuously on the move, and even if she should come up with one she was afraid of being considered a hindrance rather than a help. There were times, too, when she suffered from the most dreadful doubt. Had she allowed her love to override her common sense? Raoul was a Republican and she had acquainted no one of the fact. Had he gone to join Charette? Should she have denounced him? If harm befell the general because of her omission then she would never be able to forgive herself. It was most likely, however, that now she was aware of his duplicity Raoul had returned to Paris, to his despicable Republican masters.

At the beginning of March news had reached them of an horrendous massacre at the village les Lucs, where the Republicans had actually bombarded a church containing Vendean refugees. Nearly six hundred men, women and children had died in an event that would long be remembered for its infamy. Throughout the countryside feeling against the Republicans ran high, and any of them who ventured forth in small bodies or alone risked being taken by peasants and murdered out of hand.

As spring continued the Vendeans' fortunes took a turn for the better. Charette was joined by his friend Joly, and General Haxo, who had been hounding him through the winter, was defeated by them and killed in the area of La Roche. In the east of the region the Vendean leader, de Sapinaud, was having some success, and General Stofflet, returning from across the Loire, managed to retake Cholet.

At the end of April, when the Vendean generals gathered around the ruins of the Château de la Boulaye to again pledge their loyalty to the cause, word was sent to Henri, but it was at this time that Marie went into labour. For a while Hortense considered leaving without him, but Marie was suffering greatly and both her cousins needed her near.

Jean Henri Claviere made his entrance into the world during the last week of April. He was a sturdy infant who cried lustily and soon began to thrive. Marie was weak and weepy after her ordeal, and because of it Henri remained a little longer at her side. As spring turned to early summer Marie recovered both her spirits and her health and was able to face the imminent departure of her husband with equanimity.

'He wants to go and I won't hold him any longer,' she told Hortense as they sat together on a garden bench. 'I had intended to find a wet-nurse for the baby and go with him, but I can't bring myself to do that now. It's funny, but I had no idea how much I would love this baby until it was born. I'd still like to go with Henri, yet I know I can serve him best by remaining here. I shall have to rely on you to prevent him taking any foolish risks. I shall always be grateful for the way you sent him home after Cholet.'

Hortense was forced to remember that Raoul had assisted her in that. He had taken Henri's place and nearly died because of it. His motive then had seemed of the purest, and, even looking back, she could see no way his action could have aided the Republican cause. For just a moment she wondered if she was guilty of letting his transgressions blot out the good things that he had done.

At the beginning of June Henri and Hortense, together with some fifty local peasants, many who had taken up arms before but had returned either after Cholet or for the spring planting, went off to join Charette at his camp to the east of Lége. The journey took nearly two days and they arrived just as the sun was setting. The camp was situated beside a small farm and stretched out across a rolling meadow and into the adjacent woodland. The army was much better equipped than in the winter-time and a number of bivouacs were dotted among the usual makeshift shelters. Horses, mules, oxen and wagons were scattered throughout the camp and Hortense could even see the occasional goat. In spite of the apparent chaos, there seemed to be an air of purpose about the men, and a cheerful confidence. There was much laughter and the smells of wood-smoke and roasting meat drifted through the evening air.

Charette and his officers had made themselves

comfortable around a large farmhouse, and once they had settled the men Henri and Hortense walked over to report to him. In the farmyard itself a mobile forge was parked and a shirtless peasant was standing in the middle of the wagon bed working the enormous bellows. A blacksmith was hammering out a horseshoe on the heavy anvil beside the vehicle, and two other men were trying to calm a recalcitrant horse.

A young Vendean officer was lounging on a bench beside the door of the whitewashed farmhouse. He stood up as they approached and called out a greeting. It was with a great deal of pleasure that Hortense recognised Jacques Martin, and hurried forward to give him a hug. He swung her off her feet then, setting her down, planted a quick kiss on her cheek.

'Hey, Raoul!' he called out exuberantly, glancing towards the forge. 'Look who's here!'

Hortense felt her breath catch in her throat. Although she had acknowledged the possiblity of meeting her husband, she hadn't really expected it; if she had then she definitely wouldn't have come. A number of different emotions boiled up insider her—surprise, anger, apprehension and something more, something she did not want to consider because it made her too vulnerable. Slowly she turned around in time to see Raoul hand the reins of his horse to one of his companions and begin walking towards them, moving with the same lithe grace she had come to know so well. Butterflies fluttered in her stomach and her heart began a treacherous increased beating. Damn him, she thought, is he always going to have this effect on me?

He was clad only in a white open-necked shirt and breeches, with boots that looked shiny and new. He had lost weight, she noticed, and was carrying not an ounce of spare fat, but looked fit and as tough as old leather.

Although the summer had only just begun, he was berry-brown, which only seemed to heighten the startling blue of his eyes. The cut on his cheek had left a thin, pale scar, further adding to the impression of a hardened soldier. What a shame, she thought, and was horrified by the feeling of tenderness that washed over her. She hadn't wanted to see him again. She didn't want to face the uncertainty and indecision that being in his company would bring.

He smiled tightly, the light not reaching his eyes, and she realised with a little spurt of sorrow that he was harder and more withdrawn than before. Not surprisingly he seemed a little wary. No doubt he was wondering just how much she had told her cousin.

Beside her, Henri stiffened. He had no idea what Raoul had done to upset Hortense, but family loyalty placed him firmly on her side. She knew then that she would have to be conciliatory or the two men would like to come to blows.

'Aren't you pleased to see her?' Jacques demanded innocently, puzzled by his friend's reserve.

Raoul met her gaze and held it challengingly. 'Of course I'm pleased to see my own wife.'

Hortense paled, and anger boiled up inside her. Whatever she had been expecting him to say, it was not that. With a struggle she managed to control her churning emotions and forced a smile. 'Are you well, Raoul?'

He nodded, not adding that the sight of her was doing strange things to the rhythm of his heart. Lord, but she looked good, standing there, clad in a soft white shirt and full dark green skirt. Her hair had grown and now brushed her shoulders in a tumble of red brown curls that looked so soft that he ached to touch them.

'You dark horse!' Jacques exclaimed. 'In all these months you never said anything about marrying her, although I can't say I'm surprised.'

Raoul shrugged. 'The subject never came up, but now she's here I thought I'd better stake my claim.' Dragging his eyes away from her, he turned to Henri. 'I'm afraid I owe you an apology. I should have asked your permission; unfortunately at the time there was no way of getting in touch with you.'

Hortense was stunned by his audacity. He was acting as if their marriage were perfectly normal.

'I don't object to the match as long as you are both happy. I care about Hortense.' The words were a warning as much as a blessing. 'I'm aware that you've quarrelled. . . I won't stand by and watch her hurt.'

Raoul nodded solemnly, holding Claviere's gaze without flinching. 'I never intended to hurt her.' His gaze swung back to the girl, his expression still unreadable. 'I'm hoping we will be able to settle our differences.'

Hortense did not give him the assurance he craved and was furious with him for putting her on the spot. Henri was looking at her expectantly, Jacques in surprise. For a moment she was tempted to tell them just how matters stood.

When she said nothing Raoul turned back to Henri and, forcing a smile, asked him how many men he brought with him.

'About fifty.' Claviere relaxed a little. 'It's not enough for my own command. I don't know what your position is now, Raoul, but I'd be happy to serve under you. We are exceptionally well equipped, thanks to my uncle's legacy, and probably have more powder and shot than we will ever need.

'Charette has given me a troop and a captaincy. When you see him you can tell him that I'd be happy to have you with me. In fact, I have some of your old men under my command. Charles Letouc, for one.'

'If Raoul wants you then the general will agree,' Jacques informed them with a laugh. 'He has a soft spot for the few of us who stuck with him during January. Raoul especially, since he saved his life a couple of months ago when his horse was shot from under him.'

Hortense was surprised by this piece of information and glanced assessingly at her husband. Was it possible that he had really come over to the Vendean side? At that moment there was a commotion behind them as the horse that was due to be shod reared up and tried to pull away.

Glancing around, Raoul muttered an oath beneath his breath. 'I'll have to go. That new horse of mine hates being shod. Jacques will take you to the general.'

As he turned back to the forge Jacques and Henri moved towards the farmhouse door. For a moment the girl's eyes followed him. She was surprised when, leaving his horse for a little longer, he turned back.

I know you still don't trust me,' he said, stopping her moving away from him by holding on to her arm. 'But I can assure you that since I joined him I've remained entirely faithful to Charette.'

'It doesn't change things,' she told him furiously. 'In spite of your change of heart, there can be nothing between us now. There have been too many lies, too much duplicity. I don't know why you had to mention our marriage. There was no need for anyone but Henri to know. Now people will expect us to spend time together.'

'I'm not ashamed of it,' he rasped. 'Besides, I'll have no wife of mine wandering around the camp giving the impression that she's unattached!' He glanced towards the angry horse and his brow wrinkled in frustration. 'I've made compromises, Hortense. You can't just write our marriage off.'

'Oh, yes, I can,' she replied coldly, dragging her arm away. 'I shall never forgive you!'

Charette remembered Henri from St Fulgent. He

welcomed him warmly and readily agreed to his joining Raoul. He also, much to the girl's embarrassment, approved heartily of Raoul's marriage.

'There are a number of wives with us now,' he commented, 'and they are as brave as any of my men. Mesdames de Fief, de Monsirbier, de Bulkeley—they are all here, and strong supporters of our cause.'

The following morning the Generals de Sapinaud and Stofflet arrived at the camp together with the Chevalier de Tinteniac. Tinteniac, it was rumoured, had brought a letter from England, from the Comte d'Artois, uncle to the young King. Henri was ecstatic.

'If the Count comes to join us it will really strengthen our cause,' he declared.

That evening there was music and dancing to celebrate the envoy's arrival. As usual, Charette and many of his officers joined in with the peasants. Hortense was caught up in the excitement and danced first with Henri and then with the General himself. She partnered a succession of exuberant young peasants and then Jacques Martin. Throughout the day she had seen nothing of her husband, and she could not resist asking Jacques where he was.

'He came in late from patrol last night and went out again early this morning,' Jacques told her. 'The General gave him permission to raid a Republican camp he came across in the forest of Touvois. . . Don't worry. He'll be all right. He knows what he's doing.'

When Jacques relinquished her she danced with another officer, a swarthy young Breton who held her much too close. Throughout the evening she had drunk a deceptively large amount of wine and she was feeling quite light-headed. Her step faltered and, chuckling, he pulled her tight against him, at the same time nuzzling her ear.

'I'd like my wife back, if you don't mind, Morez.'

Raoul spoke coldly from behind her partner, and the next moment she found herself in his arms.

She didn't want to dance with him and tried to tell him so, but, ignoring her words, he dragged her close. 'If you can put up with a snake like Morez mauling you then you ought to be able to stomach me!

Through a haze of wine she realised that he was as angry as she had ever seen him. His hard, lean body was taut with it. Was he actually jealous, she wondered, or was it merely a matter of pride? He had removed his jacket and she could feel the warmth of his chest beneath her cheek and the crispness of his chest-hair through the thin cotton. It would have been so easy to forget all that was between them, to curl her fingers in the soft hair at his nape and draw his head down for a kiss.

'You're my wife, Hortense,' he continued sharply, 'and if you don't take me to your bed you'll take no one! Just because you hold my life in your hands doesn't mean I'll stand back while you make a fool of me.'

Before she could protest the music changed and they were forced to make a line with some of the other dancers. Glancing sideways at him, she was surprised at how well he mastered the lilting steps of the peasant dance. She couldn't help wondering how often he had danced it before, and with whom.

As soon as the music ended he drew her away from the dancing and flopped down on the grass, choosing an isolated spot that would offer them some privacy.

'You still don't trust me, do you?' he complained irritably.

'I don't see how you can expect me to.' Reluctantly she settled down beside him, being careful not to get too close. 'Have you seen any sign of this other assassin?'

Tiredly he shook his head.

'Perhaps he doesn't exist.' It sounded like an accusation. 'Perhaps he's given up or been killed.'

'Perhaps.' Sighing, he rubbed tiredly at the back of his neck, still not looking up at her. 'Personally I think the General is in greater danger now that more men are joining him. It is impossible to check on them all.'

'It's marvellous, though, isn't it? With so many new recruits we're bound to succeed. And if the Comte comes. . . Wouldn't it be wonderful if we could not only free the Vendée but put the young King on the throne?'

For a moment he did not answer her. 'No,' he finally replied in a flat voice. 'I don't think it would be wonderful at all. I'm fighting to free the Vendée, not to restore a King who will once more ride roughshod over his people. My only comfort is that I don't think d'Artois will come. The man lacks backbone, like the rest of his kind!'

Hortense was shocked. 'In spite of everything, you're still a Republican,' she accused.

'I'm a Vendean first,' he answered sharply.

Hortense felt any remaining trust in him slipping away. 'How do I know you won't change sides again?' she demanded. 'I begin to think I should have denounced you after all.'

The anger he felt both at events and at her made it impossible for him to reassure her. 'You don't.' He laughed cynically. 'Do you know, I begin to think mercenaries have the right idea? They don't try to decide if a cause is just, they simply fight for the side that pays the most.'

'You're despicable,' she snapped, disappointment fuelling her anger as she climbed to her feet. 'You show no loyalty at all. Well, just you remember that I'll be watching you. If you do anything at all to harm our cause not only will I denounce you—I'll shoot you myself!'

Fool, he told himself as he watched her go striding away. Why had he let his disgust and frustration provoke

him so? She was never going to forgive or trust him now.
Lying back on the grass, he closed his eyes, nearly
overcome with a sense of hopelessness. He should never
have married her. He had thought she loved him, yet
events had shown how little her love was worth.

Two days later Charette announced that they were
breaking camp in order to attack the Republican-held
town of Challans. Henri suspected it was a ploy to
impress de Tinteniac and the Comte d'Artois, but that
did not detract from his enthusiasm. Having spent the
winter and spring at home, he was anxious to distinguish
himself in battle.

The evening before they were due to march out Raoul
came to discuss the arrangements with Henri. Hortense
had not seen him since the night of the dance and,
although he glanced once or twice in her direction, he
did not speak. She thought he looked tired, and Henri
verified that he had been doing more than his share of
patrols.

'I think he's avoiding you, Horry. I do wish the two
of your would get things sorted out,' her cousin
complained.

The next day the army began its advance towards
Challans, the capital of the Marais. They were a brave
sight, some eight thousand infantry with their wide-
brimmed hats, muskets and peat-cutters, and nine
hundred cavalry. It was a fine day and the sunlight
glinted off their swords and freshly polished bayonets.
They marched confidently, to the accompaniment of
cornet and drum, their white silk flags flying challengingly in the soft breeze.

That night they camped on the edge of a thick forest.
In spite of what they knew they would face the following
day, their spirits were high. Hortense sat a little apart
from the men and carefully checked through her supply
of bandages. From time to time she glanced across and

her gaze fell on Raoul. He was stretched out beside the
camp-fire and appeared to be listening more to the others
than talking himself. It was a trait she had only recently
become aware of in him. She knew he wasn't happy, and
it bothered her more than it should have. Even when he
smiled she could see the shadows behind it and, in spite
of everything, it upset her to know she was responsible
for putting the misery in his eyes.

After an open-air mass the following morning, the
army marched out, leaving its baggage and camp-
followers behind. The wagons containing the nurses and
medical supplies continued on to the edge of the woodland, and then they too were halted. It was here that
Hortense waited, watching the fighting men march out
and waving until her arm ached.

They were all anticipating a great victory but it was
not to be. Things were going badly, they realised as soon
as the first casualties began coming in, telling horrific
tales of retreating peasants being charged down and
decapitated by Republican cavalry. By the time the first
retreating Vendeans appeared Hortense had a good idea
of what had occurred. The Vendean centre it seemed,
had failed to hold against the enemy's cavalry, and the
Republicans had been able to turn on Charette and
Stofflet commanding on the flanks.

With their wounded loaded into wagons the Vendeans
retreated further into the forest, their own cavalry covering their withdrawal. Hortense knew that both her
cousin and her husband were in the rearguard, and she
was concerned for the safety of them both.

As dusk was falling the defeated army made camp and
temporary shelters were set up among the trees to house
the wounded. They had plenty of bandages and even a
small supply of laudanum, which they kept for the very
worst cases. In fact, there were few of these, making

Hortense suspect that, of necessity, many of the most seriously wounded had been left behind.

It must have been at least ten in the evening before the last of their forces came riding in. By this time Hortense was desperately tired and, with most of the wounded cared for, was looking forward to some rest. When Raoul and Henri appeared, carrying a badly injured Jacques Martin between them, she wept. The young man's arm was a mess, an enemy sabre having opened it virtually from shoulder to wrist. The tourniquet his friends had knotted around his upper arm had undoubtedly saved his life, but for what? she wondered bitterly, knowing that there was no way they were going to be able to save the limb.

Jacques was laid down on a mattress just inside the shelter, and the doctor was summoned. He only confirmed what they had all known. Almost unemotionally he began making preparations for the amputation. Henri looked helplessly at Raoul.

'Go and check on the men,' the latter ordered. 'I'll remain here.'

When the doctor had everything ready Raoul gently moved Hortense aside. 'See to someone else,' he told her. 'I'll assist the good doctor.'

She wanted to protest that it was really her job, but she was not at all sure that her stomach was up to it.

'Go on,' he said and he surprised her by reaching out to touch her cheek.

On less than steady legs she did as he bid, grateful to escape the gory scene. When she returned half an hour later it was all over. The patient had died beneath the surgeon's knife without, mercifully, regaining consciousness. Looking around, Hortense saw her husband sitting with his back against a nearby tree. With his head resting against his knees he looked dejected and drained. She walked across to him and, giving in to instinct, ran her

hand caressingly across his hair. It was a gesture to
comfort him, to tell him that he was not alone in his
sorrow. She was surprised when, catching hold of her
hand, he pressed it against his cheek, clutching it as
tightly as a lifeline.

'Oh, Raoul,' she whispered when she felt the wetness
of his tears. 'I'm so sorry. I know you had grown close
to him.'

Forgetting the differences between them, she knelt
down beside him and the next moment he had pulled
her into his arms. For a while he just held her, drawing
on her strength, and then he took her mouth in a deep,
desperate kiss. Hortense hadn't the heart to push him
away and instead gave herself up to the pleasure of being
in his arms, of once again feeling the magic of his lips.
He was gentleness and passion, vulnerability and
strength, and, in that moment, she knew that she cared
for him still.

When she heard someone approaching she reluctantly
eased herself from his arms. Charles St Claire, another
of Charette's officers, joined them, his expression sober.

'I'm sorry about young Martin,' he said to Raoul. 'I
know you were friends. The General believes we were
betrayed. At first he thought the Republicans had been
alerted by a reconnaissance mission of Joly's. Now even
he agrees we have a traitor in our midst. But we shall
find him, Duchambray, never fear. He shall pay for the
lives he has sacrified.'

'No,' Hortense breathed as St Claire walked away.
Her stomach contracted in disappointment and she
glared at Raoul accusingly. 'How could you? Dear God,
what kind of man are you? Have you no feeling or
conscience? I should have denounced you!'

Raoul paled beneath his tan and his expression froze.
'It was not I,' he rasped, anger and hurt boiling up inside
him. He saw no softening of her expression, no inkling

of belief. 'Oh, hell! I don't don't even why I'm bothering to deny it. I'm sick of trying to convince you, of trying to live up to your impossible ideal. It might have taken a long time for it to sink in but I have finally realised just how little you really cared for me. When you tried to shoot me you made it plain how you felt but I, poor fool, refused to accept it. Denounce me and be damned! You've sacrificed everything else for your infernal cause.'

Turning on his heel, he stormed off through the trees, leaving Hortense to stare in anguish after him. His bitterness and anger had taken her by surprise and engendered a small measure of doubt. She didn't know what to believe and she was too tired to reason things out. Almost in a daze, she sought her blankets and, in spite of her misery and uncertainty, fell almost instantly asleep.

When she awoke the following morning Raoul had gone from the camp, leaving without any goodbye or explanation. By then the whole army knew of their betrayal at Challans, and Hortense was not the only one to connect the two events. She could only see Raoul's disappearance as an admission of guilt, and she felt so sick at heart that she wanted to die.

Charette was furious to find that one of his most trusted officers had decamped in the night. It could be considered desertion, he told Hortense, and when and if Raoul returned then he would think about having him shot. He felt sure she must know something of her husband's plans and she spent a gruelling half an hour trying to convince him otherwise. Even then she could not bring herself to denounce Raoul. He was no longer a danger to them, she reasoned, and there was no reason why she should sacrifice her own position. She wouldn't admit even to herself that she had retained a small measure of faith in him. He was her enemy. He had used her and she would never forgive him for it.

Henri too was seething. To begin with he steadfastly defended his friend, making Hortense long to blurt out what she knew, but then he too gave way to anger.

'He had better have a damned good reason for putting you through this,' he finally told her, 'or when I see him again I shall shoot him down like a dog!'

Raoul stared at the blackened shell of Ramboulard standing out against the rosy evening sky. The building remained imposing in spite of its ruin. It was as if its very stones had absorbed something of the pride and defiance of the countless Duchambrays who had inhabited it. Pausing just inside the wide gateway, he forced down the grief and nostalgia that threatened to engulf him, knowing it would only weaken him and cloud his judgement. He knew he needed to think clearly, something he had not been capable of for the last few days.

Someone, probably the potential assassin, had betrayed the Vendeans. Young Jacques and many others had died because of it, and Raoul had been faced with the unpleasant reality that the next time it could be Henri or Hortense. Guarding the General was no longer good enough, he'd realised. If he wanted to protect those he cared about he had to make a positive move against the spy. It was then that he'd thought of Michel Saurin. If the young lawyer had been his contact then might he not be in touch with this other man also?

Raoul had left the Vendean camp rather on impulse, knowing he would be doing so under a cloud but unable to think of any way he could explain his actions to his General without incriminating himself. His search for Michel had taken him to St Fulgent, to the home of the older Saurin, where he had ostensibly enquired about the running of the Duchambray estate.

The old lawyer had been delighted to see him and had surprised him by declaring that he was now the rightful owner. True, the house was gone, but he could still expect a healthy income from the renting of the land. Raoul had been too tired and preoccupied to discuss business but had feigned an interest and signed some papers, placing the running of the estate in the lawyer's capable hands. Then he had casually enquired after Michel. He had been surprised when Saurin had paled and turned away.

'We have quarrelled,' was all the old man would say. 'I have no idea where my son is now.'

Refusing the offer of a place to rest, Raoul had taken his leave, knowing there was no way he could accept the older Saurin's hospitality and then feel free to do what he must, namely find Michel and, if necessary, beat the required information from him. He had been on the point of leaving, Saurin's servant having shown him to the door, when the fellow urgently whispered the surprising information that Michel was camping out at Ramboulard.

After thanking him Raoul had made his way to the only inn in town, where he had rented a room for what remained of the day. He'd been too tired to think straight and, knowing he would need all his wits about him when he finally confronted his quarry, had allowed himself the afternoon to sleep. Now, with darkness fast approaching, he was still not entirely sure how to handle the Republican.

Dismounting, he led his horse off the now weed-strewn driveway and into the surrounding trees. He knew the grounds like the back of his hand and unwanted memories came back to taunt him as he wound his way towards the back of the stables. After tethering his horse to a convenient oak tree he checked his pistol, making sure that it was loaded and primed. Then, tucking it into his belt, he let himself through a postern gate and into the stable-yard.

The stable buildings stood in two blocks on either side of him, with the main entrance to the yard directly opposite him. Taking a step to the side, he paused with his back against the wall, unsure which building to investigate first. It was getting dark now and there was no movement or noise to guide him, only stillness and shadows and the continuous song of the crickets. It was funny, but he could never remember their being so loud.

Making up his mind, he moved quietly across the cobbles towards the building on his right. There was a doorway at each end of it, both standing open, and he entered the one nearest him. Inside it was even darker, and although the place had been empty for several months it still smelled of horses and leather. Drawing his pistol from his belt, he walked slowly up the corridor in front of the stalls, straining his eyes and peering carefully into each one. It was not until he reached the final stall opposite the second doorway that he saw any sign of occupancy. Here fresh straw had been thickly piled against one wall. Blankets were folded in one corner and two blackened cooking pots lay beside the ashes of a fire.

Retracing his steps, Raoul avoided the penultimate stall where, fresh horse-droppings suggested, Saurin kept his horse, and settled down to wait in the one next to it. It must have been nearly an hour and it was really dark by the time he heard a horse enter the stable-yard. After pausing to light the lantern Saurin led his horse inside and unsaddled it. Raoul waited until he had returned to his camping place before moving forward to make his presence known.

The Republican was kneeling down with his back to him, piling up twigs and straw to make a new fire. Raoul halted just outside the circle of lantern light.

'Good evening, Michel,' he said softly, looking meaningfully at the two plump pheasants lying on the cobbled floor. 'You seem to be making yourself quite at home on my land.'

'Duchambray!' The Republican tensed, then slowly stood up and turned to face him. 'I had hoped you were dead.'

'As you can see, I am very much alive,' Raoul replied, feeling his way. 'I'm surprised our compatriot didn't tell you that. I've been ingratiating myself with General Charette.'

'That's a lie!' Saurin grated, his lips curling contemptuously. 'M. . .my other informant has kept me in touch with your activities. You aren't just playing a part, you aristo bastard, you've changed sides!'

Raoul shrugged and smiled coldly as he drew the pistol from his belt. 'I need to know the name of this other informant, Michel.'

'You can't seriously expect me to tell you,' Saurin challenged. 'I'd die first!'

'Oh, no,' Raoul told him, transferring the pistol to his left hand and drawing his sword. 'You won't die, not until you have given me the information I require. I shall shoot you in the leg and then slowly carve you up. After a while you'll be only too eager to tell me.'

Beneath his sallow complexion the Republican paled. His angry bravado seemed suddenly to desert him, and his shoulders slumped in defeat.

'If I do tell you you'll kill me anyway,' he finally replied.

Raoul didn't doubt that he could force the information from him but, in truth, that was not his style. 'I'll give you my word, Michel. Let me have the name and you shall live. . . Only decide quickly; in half a minute I'm going to put a pistol ball in your knee.'

For a moment Saurin hesitated. 'Morez,' he finally answered, his eyes blazing with hatred. 'Mathurin Morez.'

Raoul swore softly in surprise. He didn't like the young Breton and hadn't thought him brave enough to take such a risk. 'Tell me, is he prepared to play the assassin as well as the spy?'

'We are not all as lily-livered as you!' Saurin's lips curled contemptuously. 'When the time is right he will do what Paris has paid him for. He has never been on a mission where he did not succeed and is more than a match for a degenerate like you, whose mother was nothing but a high-class whore!'

'Shut up, damn you, if you expect me to keep my word!' Raoul grated, only just managing to hang on to his temper. 'I haven't yet forgotten that you were responsible for my cousin's death. Now get yourself over here and put the bridle back on your horse. When I leave here I shall be taking him with me. It shouldn't take you more than a couple of hours to walk into St Fulgent.'

Glowering resentfully, the Republican moved around Raoul and over to his horse. Raoul was still watching him, but in the darkness away from the lantern light failed to notice the way his hand crept beneath his coat. Saurin felt the reassuring hardness of the knife he wore strapped beneath his arm, and he smiled. Monsieur Duchambray was in for an unpleasant shock. He was only sorry he wasn't going to be able to taunt him with his approaching demise. Bending down as if to pick up the discarded tackle, he withdrew the knife and, turning, in one swift practised motion sent it arrowing towards the man he hated more than any other. Alerted at the last moment, Raoul managed to dodge aside, gasping in relief as the blade buried itself in the wooden post only inches from his arm. Acting purely on instinct, he fired. The pistol ball took Saurin in the shoulder and he tumbled sideways, right under the plunging feet of the terrified horse.

Immediately Raoul rushed forward, but it was a moment before he could calm the animal. Finally, having guided it into the stable-yard, he fetched the lantern and checked on the fallen man. He was dead, his face bloodied beyond recognition. It was just as well, Raoul thought dispassionately. The fellow would have made an implacable enemy and he would always have had to watch his back.

Fighting down his revulsion, he dragged the Republican's body out into the thickest part of the woods and left it there; then drove the horse out on to the overgrown lawns to graze. After placing his own mount in the stall he made shameless use of Saurin's blankets, and proposed dinner and fire, exhibiting a pragmatism and lack of emotion that even his father would have admired.

# CHAPTER THIRTEEN

THE morning after Raoul's disappearance the Vendean army moved on to the town of Belleville, where Charette intended to set up camp for the rest of the summer. The majority of the soldiers set up shelters and tents in the surrounding fields, but most officers found billets in the town itself. Hortense and Henri were taken in by a pleasant widow woman, Madame Loyland, whose cottage was only a few doors away from the larger house where the General himself was staying.

Hortense found it impossible to respond to the optimism and good spirits of those around her. She felt betrayed and desperately lonely, unable to confide even in Henri. Raoul was not worth it, she told herself. She tried to hate him, reminding herself over and over of how he had betrayed and used her.

Another unpleasant result of Raoul's disappearance was that Charette had given his command to the Breton, Morez. Of necessity Hortense was often in his company, and he made her skin crawl. When Henri was around he was courteous, but on other occasions treated her quite rudely, making several nasty comments about Raoul. On the evening after their arrival in the town she had walked out to the well to fetch some water and found him waiting for her. He had grabbed her and tried to kiss her and a fierce struggle had ensued, only ending when she had managed to catch him a hefty whack with the bucket she was carrying. The matter would not have ended there had not Madame Loyland's ten-year-old son Christian appeared. Morez had left then, but his eyes had promised retribution.

Hortense felt uneasy and more than a little frightened. She could have told Henri, she supposed, but she did not want her cousin fighting her battles and, besides, Morez had quite a reputation with a sword.

On their third evening at Belleville, at Madame Loyland's request, she went into the nearby woods with Christian to gather some wild strawberries. She and the child had become good friends, and as they walked between the trees he chattered easily to her, only pasuing now and then to sample the small, succulent fruit they were picking. He was a charming child with thick dark hair and an endearing smile, and yet there was a seriousness about him that went far beyond his years. He was the head of his family now, he told her somewhat pompously, since his father had died in the fighting at Cholet.

As a result of the child's continuous eating, their basket seemed to take an eternity to fill, and after about an hour they stopped to rest on a fallen tree trunk. It was a beautiful evening, sweet-smelling and cool, rejuvenating after the intense heat of the day.

When the boy reached for another strawberry Hortense laughed and playfully smacked his hand.

'You don't laugh often enough,' he told her with a perspicacity beyond his years.

'That is because she is still pining for her unworthy husband,' said a cold voice from behind them.

Hortense turned to glare at Mathurin Morez. She was surprised by his appearance, but she had no intention of letting him intimidate her. 'I have no intention of discussing my husband with you! Come, Christian, let us finish collecting the fruit and return to your mother. She will be wondering what is keeping us.'

'The boy's mother wants him. She sent me to find him.' Morez smiled nastily. 'I will help you collect the rest of the fruit.'

'Then Christian and I will both go back,' Hortense replied, climbing to her feet.

She would have moved away but Morez caught hold of her arm. He was still smiling, but his fingers bit cruelly into her flesh.

'Go on, boy,' he snapped. 'You can tell your mother we won't be long.'

Christian hesitated, but when Hortense, not wanting to involve him in an unpleasant scene, nodded her agreement he went racing away.

Jerking her arm free, she turned to confront Morez. 'I don't particularly want your company, but if you are determined to force it on me then you can make yourself useful,' and, thrusting the basket into his arms, she moved off through the trees, not pausing to see if he followed.

Frowning, Morez walked at her shoulder. 'I need to know about your husband,' he said.

'If you are asking why he left then I don't know,' she snapped, her stomach churning. 'I told the General as much.'

'But you must know where he has gone.'

'No,' she replied uneasily, 'I don't. I don't know anything about it. In fact, I've come to realise that really I knew very little about him.'

'Not even the fact that he was a Republican!'

The girl suddenly found it difficult to breathe. How on earth had this unpleasant man come to know that? Steadying herself, she forced a laugh. 'Now you're being fanciful. If you must know I think he'd had enough of war. . .and of me.'

He sniffed derisively. ''The man's besotted with you. I've seen the way he looks at you. He's in love with you and I'm sure he must have told you where he was going. I need to know, *madame*, and one way or another I intend to find out!'

There was no mistaking the menace in his words, and Hortense felt her stomach tighten in fear. She took a nervous step away from him. 'I've told you, I know nothing! I realise there are those who think he betrayed us but——'

'He didn't betray you,' he replied coldly. 'I know that for a fact. He hasn't been in contact with the Republicans for some time.'

'But how. . .?' No sooner had she said the words than she knew. It was so terrifyingly obvious. Fear vied with remorse and an overwhelming relief. Raoul had not betrayed them, had not returned to the Republican cause.

'I need to know what he is up to, Hortense.' Her companion's eyes were boring into her, dark and hard like a snake's, and a nasty smile twisted his lips. 'If you know what's good for you you'll tell me exactly where he has gone.'

With her heart pounding she turned to run from him, but he caught her up in a matter of strides, tackling her and sending her crashing to the ground. In spite of her struggles, he turned her over and, imprisoning her wrists in one hand, cruelly grasped her chin, forcing her to look at him.

'Where has he gone?' he demanded. 'Tell me, you bitch!'

'I don't know,' she grated, and he slapped her hard.

'There'll be more of that if you don't answer me!'

'Why?' she demanded defiantly, although she was trembling with fear. 'I know what you are now. You'll have to kill me anyway!'

'Not necessarily. My business is complete here and I shall be leaving camp. . . In fact, your husband is no great danger to me. It's just that I hate leaving loose ends.'

'He left because I threatened to expose him,' she

gasped, still struggling. 'I don't. . .know. . .where. . .
he went!'

'Liar!' He slapped her again for good measure. 'You
knew he'd changed sides. What is he up to?'

Hortense had never felt as frightened or helpless in
her life. She didn't doubt that he intended to try and
beat the information from her, and she didn't even have
the means to make him stop. Hopelessness welled up
inside her and she could almost taste her fear. She tensed
herself to receive another blow, but it never came.

Instead an ice-cold voice demanded, 'Ask me, Morez.
Your quarrel is really with me, and I am more than
willing to tell you where I've been.'

She did not ask herself what her husband was doing
there as she experienced a feeling of relief so vast that it
made her light-headed. Morez rolled off her, and she sat
up shakily to view the two men as they angrily faced
each other. Raoul had drawn his sword and his
expression was livid.

'I've been to see Saurin,' he continued icily. 'I wanted
to know your identity. I found I couldn't stomach having
my friends betrayed, not when there was something I
could do about it.'

The girl's heart lifted at his words and she berated
herself for her lack of trust and the terrible things she
had said to him. Dear God, would he ever be able to
forgive her?

'Traitor!' Morez spat. 'Degenerate traitor!'

Raoul glanced at the girl and a for a moment his
expression gentled. 'Go back to the cottage, Hortense.
Madame Loyland is waiting for you. I will settle things
here.'

Getting shakily to her feet, she moved to the edge of
the clearing, and almost at once the men seemed to
forget her.

Morez laughed harshly. 'So you came back to

denounce me, turncoat dog. I had not thought you man enough!'

'Shut up!' Raoul hissed. 'Draw your sword and we'll see just how good you are.'

'No,' Hortense choked, 'don't give him a chance.' But she was already too late. Raoul stepped back, and with a satisfied smile Morez unsheathed his weapon.

For a moment the two men circled each other like sparring gods, then Morez leapt into the attack. The two swords closed like scissors, crossing with a clang, then broke apart as they began fighting in earnest. They attacked and parried, moving rapidly backwards and forwards across the grass, their blades crossing, rasping and parting once more. Morez was good, very good, but Raoul was stronger and, if anything, faster. Half a dozen times he saved himself by sheer dazzling speed, his sword proving a bright, impenetrable wall.

Hortense watched the dazzling display of swordsmanship with her heart in her mouth. If Raoul fell then she knew that she would likely die, but she could not drag herself away. She hadn't realised that her husband was that good; certainly he had never boasted of his prowess, but he was an equal match for Morez. Both men were breathing heavily now and they were both beginning to slow. Raoul had been tired and travel-weary before they had even begun, she realised, and her concern for him increased.

When he caught sight of Hortense out of the corner of his eye Raoul swore beneath his breath. Why could she never do as he asked? Conscious that her life too hung in the balance, he increased his effort, and in doing so made a mistake. With breathtaking rapidity Morez executed a sophisticated attack, Raoul countered impatiently, and in an instant the Republican was through his guard. With a last-minute twist of his wrist Raoul managed to deflect the blade, and instead of entering his chest it sliced across his left arm, ripping his sleeve but not touching his skin. Hortsense bit back a scream. Morez laughed, thinking he would now have the advantage, but the narrow escape only served to heighten Raoul's determination.

Pressing forward, he watched with steady blue eyes for the slightest opportunity. Less than a minute later the moment came. His opponent made the smallest of miscalculations, off by no more than an inch, and Raoul slipped his blade through and into the Republican's chest. Morez fell to his knees, then, as he toppled sideways, made one last desperate slash.

'Royalist bastard!' he hissed between teeth clenched in pain. 'May you rot in hell!' He laughed horribly, a rasping, gurgling sound. 'But you are too late to save your General. . . Once he tastes his wine he'll be . . .finished. . .'

Moving foward, Hortsense slipped an arm around her husband's waist. His face was chalk-white, and she could feel him trembling. When she glanced down at Morez she saw that he was dead.

'It's a good thing I returned when I did,' Raoul gasped between laboured breaths, grateful for his wife's support. The fight, combined with hard riding, had exhausted him, and only in the back of his mind did he register the fact that she seemed to care.

For a moment Hortense clung to him. Her feelings were in turmoil. She still loved him. The fact had been brought sharply home to her as she had watched him fighting for his life. If he had died then she knew she would not have wanted to survive. She loved him, and yet she was realistic enough to know that the hurt they had caused each other would not quickly heal, perhaps never. She wanted to apologise for doubting him but her pride held her back and, besides, now was definitely not the time.

'He said something about the General; something about wine. . .' Raoul forced his tired brain to function. 'My God, he's poisoned the General's wine!'

Turning, he grasped Hortense by the shoulders, his eyes burning with urgency in his pale face. 'Charette will be dining any time now. You must take me to him. There is no time to lose!'

He didn't need to explain matters further, and they returned to the town as quickly as they could. They both felt the same sense of urgency as they skirted the tents and camp-fires, moving at a brisk walk. Many of the Vendeans glanced at them curiously but, in spite of Charette's declared intention to arrest Raoul, no one tried to detain them. When Hortense began to lag behind Raoul held out his hand and, without thinking, she grasped it.

Entering the town itself, they appraoched the large two-storey house where the General was staying. They hurried up the short garden path and, finding the door open, entered without ceremony. They found themselves in a large hallway with two short corridors leading off it, one towards the rear of the house and the other to their right. At the end of the latter a door stood open, and they could hear the sound of laughter and jovial conversation.

As they moved towards the sound another door opened and a young officer stepped out into the hallway. Fortunately he did not seem to recognise Raoul.

'Whatever your business, it will have to wait,' he told them with a frown. 'The General is about to dine.'

'It's imperative we see him now,' Raoul insisted, preparing to move around him.

'Duchambray!' Major Sabatini, an arrogant grey-haired officer, also entered the hallway. 'I must say you have a cheek, coming back here.' He glanced at his young companion. 'Place him under arrest, Babette. The General will deal with him later!'

'For God's sake!' Raoul exclaimed. 'Just let me have a quick word him, then, if you still want to arrest me, you can.'

He moved towards the open door but was halted by the tip of Babette's sword pressing against his chest. Impatiently he knocked the blade aside, intending to step around the young officer. Reluctant to use the weapon, Babette tossed it down and instead tackled Raoul, sending him crashing against the wall. Hortense stifled a scream, seeing her husband wince as he slammed against the plaster. For a moment the two men struggled, before the brutal use of Raoul's knee caused his opponent to double over and crumple to the floor.

Ignoring Sabatini, Raoul hurtled into the dining-room. A handful of Vendean officers and two ladies were sitting around a long rectangular table set ready for a meal. Two roasted ducks and a plate of vegetables steamed in its centre. Charette's host was holding a carafe of wine. He had been about to pour it when the commotion in the hallway had distracted him.

'What the deveil?' exclaimed Charette, rising to his feet. 'Duchambray, what is the meaning of this?'

'The wine, my General,' Raoul panted. 'I have reason to believe it has been poisoned.'

'Poisoned!' The word echoed around the table. Then someone laughed uneasily in disbelief.

'I'm sorry, my General, I tried to stop him,' Sabatini mutterd, catching hold of Raoul by the arm. 'Do you wish me to arrest him?'

Charette made an irritable dismissive gesture and moved around the table towards Raoul. For a moment he studied him, noting the dirt and tiredness, the determination on his pale face.

'You had better have a good reason for your disappearance,' he told him not unkindly, then, turning back to
his dinner, companions, ordered them to dispose of the
wine.

No sooner had he said the words than a door at the
other end of the room, presumably leading from the
kitchens, opened and a harassed-looking woman entered.
She glanced at the still full carafe and visibly relaxed.

'Thank God!' she exclaimed. 'You have not touched
it. My son had but a taste and has been abominably sick.
I am very much afraid that the whole cask has been
contaminated!'

The diners appeared stunned.

'It seems that you have saved my life for a second
time.' The General glanced at Raoul and smiled wryly.
'Come, we had better talk.'

Leaving his meal, he led Raoul into the hallway, where
he acknowledged Hortense with a brief nod. 'I don't
know what your husband has been up to, but I am about
to find out. . . Don't look so worried. I have no intention
of having him shot.'

She could only watch as he ushered Raoul into another
room.

When Sabatini made to follow he motioned him away.
'No, I don't need you. Go and take my place at the table.
I will eat later.'

When the door closed behind them she turned to smile
apologetically at Babette, who was standing shakily
against the wall, and walked outside to wait. Sitting
down on a stone bench, she struggled to control her
anxiety. She had no idea how much Raoul would tell
Charette, and in spite of the General's reassuring words
she was worried for him. She looked up at the darkening
sky, but the beauty of the sunset was completely lost on
her. She could only remember how afraid she had been

during his fight with Morez. She hadn't stopped loving him, she realised, even when she had thought the worst. Now, having found out that he had remained entirely faithful to Charette, she did not feel the jubilation she would have expected. Instead she felt empty and more than a little afraid, afraid that for them it was already too late, that her suspicion and mistrust, no matter how understandable, had damaged their marriage beyond repair.

When Raoul came out of the house almost half an hour later it was all she could do not to throw herself into his arms. Instead she approached him cautiously, wondering what had occurred. The fading purple light picked out the deep shadows on his face and she wondered with compassion when he had last slept.

'How much did you tell him?' she asked tentatively.

He did not meet her eyes and, glancing across the street, smiled sadly to himself. 'I am tired of subterfuge, Hortense. I told him it all.'

'Yet he did not arrest you.'

He shrugged. 'He has promised to spare my life. He wants to see me again tomorrow. I had to give my word not to leave camp.'

'And me?' she asked quietly. 'Was he angry with me?'

'He does not realise how much you knew.' He glanced contemptuously at her. 'Don't worry, Hortense. Your own position is in no danger.'

'That does not concern me,' she replied, swallowing a spurt of anger. 'How could you think that?'

'To be quite honest, at the moment I'm too tired to think at all.'

His exhaustion was all too apparent, and Hortense had to fight a desire to hold him close. She ached to brush the lines of fatigue from his face, to whisper words of love and comfort, and yet she knew she had forfeited the right.

'Come,' she told him, taking his arm, 'I'll show you where you can sleep.'

She took him to Madame Loyland's and led him up to her room. The house only had three bedrooms. With *madame* and Christian using one and Henri the other, there was nowhere else for him to go, and in his present state he was in no condition to look for other lodgings. Leaving him to undress, she went to fetch him a drink and some water to wash. When she returned she found him sprawled sideways across the bed, his legs dangling over the edge. He had divested himself of his coat, and his boots lay at his feet as if he had only just managed to remove them before tiredness had overtaken him.

She was almost overwhelmed by a feeling of tenderness and, setting the ewer of water down, struggled to right him on the bed. He was a dead weight, not helping her at all, and even when she wiped some of the grime from his hands and face he did not stir. There was nothing more she could do for him. All he needed was sleep, but she found she did not want to leave him and had to force herself to go back downstairs to wait for her cousin. It was past the time, she realised, for her to confide in him.

As she had expected, he was angry and more than a little hurt by her secrecy. At first he threatened to call Raoul out, taking his duplicity as a personal affront, but, on hearing what his friend had done to save the General's life, he began to calm down.

She slept that night, fully clothed, on the same bed as Raoul. She tried to tell herself that it was because there was no alternative, yet knew it was because she wanted him near. When he awoke in the early hours, sweating and breathing heavily from an unpleasant dream, she longed to comfort him. In the grey light that filtered through the half-closed shutters she saw his face creased with a pain that was more than physical.

'Raoul?' she questioned. 'Are you all right?'

'Yes,' he replied sharply, feeling foolish and disorientated, again experiencing the soul-wrenching guilt that always accompanied a dream about the fire. In the daylight he was now able to come to terms with the emotion, could even reason it away, but at times like this it still came back to torment him.

'Would you like a drink?' she asked, ignoring his obvious irritation. 'I have some water.'

'No,' he snapped, hating the sympathy he saw in her face. His throat felt like dust but he didn't want her waiting on him. He loathed being at a disadvantage with her.

She was leaning across him in concern, her breasts within inches of his face, and suddenly his anger was tempered by an altogether different emotion.

'Raoul, don't, she protested as, curling his hand behind her neck, he drew her towards him. 'We should talk. . .'

'No,' he growled with a hint of desperation. 'This is the only thing that is right between us. Don't think, Hortense, feel, only feel. . .'

She had been lying beside him for hours, aching for him, wanting him, and pushing him away was more than she was capable of. Her doubts fled as his mouth found hers. Her fingers curled in the still damp hair at his nape, urging him even closer. The world fell away from her as warmth flooded both her body and her mind.

He murmured words of endearment, words of encouragement and praise, and yet those she so desperately wanted to hear remained unsaid. Then he was one with her and it was everything she remembered and so much more. Their union was more violent, more stirring because of the pain they had both suffered, and more desperate because they both knew it would solve nothing.

As soon as their passion was spent Raoul rolled away

from her and fell amost instantly asleep, a deep sleep
that was, for a while at least, no longer haunted by
shadows of loneliness. Would he even remember their
lovemaking when he woke up? Hortense wondered
sadly. Would it mean anything to him other than a
physical release?

She watched him quietly as the dawn light brightened
and mellowed, bringing his beloved face into a clearer
perspective. Unable to help herself, she carefully, deli-
cately, traced along the line of his jaw with her fingertip.
It was a strong face, she thought, often softened by the
humour and sensitivity that would come into his eyes.
He was still sleeping deeply, and as her fond gaze rested
upon him she had to fight the impatience that wanted
him to wake. She was anxious to find out how matters
stood between them, almost desperate to apologise and
try to make things right. More than anything she wanted
to be able to tell him that she loved him, to say those
simple, exquisite words, but she knew that he needed
his sleep.

Finally, hearing sounds from below, she crept from
the bed and quietly dressed. By the time she entered the
cosy kitchen Madame Loyland had already gone out,
and Henri was sitting at the scrubbed table drinking
coffee. Raoul's saddle-bags lay beside him and, after
asking her permission, young Christian carried them up
to her room.

'Has Raoul said much?' Henri asked once they were
alone.

Hortense shook her head and forced a smile. 'He was
asleep when I went back to the room. He still is. I don't
think even a troop of horses would waken him.'

Henri looked at her almost pityingly. 'Hortense, I
think you should face the fact that the General will likely
send him away. You will need to decide whether you are

willing to go with him, whether you're willing to share his lack of allegiance and friends.'

'I'm sure it won't come to that,' she almost snapped. 'You're forgetting that he saved the General's life.'

'And you are forgetting that he was a Republican, that he probably still holds some Republican views.'

Hortense dismissed his fears as she poured herself some coffee, but his words were to come back to haunt her later in the day. The General himself arrived at the house just before noon, explaining that, as he had little else to do, he had come to talk to Raoul. Hortense was not fooled, realising that by conducting the interview away from his headquarters he was seeking to keep matters informal. Madame Loyland, flattered by his visit, showed him into her parlour and plied him with pastries and coffee, and while he chatted to Henri Hortense went upstairs to wake Raoul.

She found him already dressed and in the act of shaving. He apologised sheepishly for oversleeping, but she hastily brushed it aside.

'You were exhausted,' she told him, smiling as she caught his eye in the mirror. 'I must say, you're looking much better now.'

He dried his face and, turning, regarded her seriously. 'You've taken good care of me. . .better than I deserved.'

'You deserved taking care of.' Taking the plunge, she added, 'Raoul, I'm sorry for being such a bitch. I should have trusted you more.'

He frowned and a shadow once more darkened his eyes, turning them a deep midnight-blue. 'No. . . I can understand why you didn't. I had no right to expect your complete trust after what I had done.'

She smiled awkwardly, wanting to tell him that he would have it in the future, yet knowing it would be a lie. 'I've come to fetch you. The General is downstairs.'

He nodded and tossed the towel he had been using down on the bed, unconsciously squaring his shoulders as he did so. 'Then we had better see what he has decided.'

'Ah, there you are, Duchambray!' Charette greeted him cheerfully, seeming not the least put out by the delay.

'I'm sorry I was not up to greet you,' Raoul apologised. 'I can't remember ever having slept for so long.'

'It doesn't matter.' Charette glanced at Henri sitting across from him. 'Claviere has been keeping me entertained.'

'We'll leave you now,' Henri said, rising to his feet and glancing meaningfully at Hortense. 'You will wish to speak with Raoul alone.'

'Sit down, Henri,' Raoul told him, then, turning to Charette, added, 'I now have no secrets from these two, General. You may speak freely in front of them.'

'Then I trust they can keep their counsel,' Charette replied seriously. 'Should the facts become widely known there are those of my officers who would demand your life. Myself, I have ever been a pragmatist and believe you might still be able to serve me. I am also conscious that I owe you my life.' He smiled. 'Not once, Raoul, but twice! I believe you when you say you have served me faithfully. Unfortunately I cannot ignore what went on before and I can let no man serve me whose loyalty is suspect. However, I have decided to give you back your command, but on one condition. . . I am not at all sure that it is a condition you will be willing to fulfil. If you are prepared to take an oath to devote your sword and your life not only to the Vendean cause, but the restoration of our rightful King, then I shall be glad to have you with me.'

The girl's relief faded when she glanced at her husband's face. His expression had frozen and he was pale beneath his tan. Dear God, she thought, he's going to refuse it, and she felt an anger and disappointment so great that she wanted to scream.

Trust Charette, thought Raoul grimly, to get right to the heart of the matter. He just couldn't do it. He had been prepared to die for the Vendée, but never, never for an accursed Capet, never for a monarchy he had helped to overthrow. In his desire to help free the province he had lost sight of the fact that they were also fighting towards that end.

'I can't,' he replied tightly. 'I would give my life for Vendean autonomy, but not for that.' He glanced at the girl, silently pleading for her understanding. 'Not even for you, Hortense, can I swear to such a thing. It is against everything I believe in. I'm sorry.'

Henri groaned and swore softly beneath his breath, although he was not at all surprised, either by the General's request or Raoul's answer.

Charette smiled sadly in resignation. 'I am sorry too, my friend, although I had anticipated your answer. Before I let you leave here, however, I require a different promise. You must swear that you will not return to the Republican cause.'

He did not say what would happen should Raoul refuse, but they were all aware of it.

'That I can promise you,' Raoul returned with a sigh.

'Then I shall expect you gone before dark.' Charette stood up to take his leave, pausing a moment to glance questioningly at Hortense.

'No, General, I shall not be leaving with him,' she supplied in a voice so strained that it did not sound like her own. 'He has chosen to stand by his principles, and I shall stand by mine.' She glanced across the General's shoulder at her husband, her eyes bright with accusation and anger. In spite of everything, he was still a Republican, still her enemy.

# CHAPTER FOURTEEN

WHEN Raoul left camp in the late afternoon it was Henri who saw him off. Hortense had kept out of his way and given him no chance to explain, not that there was any real explanation he could give her. If she had only known how tempted he had been to take the wretched oath, to compromise his principles solely for her. But he had made enough compromises, too many perhaps, and she remained just as implacable. She had refused to understand his position, and hadn't even thought enough of him to come and say goodbye.

'Where will you go?' Henri asked, uncomfortably aware of his friend's pain and isolation.

Raoul looked away. 'At first to Ramboulard. There is at least something constructive I can do there. Later, who knows?'

For a moment he hesitated, wanting to offer Henri some sort of apology; then, thinking he would only make matters worse, he swung up into the saddle. He glanced once more towards the cottage, searching for Hortense, and his mouth tightened in a grim line.

Hortense watched him ride away from behind the half-closed shutters of her room. He looked so desolate, so alone, that it was all she could do not to run after him. He had made his choice, she reminded herself. He had refused to do the one thing that would have allowed him to remain with Charette, the one thing that would have allowed him to remain with her. In rejecting the oath she couldn't help feeling that he had also rejected her.

The next few weeks passed slowly in a blur of misery. Vendean morale was high but it made little difference to

Hortense. She felt exhausted both mentally and physically and found that she ached to be with Raoul. More than once she regretted not leaving with him but, remembering how she had chased him and given herself to him, she was filled with insecurity and the heartbreaking belief that he did not love her enough. . . Besides, he was still a Republican, no matter how courageous and caring. He had put his political integrity before his marriage and, feeling as she did, she could only do likewise.

As the summer progressed the Vendean army began to relax. Gradually it became apparent that the Republicans had withdrawn from the centre of the region, although they continued to garrison troops on its periphery. Taking advantage of the lull in the fighting, many peasants returned home to work in the fields, mills and wineries.

Having already missed so much of the fighting, Henri elected to remain with Charette, although he did consider it safe enough to send for his wife and child. They arrived towards the end of August, and Hortense was amazed at the change in the baby. He was smiling and had filled out so that she no longer felt apprehensive about holding him. Suddenly she desperately wanted a child of her own, and against her will her mind conjured up an image with dark hair and brilliant blue eyes. Patriotism was a cold bedfellow, she realised, and pride could not make up for lack of children and a husband's love.

Summer gave way to autumn, and the peasants, their harvests completed, began to return to Charette. Quitting his base at Belleville, he led his army against a Republican camp near Nantes, and Henri, leaving Marie and Hortense with Madame Loyland, went with him. There followed three decisive victories in less than three weeks as Charette attacked and laid waste other Republican strongholds. When he returned to Belleville the General was jubilant. After one and a half years of war the Vendée was virtually free. No longer so naïve, Hortense wondered how hard they were going to have to fight to hold on to what they had won.

As winter approached the Republicans began to make some concessions. Vendean prisoners were released in Nantes, Saumur and Angers, and Carrier was publicly condemned for his barbarity. The pain Hortense felt at the breakdown of her marriage remained just as acute. She had heard nothing from Raoul, and yet she was unable to put him from her mind. In the loneliness of the night she longed for him and often wonderd what he was doing.

In the second week of December some friends of the General who owned a château not far from the town held a Christmas ball. The atmosphere was festive and spirits high as the Vendean nobility celebrated not only the season but the latest Republican concessions.

Hortense, who had been invited along with Marie and Henri, desperately determined to enjoy herself. There was little profit, she realised, in submerging herself in useless regret. For the occasion she had purchased a new gown of light green crêpe, and she knew she looked as well as any woman there, including the lovely Marie. Although aware of her marriage, the unattached officers swarmed around her like bees around a honey-pot, teasing her and flirting outrageously. She laughed and encouraged them, at the same time thinking that not one of them could measure up to Raoul. Try as she might, she could not forget the previous December, when they had been newly married and oh, so much in love. She felt miserable, and because of it tried even harder to enjoy herself. She seemed to sparkle beneath the grand chandeliers, and if her laugh held a hint of hysteria no one seemed to notice; they were all too intent on their own pleasure.

Halfway through the evening the General disappeared. He was gone for some time, although few noticed his absence. When he did return he made straight for Hortense. Instead of asking her to dance he told her that he wished to talk. Taking her arm, he led her from the brightly lit room and across the wide hallway, from whence rose an impressive flight of stairs.

'There is someone here who wishes to see you,' he said, pausing outside another door. 'Someone who, I believe, deserves your kindness. He came to me tonight, bringing the first overtures of peace, a peace he desires more desperately than most.'

Opening the door, he ushered her into the room, then quietly closed it behind her. She found herself in a well-stocked library, dimly lit by a single candle. A man was standing in the shadows near one of the bookshelves. Although she could not see his face, Hortense recognised the tall dark-coated figure immediately.

'Raoul?' The word caught in her throat.

'How are you, Hortense?' His throat was husky, a little uncertain, as he moved forward into the candle-light. 'I found I couldn't leave without seeing you.'

'I'm well.' Her eyes drank in the sight of him and she decided that her memory had not done him justice; he was still the most handsome man she knew. Oh, how she had missed him, longed for him, but concern welled up too. He looked tired, older somehow, and the candle-light picked out the deep shadows on his face. Deep creases bracketed his mouth, and the small scar on his cheek was a vivid stain against the chalk of his face. Hortense ached to hold him, to draw his head to her breast and stroke away the suffering her intolerance and the dreadful war had placed there.

'You're looking tired,' she murmured and was surprised how calm she sounded when, in reality, she was deeply shaken by the sight of him.

He shrugged dismissively. 'I've been doing a lot of riding.'

'Not one word, Raoul!' she blurted. 'In all these weeks I've heard nothing from you. I didn't even know if you were alive or dead!'

'I honestly didn't think you'd care,' he answered simply. 'You never even came to see me off.'

'I was angry and disappointed,' she replied, a catch in her voice. 'I behaved like a spoilt child.'

For a moment he was silent as he continued to study her intently. 'My father and I have been working for peace. . . We parted on bad terms, without even discussing our differences. Over the past weeks I haven't ceased to wonder. . . I came to see if you wanted a divorce but. . . I need to know, Hortense. Is the war all that stands between us, or is it something more?'

Hortense forced herself to look at him and saw the same pain she was feeling reflected in his face. She was surprised to find him still vulnerable to her, surprised and tender. She realised then that she loved him just as much as before, and wondered how she had ever thought she could manage without him. For the first time she began to see his failure to take the oath as something other than a lack of commitment to her. She had been self-centred, she realised, and too intolerant to see things from his point of view. She felt ashamed and unable to meet his penetrating gaze.

'No, I don't want a divorce,' she managed to say, feeling sick at the very thought of it.

'Look at me, Hortense,' he demanded softly, his confidence boosted by her apparent misery. 'Look at me and tell me to go away and I swear I won't bother you again.'

Tears filled her eyes and she covered her mouth to hold back a sob. His humility was almost more than she could bear.

'I still care for you,' she admitted huskily, knowing that she owed him the truth. 'I've tried not to, but I still do.'

For the first time in months she had opened herself to him. He saw honesty in her face and something more. Something that again allowed him to hope.

'If there is peace,' he asked quietly, 'will you come back to me? Will you try to make our marriage work?'

It was all Hortense could do not to go to him. He seemed so hesitant, so unsure. In fact his Duchambray arrogance seemed to have completely deserted him.

'Our marriage doesn't have to depend on peace,' she replied quietly. 'Do you remember what you suggested on Noirmoutier about leaving the country? I——'

'No.' His firm negative surprised her. 'I was wrong to ask it of you. You feel too strongly for your cause. You love the Vendée too much. I know now what it would cost you to leave.'

Moving forward, she looked up into his eyes, seeing the gentleness there, the understanding, and her heart expanded with love for him. He was a man, she realised, who would always be able to see the other side. It was a rare gift and she wondered why she had not appreciated it before. More than ever she wanted to run to him, to hold him and kiss him and tell him how much she cared, but there was a strange restraint between them, as if they were both afraid to strain the fragile bond they had just forged.

Slowly, almost as if he was afraid she would bolt from him, Raoul reached out to rub the back of his hand across her cheek. She wanted to hold it there, and felt bereft when he drew it away.

'I'm committed to working for peace,' he told her,

watching her face intently. 'Until a treaty is signed I will have no time for a wife. I can only beg you to bear with me. There is still a great deal to be sorted out by those more influential than I, but I too have a part to play. In fact, Charette has asked me to be on hand to advise his negotiators. He trusts me, Hortense, perhaps because I didn't take his wretched oath. I was hoping that you might bring yourself to trust me too.'

'I do trust you,' she replied, a catch in her voice. 'I trust you to be honest with me in the future, even if our views are not the same. I trust your integrity, your honour.'

Sighing, he stepped away, his expression once more sombre. She could sense the tension in him and she wondered what he was going to say.

'You know there can be no question of returning the King, don't you?' he informed her in a tight voice. She was such a fervent Royalist that he dreaded telling her, yet he knew it was essential that there be complete honesty between them now.

'Does the General know that?' she asked.

Raoul nodded, waiting for her condemnation. It never came.

'It doesn't matter.' Hortense was surprised to find that she meant it. Even a few weeks ago her answer would have been quite different. 'The Vendée needs peace.'

Raoul heaved a sigh of relief. He hadn't realised how tensely he had been waiting for her answer, not until she had given it. 'It will be a peace with honour. That I promise you. In all else I believe the Vendée will get what she wants.' He smiled a little wryly. 'I may be a Republican, Hortense, but I have discovered that I'm a Vendean first and foremost.'

Since the moment she had entered the room Hortense had been feeling the love and longing for him, so harshly repressed and denied these past months, growing inside her. She had not thought it possible to love him more, but she had been wrong. What she felt for him was a little frightening in its intensity.

The warmth and approval Raoul saw in her face made his heart race. It had been months since she had last looked at him like that, not since the flight from Noirmoutier. He longed to take her in his arms but didn't dare; once he felt her softness against him he didn't think he would ever be able to leave.

'I have to go,' he told her in a ragged voice. 'I know we still have a lot to say to each other, but my father and a commissioner are waiting for me not a mile down the road. . .' He moved towards the door, then paused and turned back. 'If I can come to you again I will.'

'We're going home for Noel,' she blurted, wondering if it would be better for her to stay at Belleville.

'Oh.' A look akin to disappointment crossed his face. 'I don't think Henri would——'

'He'd welcome you if I asked it. He likes you, Raoul, in spite of everything.'

'I'll come if I can,' he rasped.

Then he was gone, without any protestations of love or definite promises. Indeed, so brief had his visit been that Hortense could almost think him a phantom conjured up by her own desperate longing. She loved him, and yet somehow the words had remained unsaid, something she was to regret over the empty weeks to come. Nevertheless, when she returned to the ballroom her step was lighter. They had at least made a small move towards reconciliation, and again there was hope in her heart.

Two days later the Clavieres returned home. The warmth of the old château wrapped around them. Marie blossomed and Henri basked in his wife's unconditional love. That is how love should be, Hortense thought, and she realised how short she had fallen of that ideal.

Christmas Day came, bringing with it poignant memories, but no Raoul. It was nearly a week later that a travel-weary peasant delivered a letter apologising for his absence. It was a letter full of news and dutiful phrases, not at all like a lover would write, and once again she began to despair. Had she killed all the love he had felt for her? she wondered. Was he seeking a reconciliation from a sense of duty alone? It was a depressing thought. He wrote again in early February, to tell her that the peace negotiations were almost completed. Again the letter was factual rather than romantic, although he did admit that he would be glad when the treaty was signed and he was able to come to her. Then, on a chill and blustery night halfway through February, Thomas Beaulieu arrived.

The Clavieres were just thinking of retiring when the damp, travel-stained figure was shown into the drawing-room. Hortense was not at all sure how to greet the man. He was her enemy but he was also her father-in-law. Apart from that, she couldn't simply forget that she owed him her life. He was looking his age, she noted as she introduced him to her cousins, and had obviously been working as hard for the peace as Raoul.

Henri was wary of him and a little hostile, but good manners forced him to offer hospitality. Beaulieu had, after all, taken the trouble to bring Hortense a letter from Raoul. The Republican's smile was a little wry as he accepted Henri's offer of a bed for the night and apologised for the lateness of his arrival.

'I had to bring the letter tonight,' he explained, glancing at Hortense. 'Raoul did not expect it of me. In fact, I'm sure he didn't intend you to receive it until late tomorrow.' Pulling a thick packet from his coat, he handed it to her. 'If you read it you will see why I nearly killed my horse bringing it to you. The boy is a fool. I know you love him, and I think you deserve to be given a choice.'

Puzzled and a little apprehensive, Hortense split the seal and opened the sheets of parchment. Her eyes scanned the page and she forgot all about the others in the room as she read her husband's heartfelt words of love. It was not until she reached the bottom of the page that she realised they were also words of goodbye. Although the peace had been signed, he was being forced to flee France, and had no intention of taking her with him.

'I don't understand,' she muttered, glancing at Beaulieu.

His eyes were full of sympathy, and he smiled gently as he answered her. 'He's leaving because he has to, my dear; he is considered an enemy of the state.'

'Damn it,' snapped Henri. 'Are you telling me this peace doesn't grant a pardon to us all?'

'There is an amnesty for all Vendean rebels,' Beaulieu replied, 'or your General would not have agreed to it. However, my compatriots do not consider Raoul a rebel; to them he is a traitor. His forthrightness has made him some influential enemies, and now they demand his head.'

'Oh, my God!' gasped Hortense. 'That's so unfair. Is there nothing you can do?'

He shook his head sadly. 'I am not that important, my dear. All I could do was bring you the letter.'

Hortense closed her eyes to blot out her tears. Her throat ached and her breathing was distinctly unsteady. Her hope of happiness had been snatched away, and she was left with an emptiness that was more than she thought she could bear. Raoul hadn't asked her to go with him, and all his words of love and consolation were meaningless without that.

'He hasn't asked you to go because he doesn't think

you love him enough,' Beaulieu quietly explained. He was looking at her expectantly.

Did she have the courage, she asked herself, to hazard her heart and her pride? Could she bear to go to Raoul and then have him send her away? What if the loving words he had written were nothing more than a kindness, a balm for her hurt pride? Even as she asked herself these questions, she knew that she would go to him. She had no choice; he would be needing friendship and support, and she was the only one who could give it to him. He was everything to her, and she knew that she would have to take the chance or spend the rest of her life in regret, wondering what might have been.

'Where can I find him?' she asked Beaulieu. 'There must still be time or you would not have come so promptly.'

'He has gone to Ramboulard. I believe he had business to settle there, but he is leaving for La Rochelle early tomorrow. He intends to take ship for America later in the week.'

'I'll accompany you,' Henri told her. 'We'll leave in time to reach Ramboulard at first light.'

In the early hours of the morning, with her meagre supply of clothes packed in a portmanteau strapped across the withers of her horse, and the remainder of her father's jewels and the deeds to the Louisiana plantation in her saddle-bags, she and Henri set out for St Fulgent. As they rode up the wide weed-covered driveway leading to Ramboulard the sun was just rising, tinting the sky and the frost-covered grass with its rosy hue. The girl's heart was beating painfully, for she was terrified in case she had missed Raoul.

When they found his horse tethered in the stable-yard she heaved a sigh of relief.

Henri smiled understandingly. 'We are in time. . . I suppose I'd better leave you now.'

She looked at him to thank him and her eyes filled with tears. She was unlikely to see him again, she realised; at least, not for several years.

'America is not the end of the world,' he told her, although his own eyes were suspiciously bright. 'We can write.'

'What if he does not want me?' she asked in a small voice.

'Then come home. Marie and I will always be there for you. But he will want you, Hortense. He loves you, I know he does. All you have to do is convince him that you love him too. . .' He leaned across to kiss her cheek and wish her good luck.

Then he was gone, leaving her feeling very much alone. He had always been so close to her, the brother she had never had, but he was a part of her past. Raoul was her future, she realised; she had only to convince him of the fact.

Tethering her horse next to her husband's, she walked through the postern gate towards the ruined château. Frost crunched beneath her feet and it was as if she were the only living thing in a misty pink-tinged world. Pulling her cloak more tightly around herself, she shivered, sure she could feel the eyes of countless dead Duchambrays resting upon her. Even after all these months she could smell the soot and images of the great conflagration returning to her with an unwanted intensity.

She climbed the wide steps, then peered in through the open doorway, her eyes seeing nothing but rubble and rain-washed charcoal. The first floor had completely disappeared, and she was able to look up through twisted rafters and patches of blackened slate to the lightening sky above.

Realising that it would be dangerous to enter, she slowly made her way around the side of the building.

When she reached the rear terrace she finally discovered Raoul staring out across the overgrown lawns and the dead rose garden. He was wearing a greatcoat of dark grey that seemed to fit so entirely with his surroundings that at first she did not notice him. He was standing as still as a statute, and she knew instinctively that he was seeing the grounds as they had been before the fire. Her heart ached for him and for all he had lost.

Softly she called his name, hardly aware of doing so.

He turned towards her and, taken unawares, his face lit with pure joy. It was quickly masked, replaced by a look that was altogether inscrutable. For a moment she held back; he looked so distant, so unsure. The uncertainty filled her as well, and so she did not rush into his arms in the way she wanted to.

At last, still standing several steps away from her, he spoke, his voice betraying the emotion his face did not. 'What are you doing here, Hortense? I did not send for you. I had thought to spare us the pain of parting.'

'I thought to spare us too,' she answered, taking a step towards him. 'I want to come with you.'

'No!' His voice was harsh. His expression could have been carved in stone but it was an expression she had seen before, one he wore when he was at his most vulnerable. 'Circumstances have changed. . . I have nothing to offer you but uncertainty.'

'Since we first met things have been uncertain,' she told him. 'I can cope with that. . . I only need to know that you love me. You do love me, don't you, Raoul?'

He hesitated for a moment, then his chin dipped in a brief defeated nod. 'I have never stopped loving you. . . What I did for your cause, for peace, I did for you.

Her feet sped across the distance that separated them and she flung herself into his arms. Against his will he clung to her, squeezing so hard that he bruised her

tender skin. Hortense revelled in it; she was exactly
where she wanted to be.

'I still can't take you,' he said after a moment, holding
her away from him so that he could see her face. His
mouth was twisted in a melancholy smile and his eyes
looked suspiciously bright. 'I know how you love France.
I can't take you with me and have you hate me for it
later.'

'Oh, you fool,' she said softly. 'You dear, blind fool.
Yes, I love the Vendée, but I've found I love you so
much more. I'd go to the ends of the earth with you.'

When he did not immediately answer her she reached
up to cup his face in her hands. 'I love you, Raoul, more
than France, more than my life! You have to take me
with you. If you don't I'll only follow you.'

Still he seemed uncertain, and his blue eyes searched
her face. He must have been satisfied with what he saw
there, for he heaved a great sigh.

'Hortense, Hortense!' Dragging her to him, he rocked
her gently, chanting her name like a litany. 'Dear God,
you mean it! I didn't think you could ever love me that
much. I'll do my best to see that you don't regret it. . .
We won't be poor, I can promise you that. I still have
money from my grandmother, and I'm prepared to work
hard, but know this: if you come with me now then it is
for always, because I'll never have the strength to let you
go again.'

'For always,' she whispered, looking up into his face,
a face she knew she would love for all eternity.

He was her passion, her future, her reason for being,
and she vowed that she would spend the rest of her days
showing him just how much he meant to her. She had
found herself a new cause.

## EPILOGUE
### Louisiana 1805

THE lawns in front of the elegant white-painted mansion rolled down to the river, a tributary of the mighty Mississippi. At the edge of the water two boys, aged eight and ten, played, their fishing rods forgotten as they concentrated on building a castle in the soft mud.

Hortense walked across the green swathe towards them, her eyes filled with pride and love. They were so much like their father, although the younger, Julien, had inherited her grey eyes. They were filthy, she noted fondly, and would need a good scrub before dinner.

She had just collected her two grubby offspring and was walking back up to the house when Raoul came out to meet them. He was looking as tanned and fit as ever and seemed to exude happiness and well-being. His new life suited him. The plantation had prospered under his management in spite of the rather unconventional step he had taken in freeing his slaves.

He grinned and waved a piece of paper at Hortense. 'We have a letter from my father. In spite of the English blockade, some ships from France are still getting through.'

'What does he say?' she asked as they entered the house and a coloured nanny came forward to take charge of the boys.

'Henri and Marie are both well. He saw them at a reception for the Emperor in La Roche. Also the new house he is having built at Ramboulard is nearly completed.'

Hortense slipped her arm through his and studied his

251

face for some sign of resentment. After the conflict in the Vendée had finally ended Beaulieu, as a respected Republican, had been in a good position to purchase the confiscated Duchambray land.

'Don't you mind it even a little?' she asked.

He glanced at her in surprise, then gave her a smile that was brimful of love. 'Not in the least. This place means more to me now than Ramboulard. It was good of my father to make me his heir, and I dare say our sons will benefit, but I'm an American now.'

And proud of it, thought Hortense.

Unlike many of their neighbours, Raoul had favoured the American purchase of Louisiana two years previously. He firmly believed in the Declaration of Independence, seeing it as the embodiment of the Republican ideal.

'As I've refused to return to France, my father wants to visit us here,' he told her. 'Would you mind that very much? He wants to see his grandsons before he dies.'

'I wouldn't mind in the least,' she replied, standing on tiptoe to kiss his cheek. 'We owe him quite a lot, you know; not just our lives, but our happiness. He proved a most unexpected Cupid.'

Chuckling, Raoul took her in his arms and kissed her hungrily. Even after twelve years of marriage he couldn't keep his hands off her. 'Have I told you yet today how much I love you?'

'Yes,' she replied happily, 'but you can tell me again.'

# HISTORICAL NOTE

THE peace which Charette signed in February 1795 lasted only four months. Then it was the Vendeans who violated it, who at the encouragement of the English and le Comte d'Artois again took up arms. Unfortunately for Charette, the landing of English and emigrés at Quiberon in Brittany failed. In October he had his army lined up on the beach at la Tranche waiting to welcome the Comte, who had landed on the Ile d'Yeu. In spite of his promises, the man never set foot on the mainland and Charette was left to fight alone. He must have known how it would end, yet he battled on. In March of the following year he was captured by the Republicans in the woods near La Charbotterie, a small château situated between Lége and St Fulgent—now a military museum. He was executed in Nantes on the twenty-ninth of that month. He was thirty-three years old.

# MR RAVENSWORTH'S WARD

## *Petra Nash*

Having brought up her daughter in the country,
Lady Waverton knew that if Theodora was to have
the chance of a good marriage, she must have a
Season. The unexpected intrusion of Edmund, Lord
Langdale, and his guardian, Mr Alexander
Ravensworth, into their quiet lives, provided the
catalyst needed.

Alexander told himself he was simply being
unusually altruistic in discreetly arranging
Theodora's launch, though the beautiful, lively girl,
had a far greater effect on him than he was
prepared to admit – until Edmund and Theodora
announced their engagement . . .

**Look out for the two intriguing**

## MASQUERADE *Historical*

**Romances coming next month**

# LOYAL HEARTS
## *Sarah Westleigh*

The country was in turmoil this year of 1399 as Henry
Bolingbroke returned from exile to reclaim his due from
Richard II.

Lady Pippa d'Alban was in turmoil too as her betrothed,
Sir Giles d'Evreux, arrived in Henry's train. Giles had not been
in a hurry to wed her five years ago when she was still a skinny
girl, so how could the contract be honoured now, when her
family supported Richard? Astounded at her blossoming, Giles
was determined to wed her, whether she would or not!

# LADY RASCAL
## *Polly Forrester*

*Paris was aflame*

Sneaking into a dress shop, laundry maid Madeleine forgot all
about the troubles of this July 1789 as she tried on such
wonderful clothes. To her shock Englishman Philip Adamson
thought she was a lady as he snatched her to safety with his
mother. How could she refuse the chance to better herself? If
Mistress Constance wanted a young lady to be her companion,
Madeleine would *be* that lady!

Did Philip suspect her poor origins? Certainly he desired her,
though he was too well mannered to be obvious – where would
her deceit end . . .

**Available in January**